You Can Come Out Now

Erotic Lesbian Stories, Vol. 2

S. R. Cooper

Table of Contents

You Can Come Out Now

Erotic Lesbian Stories, Vol. 2

London '97

It was a rainy Friday evening in late September. The sun was beginning to fade in the background. I pulled my belt tighter on my form-fitted black trench coat; then I adjusted my black bucket hat along with the loop on my black leather clutch before I popped my collar and waited to cross the cobblestone street to catch the next cable car there. When the coast was clear, I held my clutch close to my chest as I hurried across while nearly tripping on the thin tracks embedded in the road as I approached the empty cast iron filigree bus shelter. The dimly lit lamp post inside gave off such romantic vibes; it made me wish I had a lover's lips to kiss or a hand to hold. I smiled coyly at the thought while pulling my hat down further because the rain was becoming heavier, and the wind was blowing it in all directions now.

I peeked my head out after hearing the click of the tracks indicating the cable car was nearby and became excited when I noticed the bright lights in front of the car, bursting through the fog as it made its way up the hill. I covered my eyes slightly with the palm of one hand to block its brightness and prepared myself for the board. The driver managed to stop directly in front of me…Wow, it's crowded this evening despite passengers disembarking, I thought while I moved to the side and waited for my turn to get on. Notwithstanding the crowd, I fit in, but it was tight. The driver slowly pulled off, and I grabbed a leather pull handle opposite another woman to prevent falling. At the same time, another passenger's wet umbrella dripped sky water inside my new cashmere-lined black patent leather rain booties while I grimaced.

I was married for seven years and separated for the last year. Even though my divorce proceedings were long and drawn out today, I was finally a free woman! So, I decided there was no better way to celebrate than to have food and drink at my favorite pub, The Lamb. They serve the best cask whiskey and bangers and mash on the continent! Well, at least, I'd like to think so. I hope Johnny is working tonight. He always gives me at least one drink refill on the house because he thinks I'm cute, I thought, chuckling at myself. Throughout the past year and my separation from my wife, I decided not to contest her receiving our marital house in the divorce; she deserved it. My graduate school coursework load and internship schedule didn't allow me to spend as much time with her as I would've liked. I suppose she hung in there for me for as long as she could. But whatever happened to "for better or for worse"? I was doing it for us, not just myself. Suffice it to say graduating was bittersweet. Anyway, I purchased the Tudor-style Lake cottage I had my eye on, not far from the pub; it wouldn't take me an hour anymore to get home after a night at the Pub. I secretly wished I could celebrate my victory by drinking excessively tonight, yet walking home drunk and on my lonesome didn't strike me as a good idea. After all, a lady must always keep her wits about her, especially when traveling alone. I thought while raising one eyebrow and letting out a deep sigh.

"Last stop!"

The driver yelled, startling me before letting me off a few meters from the pub.

The temperature dropped significantly, causing me to walk quickly toward the pub's entrance and rush inside. "It's a good thing I didn't remove the lining from my coat." I mumbled under my breath while hurrying to the bar and removing my bucket hat, allowing my soft brown curly locks to break free. I sat down, placing my hat and clutch on the empty seat beside me.

"Hey, Johnny! I was hoping you were working tonight."

I shouted softly at the barman at the opposite end, showing off my pearly whites as my hands shook my curls.

"Hello, beautiful! Where've you been? I haven't seen you in a month of Sundays." The barman responded gleefully.

"Oh, Johnny… I've been busy lately; I'll tell you about it later."

My smile didn't waver.

"No, no, no," he responded, waving his hand, and shaking his head quickly.

"No worries, love. Can I get you the usual?" he said,

smiling pleasantly and tucking the bar towel into his navy-blue apron pocket tied snugly around his full belly.

"Yes, please! But make that whiskey a double on the rocks for me this time, would you? I need to embrace my emotions while I warm up." I let out a hearty chuckle and rubbed my hands together briskly. I began to move my head to the blue-eyed soul singer Boz Scaggs's *"Dirty Low Down"* from the vintage jukebox in the corner while my eyes darted about.

"Sure thing, don't you worry, I gotcha, Skye." he winked.

"Hey Henry!" he shouted at the cook wearing a chef's typical lopsided white hat.

"Let me get one banger and mash straight away!"

"You betcha!" Henry yelled from the back.

"Coming right up!" Johnny then placed a lowball glass on a thin cork coaster and said, "Here ya go, darling…; one whiskey double on the rocks."

"Thanks, Johnny."

I picked up the glass and swirled the ice cubes around before taking a sip. Umm, hmm! It burns so good! I needed that. I smacked my tongue against the roof of my mouth before placing the glass back down on the coaster. I stood up to remove my trench coat, inadvertently showing off my curves and enticing Johnny. I couldn't help but burst out laughing when he started whistling at me and playfully bit his hand. I didn't intend to draw anyone's attention to myself when I wore this red cable-knit sweater dress today. The dress was hugging my curves and clearly making Johnny feel some kind of way. But I was made this way, and the women like it; so sorry, fellas. I looked over my right shoulder at him and blushed at his continuous gestures as I strode to the coat rack to hang up my coat adjacent to the bar's front window. As I strolled back to my seat, I paused when I noticed a woman casually walking in. She was wearing the iconic British brand rain hat strategically pulled down low to one side, covering her right eye while unbuttoning her matching three-quarter Khaki trench coat, while the shine of her red nails bounced off the pub's brass pendant lights. A pair of black riding breeches tucked in her red, knee-high rain boots and a black patent leather tote bag hung from her shoulder. Her walk was oddly familiar. She glided like a model on the catwalk, like someone I used to know. But nah. That woman lives in Edinburgh, and that's a long way from here in Liverpool, so I doubt it's her.

"Hmm…." I mumbled as I sucked on my bottom lip and raised an eyebrow on my way back to my seat.

"Bangers up!"

Henry yelled while repeatedly tapping the counter's bell, distracting my thoughts, and placing the food in the window for Johnny to pick up.

"Here ya go, fresh and hot for ya."

Johnny said, smiling as he placed the plate in front of me.

"Ooh, yummy!"

My mouth was salivating with anticipation. I cut into the steaming hot sausage, dipped a piece into the mashed potatoes covered in thick onion gravy, then slipped on a few peas with my knife before blowing on it and placing the forkful in my mouth. "This is delicious." I said softly, chewing with my eyes closed for a moment, then reopening them slowly while turning my head in the direction of the booths where the woman with the oddly familiar walk was sitting.

The woman's back was facing me, making it even harder to decipher whether I knew her or not. What I did know, however, was how much I liked the sheen on the woman's jet-black hair, slicked back and neatly pinned into a chignon bun. The woman sat there as still as a statue and in silence, looking straight ahead through the rain-covered window and wiping away what appeared to be a tear from her cheek.

"It looks like she had a rough day." I thought, placing another forkful of food in my mouth while Johnny went over to the woman's table after being summoned. He returned to the bar and began mixing a drink; then, he put in the woman's shepherd's pie food order. The drink he was concocting seemed strange and interesting.

"Hey, Johnny?"

"Ah, yeah?" He lifted his gaze at me bright-eyed.

"What's that drink you're making for her? It looks interesting."

I asked him, pointing in the woman's direction with my gravy-stained knife just before putting it down to retrieve a napkin to wipe my mouth.

"Oh! She's a looker, that one."

He said, taking a quick glance at the woman, then gesturing with his head in the woman's direction and chuckling, causing his belly to shake.

"This here is one of those popular old drinks making a comeback. It's called Black Velvet," he said as he poured Champagne halfway into a tall glass, then some dark stout over the back of a bar spoon.

"Wow!" I said softly as I watched Johnny closely.

"Beautiful, huh?" he asked, continuing to grin as he poured.

"Yes, it is."

"This spoon helps me create a beautiful layer of pale sparkling wine with this thick black base and this foamy head."

He continued, all while pointing to it. Afterward, he gently grabbed the glass and walked from behind the bar with the woman's food and drink order, smiling as he walked them over to her.

"Here you are, miss," he said while placing the woman's food on the table.

"Thank you." she responded bluntly after clearing her throat, without so much as looking at him.

"My pleasure, miss," he commented before walking away.

As soon as he made his way back to the bar, I asked, "Is she crying?"

"It didn't look like she was, but… maybe?" he said, shrugging his shoulders, then grabbing a towel and wiping the bar top while taking another customer's drink order.

I watched the woman as I savored my bangers and mash, all while contemplating whether to walk up to her and introduce myself. I would hate to leave without checking to see if she was all right. A small part of me also wanted to extinguish that tugging sensation of her familiarity.

"Johnny? Can I have a refill?"

Liquid courage? I thought.

As soon as my drink touched the bar, I grabbed it and headed to the woman's table.

She glanced away from the rain-stricken window and upward at me, taken aback by my proximity.

"Good night."

"You looked familiar to me when you came in, and I didn't want to leave before I found out if we knew one another." I smiled nervously.

"Oh, my goodness, Skye… is that you?"

The woman gasped surprisingly, looking me up and down, leaning back to get a better focus, and blinking out the tears that filled her eyes. "Bridgette! I thought I recognized that walk! How are you? Oh my gosh! What brings you to this side of town?" I asked cheerfully while bending down to hug her with my free hand. Bridgette returned my embrace.

"I can't believe this!" Bridgette said, wiping her falling tears and trying to muster up a smile. "I haven't seen you since we graduated from the university!"

"I know! Do you mind if I sit down?" I asked anxiously.

"Of course! Are you kidding? Please sit." Bridgette said, clearing her throat and patting both sides of her face with her fingertips.

"Is everything all right, sweetheart?

You look upset," I asked in a concerned tone while I scooted into the booth, spilling some of my whiskey on the table before placing it down.

"Yes…I mean, no." She paused, then said, "No. Well…today would've been my tenth anniversary, but…" Tears streamed down her face, yet her voice was devoid of sound. "Skye, you'll have to excuse me."

She coughed softly and picked up her drink to take a sip before turning her gaze toward the window again.

"This weather is very much reflective of my inner turmoil," she said seriously.

"Sweetheart…It's all right if you don't want to discuss it now. I totally understand. How long will you be in town, love?"

I pulled a napkin from the black metal napkin holder on the table and held it out to her.

"I'm staying at the Cottage Inn on Main Street, but I leave in the morning."

She grabbed the napkin from my hand and dabbed it under her eyes.

"Oh no!" I frowned.

I wish I knew you were in town. I would've loved to spend time together… like in the old days. I grazed her hand empathetically, and she clutched my fingers tightly.

"Me too."

She said, taking another sip of her drink, then patting foam off the tip of her nose with the napkin before pushing her half-eaten shepherd's pie to the side. Then she looked down shyly at the table.

"Well… you're still as beautiful as ever. How do you keep that toffee complexion so blemish-free?" I asked her, hoping to uplift her mood. Our hands were still tightly intertwined while I took another sip of my whiskey.

"No, you are!" she responded gleefully, looking up from the table, finally genuinely smiling. "Your "golden-brown" complexion isn't anything to sneeze at, my dear.

"Oh, and your skin loves this light, by the way."

"Who me?" I responded playfully, my hands voguing my face while I batted my eyes. We both burst out laughing.

"Well… to answer your question…, it must be in my genes because I don't do anything special to my skin."

She shrugged her shoulders modestly and blushed.

"Here, here!" I sang, my voice almost a whisper, at the same time raising my glass in a toast-like manner as Bridgette continued to blush.

Our eyes connected momentarily, causing my heart to skip a beat. I awkwardly tapped the table and changed the subject.

"Uh, so. Are you married? Have any children?" I asked, hoping the subject change was successful because the eye contact felt inappropriate to me somehow. I picked up my glass to get a piece of ice, then began to chew on it, waiting for Bridgette's response. Bridgette fidgeted in her seat uncomfortably, and the tears welled up in her eyes again. *Wrong move,* I thought nervously.

"Bridgette, I'm sorry…. I didn't mean to."

"Today…" she interrupted me. "Today," she reiterated, choking up.

I remained silent, afraid to say the wrong thing and reopen a hidden scar.

"Today would've been my tenth wedding anniversary,

but my husband died in a motorcycle accident thirteen months ago. I wasn't fortunate enough to have his children. We did come here once… to this town. I thought it appropriate to… reenact our trip. How about you? Tell me about you."

She licked away a fallen tear from her top lip before picking up her drink.

"Oh boy… Bridgette. I'm sorry, love I said sincerely while reaching out for her hand. I sighed and said, I don't have children, and I was married. My divorce was finalized just today, so I'm here this evening celebrating if you will. I told her, smirking.

"Oh, no! I'm sorry to hear that."

Bridgette responded softly and then finished her drink elegantly, raising her hand for waiter assistance. Johnny immediately received the message and began mixing her another drink.

"You wouldn't believe who I married."

I said with a cheeky grin just before finishing my drink.

Her eyes bulged, and she asked, "Who?" with a wrinkle on her brow.

"Who?" She repeated anxiously.

"Patricia, my roommate at the university. Remember her?"

I responded, grinning.

"Really! Well, God bless the Queen!"

Bridgette's voice was cheerful and upbeat now.

"Indeed! I said, giggling heartily at her reaction.

"We were among the first couples to marry after the Queen approved."

"I'm not surprised… You guys were kind of all over each other. You were two peas in a pod. Everyone suspected it, but I knew."

She said, playing with her napkin before tapping her high-gloss red nails outside her empty glass. "But wow! You guys were married and everything, huh?

"That's beautiful," she whispered.

"Yeah… We had a private ceremony in our home. It was beautiful and romantic."

Quite pensive, I paused and began tapping my nails on the side of my glass. "But with graduate school and my internship, Patricia felt that I didn't spend enough time with her, so she asked me for a divorce during the first term of my second year. She broke my heart, but I didn't have the strength to fight with her, so we separated until the divorce was final."

"Oh no! I'm so sorry, Skye."

Bridgette replied softly, raising her empty glass yet again.

"Thank you, love, but it was best we went our separate ways."

"Yeah, I understand," Bridgette responded, shaking her head slowly. Johnny approached our table with another drink and a little out of breath and said, "Here you are, Miss.

Can I get something else for ya this evening?"

"No, thank you. That'll be all."

She told him with a smile while handing him her empty glass.

"Excuse me, what's your name?"

"The name is Johnny." he told her, smiling from ear to ear before looking at me, nodding and winking playfully.

"Just raise your hand if you need me again!"

"I will. Thank you, Johnny."

She winked, sipping her drink. Johnny chuckled as he hurried off.

"I'm sorry, Skye. You were saying."

"Oh sure, no worries, love. I said, tapping my foot underneath the table on the flagstone floor and swirling around the one barely-there ice cube in my glass.

"So, where was I? Oh!"

I said, putting my glass down.

"I let Patricia keep the house in the divorce and moved a few streets from here."

"Really? How convenient."

Bridgette mumbled before turning her head to look out of the window again.

"I love the rain most days, but It seems like it's slowing down right now." she said softly, wiping the condensation off the window with her bare hand. I just sat and watched her. "I would love to catch up with you, Bridgette. Let me give you, my number. You can call me anytime."

I turned over the paper menu and wrote my phone number on it. I tore the number off and handed it to her.

"I have an idea…" she said quickly as if a lightbulb had illuminated in her mind...

"What do you say we get out of here and go to your place? It's still early, and we can catch up. Besides, I'm in no rush to go back to the inn and be alone with my thoughts tonight." she said, emphasizing with her palms and shoulders up."

"Of course! I would love that! Let me get my coat, and we can be on our way!"

I said, grinning, scooting out of the booth, and quickly walking to the bar.

"See ya later, Johnny!"

I shouted over Ambrosia's *"Biggest Part of Me"* while leaning over the padded bar top before hurrying and removing my coat from the rack.

"Goodnight, Skye. Be careful, love!"

Johnny shouted back with a smile as he waved goodbye with his bar towel. Bridgette left money for her bill under the glass before putting on her trench coat, hat, and tote to catch up with me. Bridgette could feel the heat from Johnny's watchful eyes following her as she walked past the bar.

"So long, Johnny," she teased in a schoolgirl tone, winking and wiggling her fingers at him on her way out the door, causing Johnny's eyes to widen and his smile to broaden like he hit the lottery jackpot or something!

"So long, Miss. Come back soon!" he shouted, waving both hands at her as she chuckled at him.

Once outside, the misty rain kissed both our faces as we walked along the narrow pathway toward my grey brick, Tudor-styled Lake cottage. Bridgette took my right arm nonchalantly and rested her head on my shoulder like it was the most natural thing in the world. We both strolled silently until we arrived at the foot of the concrete staircase that only accommodated one person at a time. I went first; then, I waited until Bridgette reached the top where my home's white-washed oak entry door faced us. The grey and white brick-paved walkway was lined with pink English rose bushes, and lush topiary sculptures in stone urns sat on each side of the front door while the warm white glow of the porch lights invited us to come closer.

"Welcome to my home."

I sang as I opened the heavy oak door and stepped aside to let Bridgette in.

"Let me take your coat, love. You can put your boots in that black metal shoe tray over there."

I pointed at the corner after turning on the hallway light.

"I love how cozy your place is!" Bridgette commented while taking off her coat and hat and handing them to me. She removed her boots before pulling her white cable-knit socks over her dark denim jeans, then walked past me towards the living space.

"Thanks, love. Would you like a cup of tea with a splash of blackberry brandy?"

I yelled through the pass-through window in the kitchen while pulling down the ever-rising silk slip I wore under my sweater dress.

"Yes, please. "I'd love some," Bridgette responded before plopping herself down on the fluffy mustard-colored fabric sofa in front of the stacked stone fireplace, admiring the home's décor and holding one of the sofa pillows on her lap. I prepared our tea and added a few butter cookies to the serving tray before carrying it tentatively to the living space.

"Here we go...,"

I sighed, placing the tray on the brown leather ottoman that doubled as a coffee table before I handed Bridgette her teacup.

"I'm so happy to see you, Bridgette!"

I squealed.

"We have so much to catch up on!"

My voice became increasingly high-pitched; I couldn't contain my excitement.

"Indeed, we do! Where do we begin? So many years have passed."

Bridgette blew on her tea before taking a cautious sip.

"I know!... Let's start with… what you do for work?"

I reached for a butter cookie and folded one of my legs underneath my buttocks as I listened eagerly.

"Well… I'm currently the director of instruction at the Ballet company in Edinburgh after ten years of professional dancing there."

She chuckled softly at my obvious excitement.

"Wow! You must've lived a fascinating life traveling the world and everything, huh? I bet you've been to lots of places as well."

I asked, sitting on the edge of my seat and enjoying another butter cookie.

"Oh yes, it was wonderful! Let's see now... I performed in Madrid, Morocco, Sydney, Prague, and Rome," she looked childlike as she counted the places on her fingers while she listed them with a pleasantly broad smile splattered across her face.

"We stayed in Rome for eight months! Would you believe that?"

Rome is where I met my husband."

Her smile slowly faded, and her head dropped slightly. Seconds later… Bridgette stood slowly and walked over to the four-paneled window on the rustic mahogany back door. The gusty wind blew the misty rainwater onto the glass softly.

I sat there silently sipping my tea, allowing her to connect with her emotions in silence.

"That is glorious!"

Bridgette suddenly commented after noticing the fairy lights on the ceiling of the backyard's waterfront gazebo; its twinkling lights were dancing on the still water.

"That's a thing of beauty," she said as she continued to admire it.

Isn't it wonderful?"

I entertained her fascination, smiling proudly and putting down my teacup to twirl my curls.

"I'm a horrible guest, aren't I?"

Bridgette said, turning around and heading back to the sofa.

"No, I wouldn't say that. You weren't expecting to run into me tonight.'

I alleviated her doubts and reached for her hand, squeezing it gently before releasing it.

So…" Bridgette deeply sighed, patting my leg as she sat down.

"I remember you saying you went to graduate school. Tell me, what have you been doing with *your* life? Please fill me in on the gory details!" she asked, picking up a butter cookie and eating it whole, trying to hold back her tears.

"Believe it or not, I'm a marriage counselor." I responded, chuckling.

"No way!"

Bridgette covered her mouth with one hand to keep the crumbs from falling while picking up her teacup with the other.

I noticed a tear casually escaping from her left eye.

"Yeah," I chuckled. "Ironic, right? The divorced marriage counselor. I thought I had it all figured out."

I said, slowly shaking my head.

"Perhaps my marriage would've survived had I used counseling outside of my office."

I spaced out for a moment.

"Oh, my goodness, enough about that!"

I smirked and scratched my head.

"Look at the time!"

I exclaimed after glancing down at my wristwatch.

"Should I call a taxi, Bridgette? What time does your flight leave in the morning?"

I reached for the telephone on the rustic wood table beside the sofa.

"You know what?" Bridgette pondered before slurping her last bit of tea. "I can always change my ticket. I took the train into town because I truly enjoy looking out of the windows at the beautiful countryside this time of year, *and* I still have a week left of my holiday… Besides, I want to make up for my gloomy attitude tonight." She said, returning her teacup to the tray and pouring herself another cup of tea. "I promise I'll feel better after a good night's sleep at an old friend's house if… you'll have me, of course," she said playfully, pretending to look away.

"Are you serious? I'd love for you to stay! We can get reacquainted in the morning!" I have a spare room upstairs; I'll turn down the bed for you. Just let me clean this up first!" I downed the rest of my tea and sprang into action.

"No, no! You go, and I'll clean this up. I'll meet you upstairs in a moment." Bridgette playfully "hip" bumped me out of the way and then picked up the tray.

"Are you sure? I asked, placing my hands into my hair to shake my curls again.

"Yes, I insist! I'll meet you upstairs. Go, go!" she said, shooing me away jokingly. "Fabulous!" I said with a smile, pulling my sweater dress over her head and running up the rustic staircase. I then threw the dress over the wrought iron banister as my brown curls bounced with their static ends.

Bridgette smiled broadly at my youthful behavior while simultaneously turning her head to watch me run up the stairs. She was so surprised to find herself aroused upon noticing my perfectly round golden-brown cheeks peeking out of my white cotton panties wedged between them as the silk slip continued to rise with every step I took. She unconsciously licked her lips and stared until I was out of sight. Then she walked toward the kitchen, turned on the lights, washed out the teacups and teapot, and placed them on the pinewood dishrack on the counter. She then wiped the crumbs off the tray with a dry dishtowel she found hanging on the lower cabinet door, but not before she ate the two leftover butter cookies there. She ensured the faucet was shut off completely before turning off the kitchen light and climbing the stairs, searching for the bedroom I set up for her. Clueless, she went into the first room she saw to the right of the staircase; it was dimly lit and huge with its high-polished black hardwood floors, a colonial-style ebony king-sized four-poster bed with a canopy and sheer black curtains draped around it, and grey-colored cotton sheets on the mattress. On either side of the bed was a matching ebony nightstand with brass drawer pulls, each with a gold mercury teardrop glass lamp with black linen shades in the center of it. All the darkness in the room made the mattress appear to float. *This is nice*, she thought. In front of the bed was a large, mirrored chest of drawers with black matte glass flower knobs. There was a tall ebony wooden armoire with brass drawer knobs to the far right, sandwiched between two distressed wood, grey windows. To the room's left was an identical window with a silver gilded mirror resting against the adjacent wall. Bridgette walked toward the bed, unzipping her jeans in amazement, and pulling off her cable-knit socks just as I opened the bathroom door, walking out stark naked.

"Oh! I'm sorry." Bridgette gasped with her hand on her chest as she looked away bashfully.

"No worries, love, we both have the same private parts, don't we?" I teased, winking and pulling my hair up, tying it with a large red silk ribbon. My breasts were full and firm, and my little belly pooch still had a few beads of water on it. My hips were wide, and my pubic hair was plenty.

"Let me show you to your room." I retrieved the cotton floral robe behind my bedroom door and led the way with my lavender-painted toenails. I flicked on the lights in the guest room to reveal its large octagon shape, housing a queen-sized natural wood cove bed with four pillows up against the wall. There was also one faux wax battery-operated candlestick placed in a brass candle holder on the windowsill of all four triangle-shaped windows, and nude-colored panels hung between the wine-colored drapes, slightly above the plush tan-colored carpeted floor.

"Oh, my God! This is beautiful, Skye." Bridgette commented, her socks in hand and her toes tugging at the carpet. "I want to unwind and take a nice hot bath." She yawned and placed her socks on the bed. She yawned again deeper, causing tears to stream down her face.

"Of course, love." I said softly while escorting her to a charming little guest bathroom next door. "You can use this bathroom." The bathroom had natural walnut hardwood heated flooring, a hammered copper bowl basin sink, and a brass faucet. It also harbored a free-standing copper soaker tub with a white porcelain inlay, a white wall-hung commode, and three copper pendant track lights.

"Wow, babe," Bridgette mumbled, taking it all in. "Did you decorate this yourself?"

"Aww, thanks, love. I did! I purchased a few designer magazines to find inspiration." I said blushingly. "Look.... here's a dimmer switch in case you want to take the lights down. I played with the switch to demonstrate the lighting's differences.

"Call if you need anything, anything at all, okay?" I said sincerely.

"Okay, I will." Bridgette said, letting out yet another yawn while she walked behind me towards the door to close it. She took her time, observing me walk away, confused at this sudden urge to admire my curves. She watched my buttocks bounce through my robe until I was finally through the entrance and on my way back to the room. Bridgette replayed the scene in her mind as she slowly removed her jeans and let the sexual fantasies run unrestrained through her mind. She licked her lips before shaking her head in disbelief at these unexpected desires before completely closing the door and dimming the lights. She walked closer to the tub, stepped on the woven grass bathmat, and turned on the water. Out of the corner of her eye, she noticed a two-tier white metal bath cart that held three large, covered amber glass apothecary jars on the top tier with the contents inscribed on them with a silver metallic pen. One of the jars was filled with rose petal powder, the second with dried fragrant goat's milk, and the last with jasmine-scented Epsom salts. There was also a clear glass honey pot with a honey dipper and two bars of honey glycerin soap. The bottom tier held a bath pillow, a cellophane-wrapped bath sponge, and three fluffy white bath towels. Bridgette re-adjusted the water temperature to her satisfaction and poured some dried goat's milk with five dippers of honey. She dipped her toe in the water before getting in, picked up the bath pillow, placed the suction cups where her head would be, and then sat in the tub listening to the rain's music. The soft sounds of the rain caused her to dose off for a few moments, but she awakened just as quickly after choking on the bathwater. She wiped the water from her face with her hand and then grabbed a bar of the honey glycerin soap to wash it with before rubbing the soap's lush lather across the rest of her body, adding more hot water before she began to shiver. The goat milk did a great job with exfoliation, and the honey moisturized her skin so well that there was no need for body cream. She patted herself dry, wrapped up in one of the other fluffy white towels, and walked back into the guest bedroom, where she found a white cotton nightgown and matching robe placed diagonally across the bed, her socks folded and placed in the small natural wicker basket next to it. *She's so sweet.* Bridgette thought as she looked over her shoulder at the door, smiling as she wore the fresh-smelling gown.

She walked over to the door to turn off the lights before climbing under the fluffy beige satin comforter and soft white cotton sheets enveloped with lavender's calming scent. She surrounded herself with the bed pillows but put one of them between her legs because she was still unfamiliar with sleeping alone. The rain was soft and hitting the windows ever so slightly, lulling her to sleep peacefully while the glow of the candlelight diminished as her eyes closed. A few hours later…BOOM! CRACK! went the thunder and lightning, startling Bridgette, who, for a moment, forgot where she was. She pulled the comforter up and over her head. The wind was strong and whistling now, causing the heavy rain to beat on the windows with such force that it rattled the frames. What was soothing at first became disturbing. She put on her robe and dashed to my room, knocking on the door softly yet frantically before turning the doorknob and opening it. The squeaky door hinges awakened me.

"Hey love, is everything all right?" I raised my head curiously, my voice just above a whisper. When I turned in her direction, lightning flashed from the window, highlighting my delicate facial features.

"Actually… It's not." Bridgette responded nervously, closing the door behind her. "Thunder frightens me. I'm sorry to wake you, but can I sleep with you tonight?" she asked, wrapping both sides of the robe around herself while walking swiftly toward the bed, respectfully standing outside the sheer curtains, and waiting for permission to enter. "Of course, love, get in!" I responded pleasantly, attempting to pull back the bed linen on Bridgette's side. "I needed to use the toilet anyways," I removed the bed's linen off me and jumped out of bed. I was still naked and squinting my eyes from the brightness of the lighting as I hurried across the heated wooden floors toward the bathroom. Bridgette's eyes were glued to my firm, bouncing breasts until I entered the bathroom and closed the door. Then she refocused her thoughts and moved aside the sheer curtain, removing her robe, and placing it at the foot of the king-sized bed before pulling the dark purple comforter and grey eyelet top sheet back. She sank into the feather pillow top mattress, pulling the bed linen over her nose. *Mm, it's so warm and cozy… and smells like orange blossoms,* she thought to herself before taking a deep breath in.

BOOM! went the thunder once again as I approached the bed. The loud sound caused me to hop in bed quickly, pretending to be afraid while scrambling underneath the cozy orange blossom-smelling linens, pulling them up to my neck and rubbing my feet together briskly as I giggled sweetly. "Oh, the sweet warmth."

The crackling thunder encouraged Bridgette to inch her body closer to my side of the bed. "Hold me… please." she asked softly, still facing forward.

I hesitated initially because I hadn't been with a woman in over two years and longed for the satisfaction of a woman's touch, almost fearing what it would bring me. Still, I didn't want to be accused of taking advantage of Bridgette in her vulnerable state. However, I quickly put those thoughts and desires aside since Bridgette was a friend, but most of all, a friend in need of comfort, and I decided to grant Bridgette's request. I moved in closer and placed my arm across her belly, my bare nipples inches away from her nightgown, with my head resting atop the pillow directly above her head. Bridgette sighed softly just before wiggling her body closer to mine, causing my nipples to harden as they were pressed snugly against her back.

"Sweet lord," I mumbled while trying to maintain my composure.

Bridgette took my hand in hers and placed it on her chest before falling asleep as peacefully as a baby. Four hours later, the slight dampness of Bridgette's perspiration made the cotton gown stick to her skin, waking her up from discomfort. She eased her way out of my embrace and removed her gown, throwing it to the foot of the bed, revealing her naked and toned dancer's body before returning to the comfort of my arms. I woke up enticed by the dewy warmth of her naked back and butt against my warm thighs and swollen nipples. Her carefree attitude compelled me to grab hold of her right hip, concurrently grinding on her buttocks until I realized what I was doing, and then I slowly backed away. I convinced myself she was vulnerable; perhaps it wasn't the best time to grind on her. Besides, there was no longer any thunder, lightning, or even rain falling, so there was no reason to continue holding her. Yet, when I moved away…Bridgette did the unexpected; she turned around and inched her way over slowly towards me, practically mouth to mouth and breathing heavily onto my lips before leaning in and kissing my lips softly, twice.

"Are you sure you want to do this, love?" I asked her in a low tone, returning her kisses and running my hand gently across her hair.

"Yes…Yes, I'm sure." As if to confirm her certainty, she leaned in for another kiss, her lips trembling slightly. "I need to be touched in the worst way, Skye. Please make love to me.' she whispered, throwing her leg over my hip, her eyes barely opened.

I rolled over on top of her, kissing her tenderly as our eyes connected briefly in the moonlight's glow beaming through the sheer curtains surrounding the bed. The rain began to downpour as if on cue, hitting the windows as rapidly as the wind blew. My thigh was wedged between hers now, and we both began moaning with pleasure as we grinded on each other. The ribbon fell from my hair, allowing my soft curls to sweep across her beautiful toffee-colored face. With my left hand, I pulled my hair back from her face as our grinding picked up tempo, causing us to breathe heavily.

I placed my right hand lightly around her throat while she sucked on her bottom lip before I passionately put my tongue in and out of her mouth. We both longed for human touch tonight, something a masturbation session would not fulfill. Bridgette squeezed one of my firm breasts, causing me to arch my back before gently placing my swollen nipple into her mouth while enjoying the soft friction of my curly pubic hairs tickling the lips between her legs. Suddenly, Bridgette reciprocated, rolling me over and climbing on top of me. She held the back of my head in one of her hands before placing the other between my thighs and softly stroked my hairy box while her middle finger teased my peek-a-boo clit. This caused my body to pause as I gasped, simultaneously grabbing a handful of skin on her back and her right ass cheek firmly.

"Your skin is so soft," I whispered, pulling her completely into me while bowing my head to nibble on her right shoulder.

Bridgette pulled air through her teeth slowly and seductively before sticking her tongue in and out of my ear because of the sensations my nibbling created inside her. She licked, kissed, sucked, and bit on my neck softly before nibbling down my breasts and stopping at my enlarged nipples. She feasted on them hungrily, breathing deep and lustfully. "Pinch me, baby. I wanna make sure I'm not dreaming." Bridgette sang softly as she came up for air with her thigh between mine, causing us to slow dance rhythmically to the beat of the rain.

"I gotta know what you taste like." I said in a deep, sexy voice while raising her leg with my thigh and wedging it tightly against her crotch before I flipped her over and kicked the comforter to the floor. I started kissing and licking the front of her body rapidly, making her nipples shrivel in ecstasy while I wedged my head between her thighs. I kissed her furry, thin lips while my tongue separated them to taste the warm, savory nectar pooling there.

Bridgette gasped and panted quickly. "Please don't stop!" she cried, widening her legs and lifting her head slightly off the pillow to watch me enjoy myself, then taking a handful of my curls between her fingers and laying her head back down.

"Oh my god…" Bridgette squealed, climaxing repeatedly and simultaneously with the crackling thunder. "Yes, baby! Oh my god… yes, baby!" Bridgette continued to yell out as her body jerked, eventually jerking her clit from my mouth. I looked up at her and just smiled.

"Damn, babe…" she said as her body began to calm down. "You. Are. So… Good," Bridgette whispered, breathing deeply, and running her hands through my hair. I let out a sexy chuckle before pushing myself up to lay on her belly, reaching out and taking her hand.

"My turn." Bridgette said seductively, taking my hand and interlocking our fingers before flipping me over. She straddled me, planting tender kisses on my lips while sucking on my tongue and continuing down to my moist, hairy love box. She opened my lips gently with her thumbs before sticking her tongue in for a taste. "Mm, such salty goodness." she whispered as she savored my clit, looking up at me even though the darkness blinded us. "I've never tasted a woman before… but my thirst for you tonight must be quenched!" Her voice was soft, but there was a hint of aggression.

I let my feelings flow; my moans were sweet and intoxicating to Bridgette's ears, causing her tongue to slowly travel in and out of my canal, retracting my sticky, salty goodness. "I'm cumming…baby…" I said softly, my body quivering as my sweet cream dripped slowly onto Bridgette's bottom lip and the bed.

"Why do you taste so good to me?" Bridgette asked rhetorically, sucking her bottom lip moments before returning her mouth to my clit, licking it quickly to savor what remained. "Okay, baby, okay." I cried repeatedly, rapidly tapping Bridgette on her head. Bridgette obliged and slowly stopped, climbing onto my body until she reached my mouth, kissing it passionately before laying her body across mine.

When we locked our eyes, we both said, "Thank you" to each other, and then we fell blissfully asleep to the soothing sounds of our breathing.

The following morning… I found myself alone in bed and was surprisingly disappointed about it. However, the sound of Vivaldi's *"Four Seasons"* was beginning to echo throughout the house, while the scent of fresh coffee brewing was also making its way upstairs. I smiled widely as I jumped out of bed.

I looked inside my silver trinket box on the dresser for a hair clip before throwing on my flowered robe, pining my hair up, and going downstairs to be closer to it all.

"Good morning, love!" I chirped as I tied my robe and walked into the kitchen. Bridgette returned the pleasantries with the widest grin her face could hold, showing off her pearly whites and angelic look in the white cotton gown and robe I so graciously let her wear. "Aren't we in a good mood this morning?" I said playfully as I reached into the cupboard to get a cup to pour myself some coffee.

"Indeed, I am! And… Thank you again for last night," she said, kissing me softly, then biting my lower lip.

"No… thank you," I teased.

We were both blushing like giddy teenagers while maintaining eye contact.

"You know what?"

Bridgette asked cheerfully as she slowly backed away.

"What's that love?"

I removed the carafe from the coffee maker and poured the fresh brew into my cup.

"I'm going to make you a fry-up this morning. Would you like that?" She asked, removing two copper pans from the hanging pan rack over the black butcher block island and placing them on the stove burners.

"Wow! I can't remember the last time a beautiful woman cooked me breakfast; I look forward to it!"

Holding my coffee cup with both hands, I smiled while looking at Bridgette lovingly.

"Well… I'll have to fix that now, won't I?" she said with

a wink as she opened the refrigerator door. "Let's see. It looks like you have everything," she remarked cheerfully, humming slightly as she began taking some food items out.

"Eggs, hmm…what's this?" she asked rhetorically as she picked up the brown butcher paper-wrapped meat and opened it. "Ah, yes…. blood sausage, perfect! Now… mushrooms check, tomatoes check, bread check, and bacon check! Yes!" She placed the food on the counter one item at a time. "Wait…" she said, turning around quickly with a stick of butter in her hand and a wrinkle on her brow.

"Please tell me you have baked beans!"

"I should have some…I chuckled at her quirky behavior. It was a side of her I hadn't seen the night before; it was refreshing. I opened the cupboard door and said, "Here you go, love…, baked beans." I passed the can over to her.

"Fantastic!"

Oh! I almost forgot, I said, snapping my fingers and placing my coffee cup on the counter. "Would you mind putting the food on these dishes? My dad brought these for my wife and me as a wedding gift when he visited Buckingham Palace. Patricia didn't want them, so I kept them with me, and I barely got a chance to use them when we were married." I told her, re-opening the cupboard.

"Of course! Pass them to me."

I handed her two blue and white Churchill Willow ironstone plates with matching bowls. "These are beautiful, Skye," she told me, looking intriguingly at the plate's design. "All right, I picked up your *Times* from the porch and placed it on the table for you, so go have a seat, drink your coffee, and read your paper with Vivaldi while I prepare breakfast, sweetheart."

"Aww, that was so sweet…Okay, gorgeous, but can I get a kiss for the road?"

"Indeed… Bridgette replied softly, biting her bottom lip as she walked over to me and threw her arms around my neck, giving me a wet, lusciously deep tongue kiss.

"Wow… that made me lightheaded." I commented, blinking slowly. "Okay, I'll be… over… there…" I pointed playfully toward the living space as I backed out of the kitchen.

Twenty minutes later…Bridgette finished preparing breakfast, rinsed off the plates and bowls, and began plating while humming to the song "*Spring*" from Vivaldi. She placed the food on the serving tray I used earlier for tea, picked up some black currant jam from the counter, walked it out into the dining area, and placed it on the square oak dining table adjacent to the stone fireplace.

"The view of the lake is stunning," Bridgette said as she sat across from me; then she picked up a piece of fried bread and placed some baked beans on it from the bowl before handing it to me.

I eagerly put down the newspaper. "My, my…" I whispered, smiling affectionately at her. "It's so refreshing to have a woman cater to me this way; it's been such a long time that I forgot how it felt."

"What about having Barry White join us for breakfast now?" I asked.

"Sounds good to me, babe," Bridgette responded, rearranging the food on her plate.

I got up from the table and put on Barry White's *"Can't Get Enough of Your Love Babe"* and returned to the table, where Bridgette chewed and tapped her foot to the beat.

"I'm glad you're happier this morning, Bridgette."

"Well, I have you to thank for that!" she responded gleefully.

"You're an excellent cook, by the way." I moaned after biting the perfectly seasoned fried eggs with the skillet-charred tomato.

'Thank you, sweetheart." She replied just before taking a sip of her coffee. "Hey! Do you remember Professor Willoughby?" Bridgette asked, now taking a big bite of blood sausage.

"I most certainly do! He made going to psychology class exciting, I responded, placing a forkful of mushrooms and bacon into my mouth.

"Yeah! You're so right…., His toupee would lift every time he sneezed!" Bridgette yelled, causing both of us to laugh hysterically as we reminisced.

"I think he did it intentionally for laughs, though, I commented, wiping the tears from my eyes.

"Oh yeah, why's that?" Bridgette asked, licking bean gravy off her pinky.

"Well… because I never met anyone else who could sneeze on cue…, Have you?"

"No, I haven't," she softly chuckled. "Oh! Oh… Do you remember Professor Hammond, who taught Humanities?" She tapped my hand excitedly. "He was so handsome, wasn't he?" Bridgette continued as she batted her eyes, mixing her sausage with the eggs.

"Of course, I do! All of you girls took his class so that you could stare into his beautiful green eyes!" I returned the batting eye gesture and stuffed my last bite of beans and fried bread into my mouth.

"Didn't you think he was handsome?" she asked, raising an eyebrow, and looking at me over her coffee cup.

"Absolutely! But I was looking at women like he was, my love. I winked, and she chuckled.

"Have you ever been intimate with a man before, Skye?"

"No, I have not." My elbows rested on the table while I held the coffee cup.

"So.... are you a virgin, then?" she asked cautiously, putting the black currant jam on her fried bread.

"Yes, I'm a virgin to men, but my wife penetrated me on our wedding night." I grinned. "Wow! That's fascinatingly beautiful!" she yelled gleefully.

"Yeah, it was, but… that was another time," I said, staring off into the distance.

"Well then…" Bridgette said, her fist pounding down on the table quickly to change the subject. "I must say… I made a wonderful breakfast, didn't I?" she asked, rubbing her belly pooch.

"Indeed!" I shouted, rubbing my belly with her.

We both laughed, and then I stood up to clear the table.

"Let me help you with that," she offered.

"Nope!" I immediately said, clutching the tray and making a half-turn to prevent her from taking it out of my hands. "Love! you cooked! I'll clean!" I glided back to the kitchen, put the tray down, and glanced at her through the pass-through window. "Aht, aht. Leave those cups there; I told you I'd clean up, love." I commanded as I walked back into the dining area, my robe flying in the wind behind me. "Sit down and relax; I'll be back after I clean the dishes." I picked up the coffee cups and returned to the kitchen, turning my head backward to blow quick air kisses to her while blowing away the curl that fell on my upper lip. After I washed, dried, and put away the dishes, I returned to the dining area to find Bridgette sprawled across the sofa in the living space.

"Hey there, love. Are you still tired?"

"No, just stuffed!" she chuckled. "Come sit down." She sat up to make room for me.

"No! Make yourself comfortable, sweetheart; I'll sit over here."

I pointed to the loveseat.

"You're so sweet, but come here." She patted one of the sofa cushions, "I want to rest my head on your lap."

"Aww…Okay, I'm sold." I tied my robe and lounged next to her.

"Your love is so soft and easygoing." Then she gently placed the right side of her face on my thigh. "I can't imagine why someone would want to divorce you." She whispered while rubbing her hand across my thigh.

We sat in silence briefly, listening to Barry White's *"Love Serenade."*

"I guess I was supposed to be here with you. I said softly, glancing down at her and stroking her hair.

She turned on her back and looked up at me lovingly before sitting up and lifting her gown to straddle me. "We could make a good combination, couldn't we?" Bridgette asked me while looking directly into my eyes.

"We could." I blushed as she held my face tenderly with both hands and kissed me gently before rubbing our noses together playfully, mimicking Eskimos. "We do indeed… we do indeed."

We both chuckled as she leaned in for another kiss. I cupped her butt cheeks and slowly stood up, kissing her while walking towards the staircase.

"Wait…Hold on, baby." she said, pausing our kiss and looking at the back door.

"What is it, love?" I asked, my tone low and sexy while I stared at her lustfully.

"I want to make love outside in the gazebo." She said, placing her thumb seductively between her teeth. I walked to the back door without hesitation and slipped into my tan, shearling moccasins. Afterward, Bridgette reached down and turned the vintage black cast iron doorknob, opening it. I walked out slowly across the damp lawn with Bridgette's arms wrapped loosely around my neck and her legs lightly wrapped around my waist. We looked at the still lake until we reached the gazebo, where I sat Bridgette on the wide-shellacked mahogany tree trunk table. The morning air was lukewarm, and the sun was sitting high in the sky without a drop of rain in sight. The gazebo's roof blocked the direct sunlight, making it another perfect setting to enjoy one another. Bridgette removed her robe while my robe fell to the gazebo floor. I helped Bridgette out of her gown before we both began kissing each other more passionately than the night before, simultaneously running our fingers through each other's hair. I gently pulled Bridgette closer to the table's edge before stooping down and separating her legs, craving the sweetness between them.

"Wow, baby!" Bridgette said softly while placing her feet on the table for stability. She reached down and held onto my head to ensure I received all her sweetness, throwing her head back and moaning in ecstasy as her juices flowed. I sopped up her sweetness with absolute delight, moaning as I went along. Bridgette's final climax was long and steady, completely relaxing her and causing her legs to collapse and her feet to dangle from the table.

When she sat up, she gingerly pulled me closer, delicately sucking her sweetness off my lips softly and slowly before nudging me down to the gazebo floor. She laid me down, kissing me intensely while removing my moccasins as she raised my legs. She held my legs up and knelt to smack, kiss, and bite my butt cheeks just before licking between the crack that divided them. She licked my moist crack from the back to the front before savagely sucking on my clit. Then she slowly stood, placing my body in a semi-headstand, causing my thighs to squeeze her head as my clit swelled. Her dirty talk had me climaxing repeatedly.

"Yes, baby, that's it, don't leave any behind, drink it all… got damn it." I repeated seductively, my teeth clenched.

Bridgette continued to slurp inside my hairy box, slowly easing my body down onto the gazebo's floor, my body completely relaxing. We were both satisfied and breathing heavily. I slumped on my back with Bridgette crawling up beside me to lay on her belly, her head resting on her hands. The cool and dewy wood slats of the gazebo's floor felt pleasant against our skin. It helped cool us down, encouraging us to kiss and caress each other more.

Moments later…I withdrew my affection.

"Hey, sweetheart, did I do something wrong? You look, I don't know… different?" There was concern plastered on her face.

"Well…" I paused with a sigh, pulling the dandelion weed through the wood slat. "I usually visit my mum on Saturday." I sat upright completely now.

"Oh, my goodness!" Bridgette gasped, placing her hand across her moist breast in a gesture of relief. "So, what's the problem, Hun?" She asked, returning her belly to the floor.

"My mum lives in Oxfordshire." I said, turning to face her. "Okay…"

Bridgette said, looking confused and raising her eyebrow while leaning on her elbows. "Oxfordshire is three hours away, love. I spend the whole day and night with her before returning home on Sunday afternoon." I admitted in a disappointed tone. "But… I guess she could do without me for one Saturday." I told her, smiling uncomfortably.

"Why should she?" Bridgette asked, still looking puzzled. "I want to go with you." She said, looking at me cautiously optimistic, hoping I wanted her company.

My eyes lit up.

"Oh my God… that sounds like music to my ears…of course, you can! Let's get dressed!" I rapidly played the drums on Bridgette's butt cheeks before jumping to my feet. "Come on, love… we gotta buy some veggies at the farmers market before all the good stuff is gone!" I sang as I ran into the house and up the staircase excitedly.

"Ouch!" Bridgette smirked, rubbing her butt with both hands. "You're lucky I like a little pain," she yelled playfully before running up the stairs behind me. We bathed, dressed, and made our beds before heading to the market. My silver four-wheel-drive pick-up truck was left running in the driveway on the side of the house because it hadn't been driven in a week, and I didn't want to have Bridgette waiting for it to warm up. After I put a few things in the pick-up tray, I got in the driver's seat and took off for the countryside of Oxfordshire. At the farmers market…I located my favorite farmer, Jenny, with the gold front tooth and strawberry blonde locs in her hair. Jenny was the only farmer with the freshest free-range duck and quail eggs.

"Good morning, Skye!" Jenny shouted. "I have a dozen just laid fresh eggs for you today, love." She smiled, revealing her gold tooth that reflected the sunlight. "Good morning, Jenny!" I shouted, waving cheerfully "That's just what I was hoping for today!" I picked up the cartons of quail and duck eggs I wanted and handed them to her.

"I'll bag those up for ya; that'll be twenty-four dollars, love." Jenny told me while handing back the eggs in a burlap shopping bag.

"No problem, here ya go, twenty-five dollars…; keep the change and have a wonderful day!" I cheered softly as

I walked away, with Bridgette in tow, toward the fruit and vegetable stands.

"Thank you!" Jenny said, waving goodbye.

At the stand, I purchased green and purple cabbages, yellow squash, two small pumpkins, yellow and green string beans, tomatoes, pomegranates, eggplants, beets, and a couple of jars of Blackcurrant and Gooseberry jams. Bridgette wanted something to drink and walked to the freshly squeezed juice stand while I continued to shop.

"I'll be over there," Bridgette pointed, stabbing in the air as she hurried off.

"Okay, love," I nodded and walked to the flower cart to purchase a bouquet of forget-me-nots. I had the farmer wrap it with twine and clear cellophane paper before putting them in my burlap shopping bag with the eggs just seconds before Bridgette returned, eating a delicious golden apple.

"Oh, that looks good and juicy!" I remarked while licking my lips.

"It does. doesn't it?" Bridgette smirked. "Here… I bought you one, too," she said, handing an apple to me.

"Aww, thank you!"   "Here… I also bought you something," I reached into the burlap shopping bag.

"Oh! My goodness!" Bridgette said, almost dropping her apple. "These are beautiful." She stared at the flowers lovingly before licking the apple's juice from her lips, then putting them up to her nose and taking a deep breath. "Forget-me-nots are so beautiful…. "Did you know they symbolize love and respect for the person who receives them?" she asked me, blushing.

"No… I didn't know, but now I do." I chuckled genuinely, enjoying Bridgette's reaction. "Thank you, Skye," she said sweetly, her nose still in the bouquet and her eyes on me. "You're welcome, love. I'm glad you like them."

"This was so thoughtful of you." she said, continuing to blush. "No one has bought me flowers in a long time."

Just then, I reached out my hand for her to take, and we began walking towards the truck. I was carrying the bags of produce, feeling like the captain of Bridgette's heart, while she admired her bouquet.

After I put the produce in the vehicle, I drove the scenic route down hills of green on the road less traveled to my favorite strawberry farm. I preferred picking my strawberries and thought Bridgette would enjoy doing the same. I parked on the dirt road to the right of the farm, and we both proceeded to the farm stand, Bridgette leaving her bouquet on the seat. I paid for two baskets to put the strawberries in before noticing the sign advertising redcurrants. "My mum makes the best redcurrant jam!" I exclaimed, paying for four baskets instead of two. We walked to the strawberry patch arm in arm before going our separate ways and agreeing to meet back at the stand in forty-five minutes or less. Almost an hour later, Bridgette arrived at the stand munching on a strawberry when I appeared moments later, my lips stained with red currants.

"I ought to kiss you right now, " she said seductively, staring at my lips and slowly licking hers.

"What's stopping you?" I asked her daringly while slightly raising an eyebrow.

Bridgette inched toward me, placing the fruit baskets on the farmstand table, then gently grabbed my forearm, pulling me in close and pressing her lips firmly into mine, twice leaving me breathless. Then she turned around slowly, picked up her basket, and began walking toward the vehicle, intermittingly looking back at me alluringly. At the same time, I picked up mine and jogged lightly behind to catch up. On the strawberry farm grounds, to the far left, was a picnic area I was all too familiar with since I picnicked there alone several times in the past six months.

"Do you want to picnic here before continuing the journey to my mum's?"

"I would love to have a picnic with you, sweetheart."

She answered sweetly, causing me to smile so hard it hurt my cheeks. We got in the truck, and I placed my fruit on the console, then drove to the picnic area, parking alongside it. "I'll be right back." I said before putting the vehicle in park and hopping out. I went to the back of the truck, let down the tray, and pulled out a wicker picnic basket I filled with goodies when Bridgette was in the bath. I removed a bottle of apple prosecco and a patchwork quilt before walking to the passenger side and tapping lightly on the window, motioning for Bridgette to come out.

"What's this?" she asked excitedly as she opened the vehicle door and stepped out, leaving her fruit basket next to the bouquet on her seat, her eyes widening as she observed the items in my hands.

"I was hoping you'd say yes to having a picnic with me today, love." I told her, with a smile so broad it shamed the sun.

"Oh, my goodness! Wait…when did you find the time to do this?" she asked me puzzlingly.

"I had already gone to the market and bakery this week. So, I thought it would be appropriate for us to have a picnic! so I ran downstairs and prepped everything while you were still bathing."

"You're exquisitely charming, my lady." she told me as she playfully curtsied before taking the wine bottle from my hand.

"And you, my lady, are sensational." I curtsied, took her hand, and escorted her toward the picnic area. We set up in a beautifully shaded area where another couple had their blankets spread out, feeding each other fruit and kissing. Bridgette smiled admirably at the couple as she sat on the blanket in the lotus position. I placed the wine bottle and the basket down before I sat.

"It's just so beautiful and picturesque here," Bridgette said, taking in the scene then, eagerly looking inside the basket to see what I packed for us.

I chuckled softly before removing the two wine glasses strapped to the cushioned top, a corkscrew, two white cotton handkerchiefs, and a spreading knife.

"Oh wow…. You thought of everything." she said, taking out one chocolate and one orange-cranberry scone wrapped in a red and white checkered cloth, an array of pre-sliced cheeses on a dome-covered tray, a bunch of dark blue grapes, sun-dried tomato hummus with sesame seed breadsticks, and a small container of clotted cream.

"You certainly know how to throw a picnic!" "I take it you've done this before." she teased, winking at me.

"Indeed, I have." I smiled, turning the corkscrew into the wine bottle, popping the cork, then pouring us a glass.

"Cheers!"

I shouted softly, raising my glass to Bridgette's.

"Cheers! Here's to more sex!" Bridgette shouted back before tipping the glass to her lips. I was practically choking at her comment, and then I laughed shyly. We stretched out across the blanket for a couple of hours, eating, drinking, and laughing at each other's jokes and sharing tales of past years. Then, we fed each other scones with mounds of clotted cream on them. I seductively licked the extra cream off her lips, causing her to moan before returning the favor.

"Oops! I think I creamed myself, too." she whispered while staring at me seductively and putting one of her hands between her legs. "You should be ashamed of yourself for doing this to me." she teased, pretending to be bashful yet alluring. "Now, I need to use the restroom to clean myself up." She crawled over to me slowly, holding the right side of her bottom lip in her mouth.

"Oh my god... You look so sexy." I whispered, becoming moist myself.

Bridgette came face to face with me, breathing deeply and holding her lips parallel to mine but not kissing me yet, taking my breath away. My breast rose and fell rapidly as I watched her slowly stand.

"There's a restroom over there next to that vending machine." I said softly after clearing my throat and pointing in that direction. "I need to use it, but I'll go when you come back. I don't want to rest the basket down in the loo."

"Okay! I'll be right back!" she responded, air-kissing and trotting to the restroom.

"Mph!" I commented, munching on a breadstick and shaking my head to distract my thoughts. I gathered the leftovers and put them back into the basket before taking another swig of the wine and tossing the half-empty bottle in the trash.

Bridgette returned and took the basket and quilt back to the vehicle while I used the bathroom. Once I returned, I hopped into the vehicle, leaned over the console, and kissed her on the cheek quickly before putting on my seatbelt and glancing at her, blushing. "Your lips are so soft." She whispered while looking lovingly over at me, causing me to blush as I slowly drove off. I picked up the speed and then yielded a mile down the road to the vehicles that were approaching from the other direction. I waited to get onto the winding road with a sign that read "Oxfordshire six miles."

"Hey Skye… I have a question for you." Bridgette rested her arm on the open window frame.

"Sure, what is it, love?"

"Do your parents know you like women?"

"Of course, they do, sweetheart… I was married to one, remember?" I softly chuckled with a look of confusion on my face quickly glancing over at her.

"Not only do they know, but they also came to the wedding, and my dad gave me away." I responded without taking my eyes off the road.

"Really?" Bridgette responded, her voice low and

shaky as we drove over a patch of road filled with gravel and small rocks, causing her to grasp onto the window frame now. 'Yup. My dad came all the way up from Yorkshire just to give me away." I informed her smiling slightly.

"Oh, your parents are divorced?" she asked surprisingly.

"Yeah, they divorced when I went to the university."

"Interesting."

We both remained silent as we listened to Donald Fagen's *"What a beautiful world this would be"* while my right hand rested on Bridgette's thigh. We arrived in Oxfordshire fifteen minutes later. I decided to break the silence with a question of my own. "Hey Bridge…do Your parents still live in Wales?"

"Oh no! My parents moved to the States about five years ago now. I'll visit with them sometime in the summer.

"Oh my God, you should come!" she squealed.

"Perhaps I will, I've never been to the states." I chuckled pulling into the small dirt driveway of my mum's fairytale English two-bedroom cottage in one of the most remote areas in Oxfordshire.

We climbed out of the truck and immediately began unloading the groceries. I lead the way to the front door located beyond a four-stair porch. I lifted the black iron door knocker on the forest green-painted wooden door decorated with yellow butterflies on a twig wreath. *Knock, knock, Knock, knock!*

"Wait a minute, wait a minute!" A high-pitched voice

shouted like that of a songbird emanated from the opposite side of the door before it opened slowly. "Skye! You naughty girl, you're late!" A large framed older woman whose voice didn't match her looks shouted. She was wearing a flower print apron around her waist, her hair was a reddish-brown curly bush, and her features were as soft as her smile. She had an oval shaped face that was slightly wrinkled, a few freckles on her cheeks and nose, and a fair complexion. My Mum reached out and hugged me so tightly, it caused me to beg for my release. "Hello mum." I beamed as I kissed her cheek.

It didn't take long for her to take notice of Bridgette, after which she leaned back and said, "Well, who's this beauty?" while trying to move her curly bush from one side of her head to the other.

"Hello!" Bridgette said pleasantly.

"Oh! Excuse my manners!" I exclaimed, turning around quickly. "Bridgette, this is my mum Anne, mum this is my good friend Bridgette; we went to university together."

"Oh! I hardly get to meet any of your university friends, pleasant meeting you sweetheart." she said, planting a kiss on both of Bridgette's cheeks. "Let's head inside, shall we?" She crossed the distressed wood threshold. "You girls come into the kitchen; I was just making tea."

"Pleasant meeting you as well." Bridgette replied shyly, closing the door behind her, and following us down the modest-sized terracotta tiled hallway.

There was a ton of natural light illuminating our way to the back of the house through a cluster of stained-glass arched windows, leading to the kitchen. We sighed in relief after finally putting down the groceries on top of the marble butcher block kitchen island. "Here mum." I said, handing her the basket of red currants then softly patting the burlap bag of quail and duck eggs, and all the vegetables.

"Oh! They had yellow beans this time I see." she said, peering into the bag. "They're lovely! Thank you, sweetheart. I'll preserve the currants tomorrow." She took a handful and began eating them, right before putting the eggs in the fridge.

"If you don't mind me saying… Bridgette said as she leaned on the isle observing mother and daughter. "I see where Skye gets her beauty from Anne." My mum and I blushed equally at her.

"I like this one." Anne teased, pointing at Bridgette before elbowing me and moving over to the stove and retrieving the freshly steeped tea inside her favorite English rose-designed teapot. Just after that, she placed six cucumbers, six eggs with watercress and six smoked salmon finger sandwiches neatly on a floral tier plate stand. "Let's take this outback, shall we?" Her mum placed her bone China milk and sugar bowls on the serving tray and walked to her backyard garden.

I took a handful of assorted butter mints from the crystal candy dish on the counter next to the sink before picking up the tier plate stand by its gold leaf shaped handle and followed her. Bridgette playfully snatched a few of the mints from my hand, hurrying before me; through the living space. Standing tall in the living space were exposed wood beams that ran horizontally across the length of the ceiling, with a tastefully worn-out upholstered green flower print armchair placed next to a small round reading table and lamp. The fluted wood burning fireplace stood alone but there was a collection of books displayed neatly on a small built-in shelf to the right of it. A variety of throw pillows were neatly arranged on a large contrasting white floral sofa under the window with matching flower curtains.

We were quite giggly as we reached the midsized backyard garden, which was as quaint as the inside of the cottage. There was lush green grass growing in between the stone pavers, and a beautiful array of colorful geraniums in front of a cracked, old masonry brick wall. I sat down next to my mum at the white metal two-seat bistro table while Bridgette admired the black metal rocking bench with an arch pergola trellis at the back of the garden, where climbing clusters of small fragrant red roses sat inside larger ones encouraging pollinating butterflies, and hummingbirds to feast. Crawling vines and moss-covered bricks on the back of the cottage wall completed the backyard's traditional old-world charm.

"How many sugars would you like, sweetheart?" Mum asked Bridgette as she splashed a bit of milk in my teacup.

"Just one, please." Bridgette responded, walking over to retrieve it.

I watched Bridgette's every move; I couldn't take my eyes off her no matter how hard I tried.

"So, Bridgette, my dear…, you live in Liverpool, I take it?" Anne asked, sipping her tea. "No, I don't." Bridgette cleared her throat as she got comfortable on the ceramic, turquoise garden stool next to the table. She held her teacup with one hand and spoke. "I live in Edinburgh; I just came to Liverpool to visit."

Our eyes locked momentarily with an unspoken understanding to say no more.

"Oh, that's nice. Well, welcome, love!" Anne exclaimed, placing her teacup on its' saucer. "Thank you," Bridgette commented as she chuckled.

We continued to chat, drink tea, and eat the tea sandwiches when Bridgette suddenly professed.

"I know you were probably expecting Skye to come alone, so, thank you for taking the time to make the extra sandwiches, Anne."

"Oh! it was no trouble at all, sweetheart." she picked up the last egg and watercress sandwich. "I tend to make more than I should anyways." she chuckled, taking a bite of the sandwich.

Bridgette felt so comfortable and welcome, it caused her to relax even more. She looked over at me bashfully before lowering her head. The evening was setting in, turning the sky into a purple haze with a burnt orange background, its' beauty silencing us as we gazed upon it. *This couldn't be a more perfect day.* I thought as I looked over and winked at Bridgette. Anne noticed my reflective mood and decided to call it a night to give us some privacy.

"Oh my!" Anne commented, after letting out a long and hearty burp, and patting her chest softly while giggling at herself.

"Mum, we'll tidy up," I assured her as we started to

gather the tray and plate tier. "Thanks love. I want to finish the last chapter of my whodunit novel before I go to bed, although I have a sneaky suspicion, I know who the killer is." She grabbed her chin repeatedly with a look of satisfaction on her face.

"Here now!" I tidied up your bedroom for ya…; so, whenever you're ready to turn in, be my guest."

"No, mum, I don't plan on staying this time."

"Nonsense! It'll be dark soon. It's too dangerous to drive on that winding road in the dark. "Besides, you always stay the night with me. You two will stay in your bedroom, and that's that!" She huffed while walking into the house and kicking off her slippers. I glanced at Bridgette and shrugged my shoulders in surrender.

"Oh well" Bridgette smiled before we followed her into the house to tidy up. "I'm going upstairs to freshen up."

She told us. When she came back, she was wearing her dressing gown and sat in her reading chair. She eagerly opened her book to the last chapter; and began reading. We put away the last dish, and I decided to make mum another cup of tea and bring it over to her before I went to bed.

"Oh, thank you, love."

She cautiously took the cup from me and placed it on the table.

"Of course. Goodnight Mum."

I kissed her on the cheek.

"Goodnight, Anne," Bridgette repeated pleasantly.

"Goodnight loves, I'll see you in the morning."

She sang with a soft smile, returning to her novel. We climbed the stairs to my bedroom at the same time

Bridgette softly smacked me on her right butt cheek.

"Oops!"

I responded unexpectedly shocked, looking back at Bridgette as she giggled. "Watch your head sweetheart. The arch is low in the hallway. Sometimes, I swear this house is shrinking! I don't remember having to watch my head as a young girl." We chuckled softly, while I shook my head. As we approached the bedroom door; I opened it to reveal a soft pink colored room with red toile patterned curtains hanging from both windows and an African violet in a small terra cotta pot on one of the window seals. There was a queen-sized bed with a matching red toile upholstered headboard and four neatly stacked bed pillows, two on either side, on top of crisp white French laced bed linen with matching bed skirt. A small white side table stood to the left of the bed with a red candlestick lamp and white shade in the center of it. There was a pine storage bench at the foot of the bed and a working wood burning fireplace directly in front of that. The chest of drawers, desk, chair, and the built-in wardrobes were all a distressed white. In the far corner of the room was a multi floral fabric, Queen Anne wingback chair; with a white crochet blanket thrown over the back of it.

"This was your room as a teen?" Bridgette asked smiling and looking around the room. "Yes. You don't like it?" I asked her with a worried look on my face.

"No, on the contrary, I think it's beautiful and well kept!" Bridgette began removing her pants and placed them on the storage bench before sitting on the bed.

"Whew!' I sighed melodramatically, wiping away the

imaginary sweat from my brow. "You can bathe first, and I'll get us a fire going, okay?"

"Absolutely! Where's the bathroom sweetheart?"

"Just next door. "I'll bring you some bed clothes in a sec. I don't want you to catch a chill on your way back." I walked over to the chest of drawers.

"You're such a sweetheart." Bridgette climbed off the bed and softly grabbed my arm, turning me around and tiptoeing for a kiss.

"Funny you say that since I think you're sweet yourself." I responded, with a slight smile, returning Bridgette's kiss and slipping my tongue in and out of her mouth while gently grabbing her hand.

"Ooh La la," … Bridgette whispered, stealing one last kiss before she backed away, releasing my hand slowly then removing her shirt, and placing it on the bed. Afterward, she pulled her hair up into a high bun; all the while looking lustfully at me then walking off to the bathroom.

I smiled coyly at her eccentric behavior and walked over to the fireplace to get the fire started. I pulled my hair back into a bun, removed my clothes, then retrieved my bathrobe from the wardrobe. "Okay, time to get Bridgette her bed clothes! I mumbled to myself animatedly. *Tap, tap, tap.*

"Hey, love," I said softly as I opened the bathroom door.

"Hey yourself."

Her eyes were closed and her face all a glow from the small beads of sweat lying on it. "I'll be out in a moment."

she mumbled. Both of her arms were dangling over the sides of the white porcelain tub, while nestling the rest of her body further down in the hot bath water.

"No worries love, take your time."

I placed the bed clothes on the closed commode cover, closed the door, and glided back to my bedroom. I decided to go downstairs for a carafe of water since the room tended to get very dry with the fireplace consistently burning throughout the night. I found my mother asleep in her reading chair with her book opened across her chest. "I *wonder whodunit.*" I thought, chuckling to myself, and removing the book to place it face down on the reading table. I took the throw blanket from the sofa and covered her with it before turning off the reading lamp and kissing her on the forehead. Then, I headed to the kitchen to fill the carafe with ice cold water. In the bedroom…. I put the carafe on the nightstand, then took the ruffled rosette applique quilt from the pine storage bench and waited patiently for Bridgette to return from her bath. Thirty minutes later…. Bridgette walked in wearing only a towel wrapped around her, and holding the bed clothes while I was lounging across the bed. "Hey love," she greeted me softly, placing the bed clothes on the storage bench as she crawled up next to me. "The bathroom is all yours." I smiled and then scooted myself to the edge of the bed. "Oh! You didn't like the bed clothes I see." "No, it isn't that… I just thought it would be too warm with the fire going and everything. I hope you don't mind." She sat up, gripped the edge of the towel, her expression doubtful.

"Of course, I don't mind. I just want you to be

comfortable…always."

After all, it *is* warm in the room now, besides, you know I sleep in the nude," I teased, swatting at Bridgette playfully. "And I can't wait to join you." I winked.

"Sounds good to me!" Bridgette replied, laying on her side now. "Hurry back, I wanna cuddle." Her voice was whinny, reflecting her unsatiable desire while she picked at the rosettes on the quilt.

I blew her an air-kiss with my butt protruding in her direction and made my way to the bathroom. Forty minutes later… I was back with my damp hair wrapped in a towel and my robe opened, exposing my curvaceous body without an ounce of shame.

"I'm back and ready to cuddle love." I whispered.

"Good, because I missed you." She whispered back, opening her eyes slowly and turning her head mesmerized at the sight of me.

I removed my head towel and pulled back the quilt, nudging my body into the warmth of the bed. I scurried over to snuggle under her. She caressed my face tenderly before sitting up to kiss and nibble on my lips in a teasing manner. I pulled her closer, holding her tightly in my arms. I started licking her lips seductively and then placed my tongue hungrily, inside her warm mouth. I moved on to her supple neck, sucking and nibbling on it passionately as she dropped her head back moaning, while one of her hands tugged at my hair. I positioned my body on top of hers while I kissed her face softly and repeatedly, running my fingers along her arm, then between her legs; making her widen them for me. I put the first two fingers of my right hand into my mouth while staring directly into her eyes, then I traced them across her sweaty belly, finally entering them inside her, slowly and steadily.

"Oh my god!" Bridgette gasped, arching her back in ecstasy while whispering…" place one more baby." I obeyed, pumping three of my fingers inside her, and simultaneously nibbling on her earlobes. "Shhh." I whispered as her moans grew louder. "Shhh love." I repeated, becoming increasingly more excited at the thrill of sneaking it.

Bridgette's flow was warm and never ending, causing me to moan into her ear and nibble on her earlobes some more, while my fingers continued to move in and out of her with a mind of their own.

"Oh my God." she crooned, grabbing onto me tightly. "Talk to me, like lovers do." she whispered. Her moans were growing increasingly more intense-and loud.

"Mm…Yes, baby, you like this, don't you?" I teased. "I can't hear you baby." I stuck my tongue in and out of her ear now.

"Yes baby! Yes! "What are you doing to me?" "It feels SOOO good." "Oh. My. God. Skye."

She was moving about wildly with pleasure, trying not to make too much noise. "Don't run love, don't run." I told her seductively. "Fuckin' take it all, baby." "You can have it." she cried to me as I buried my head in her chest all while penetrating her more passionately, prompting her to grab a pillow with all her might. She even bit into it as she climaxed, her muffled screams made me climax along with her. "Oh my god… Oh my god!" Bridgette shut her eyes, out of breath. Then she grabbed my wrist. She swallowed hard in an attempt to moisten her dry mouth.

"Hold on, love… let me pour you a glass of water."

I kissed her sweaty face while removing the hair from mine, then I reached over to the side table and poured her a glass of cold water from the carafe and handed it to her.

"Here you go sweetheart. Thank you."

She took a long gulp, then she looked at me and said, "You're incredible, you know that?" She held my right palm to her cheek. "Give me five minutes, sweetheart." She said, placing the glass on the table, then gently pushed me down to lay in my arms and falling fast asleep. I was sexually satisfied and giggled at her soft snores before falling asleep myself.

The next morning… Bridgette was awakened by the beautiful sounds of birds chirping and the smell of freshly baked bread, while she still laid in my arms.

"This feels too good to be true," she mumbled.

I chuckled and lightly pinched her cheek.

"Good morning gorgeous."

She greeted me looking up just as I was opening my eyes.

"Good morning to you, sweetheart."

I glided my hand along the side of her waist. "Did you sleep well?"

"I did, I slept like a baby!" She stretched her arm back, paused, then quickly sat up. "Oh, my goodness!" she suddenly screamed.

"What!? What is it?" I asked shockingly.

"I fell asleep on you, didn't I?" Her hand covering her

mouth in disappointment at herself.

"Don't worry about that, love. I fell asleep with you" I chuckled winking softly.

"There's such a beautiful gentleness about you Skye."

A gentleness that transcends gender. She told me with a look of admiration in her eyes. "Thank you love." I played with my curls bashfully, pondering her words. "Mm, smells like Anne is baking bread."

She began sniffing the air as she got out of bed to put on the clothes meant for the night before.

"She is!"

I told her gleefully, rolling out of the bed and putting on my robe. "She always bakes bread for us on Sunday. Let's go downstairs and get some!" I'm right behind you! We hurried downstairs to the kitchen to find mum pulling a loaf of bread out of the oven. "Good morning, loves! Did ya sleep well?"

Mum carefully placed the hot pan on the island.

"Yes, we did!"

We said in unison then looked at each other and giggled like schoolgirls. The kitchen table was adorned with a dish of soft sweet butter, a small platter of fried quail eggs, apricot and blueberry preserves, a jar of lemon curd, clotted cream, and a pile of thickly sliced baked bread covered by a white lace silk cloth. In the corner was a basket of hot crossed buns and a small tray of rustic lemon poppy seed scones, a pitcher of fresh squeezed orange juice, and a teapot of English breakfast tea with an old ceramic milk jug full of wildflowers from the garden in the center of it all.

"It's so nice to have someone around that I can look

after." Anne gave us the warmest smile one could give.

"Wow, this is certainly a feast!" Bridgette stated.

"Yes, I bake enough for the friends at church."

As we sat down to eat breakfast, we talked about the whodunit novel, laughing at mum's detailed description of the ending until it was almost time to take her to Sunday service. "Alright, ladies, the roast is in the oven." she said, excusing herself from the table.

"You are staying for lunch aren't you, loves?" mum asked us with a worried look on her face while bagging up the leftovers she was taking with her. I looked over at Bridgette who immediately replied...

"Of course! I'd love to have lunch with you, Anne"

"Good! Then it's settled!"

Mum was smiling from ear to ear before we all went upstairs to get dressed, mum returning downstairs to meet us in her Sunday best.

"I'm ready!" she sang, her arms spread wide awaiting compliments on her outfit.

"You look beautiful."

Bridgette told her.

"Indeed!"

I chimed in, making my mum's cheeks turn red before we made our way to the truck.

"Oh! What's this?"

Mum picked up the basket of strawberries Bridgette left on the passenger seat.

"Oh!"

Bridgette exclaimed. I forgot about those. Mum handed her the basket; she grabbed one and nibbled on it. After we dropped mum off, we returned to the cottage to tidy up, storing the remaining strawberries in the fridge. Then we fooled around, and listened to music until it was time to pick mum up from the service. Bridgette laid on her back with her head on my lap as we listened to Leo Sayer's *"When I need you"* My head resting on the back of the sofa, with my hand gently resting on the top of Bridgette's head.

"Hey Bridge." I spoke up randomly as I lifted my head.

"May I ask you a question." My tone was uncommonly serious.

"Sure, go-ahead sweetheart." Bridgette stared at the ceiling as she waited for me to break the silence.

"I know you're going home soon…" I started stroking her hair. "But I just wanted to know if…"

"Damn it! Bridgette belted out, interrupting me, and sitting up rapidly. "I was having so much fun with you that I forgot to call the Inn to extend my stay!"

"That's right! I mumbled, taken aback by her sudden intensity.

"Right, right… I forgot about that myself"

"They have my credit card on file, but I think I ought to call them. I don't want them to think I abandoned my things." She said, her hand resting on my thigh while biting at the skin on her bottom lip in contemplation.

"Where's the phone Hun?" she asked, tapping my thigh rapidly.

"It's over there," I pointed. "On the table by the staircase."

"Thanks, love, it'll just take a minute." She said, walking swiftly to the phone.

"No worries, Hun. Take your time."

I smiled.

"I *wonder if she realizes how rude she can be sometimes.*" I thought. I was awoken from my reverie by the oven's timer going off, alerting me the roast was done. I turned the stove off, and then used the bathroom next to the pantry. When I glanced at the time, I realized it was time to pick up mum. Bridgette was finished with her phone call, so, we got in the vehicle and within ten minutes, pulled up to the church just as the parishioners and the Pastor were heading out.

I spotted my mum gesturing for me to come over.

"I'll be right back sweetheart." I told Bridgette as I got out of the truck and closed the door.

"I'll be here!" she shouted playfully getting into the back seat, softly chuckling. I looked back at her and winked, blowing an air-kiss.

"You remember my daughter Skye, don't you pastor Ogilvie?"

"Why of course I do! How are you, young lady?"

"I'm doing well! Thank you, Pastor Ogilvie."

"Will I see you next Sunday then?"

"No, I'm afraid not Pastor."

"Well, why not?"

He looked at me with a puzzled expression, clutching his bible, while my mum pretended to cough, looking away. "Well, I live in Liverpool now. I smiled softly while putting my hair behind my right ear. "Besides, I don't go to church much anymore."

"Oh! I'm sorry to hear that, Skye. But if you ever change your mind, our doors are always open." He reached over to hug me. I thanked him, then began walking back to the truck while mum told him she'll see him next Sunday. "It was a wonderful service." Mum told us, adjusting herself in the seat. "You should try and come with me next Sunday when you visit, Skye… it's just like it was when you were a girl.

"Yeah Skye, you should go next Sunday when you visit."

Bridgette teased. I smiled at her through the rearview mirror then chuckled.

"Perhaps I will mum, but I'm not promising you anything, and I'm pretty sure it's nothing like it was when I was a girl."

My mum smiled at me, then said... "Oh! You're more than welcome to come along Bridgette!"

"Thank you, Anne! I'll consider it." At the cottage…. "Alright girls, I'll get out of these clothes and freshen up. If you don't mind setting the table, we can have lunch before you head back home." Of course, we will mum."

"Oh!" she said, pausing midway up the stairs and looking at me.

"I made your favorite dessert."

"Yes!" I licked my lips and started taking out the dinnerware.

"You guys can't seriously be this sweet? can you?"

Bridgette teased with one eyebrow raised. "Well…" I said in a high-pitched voice while hunching my shoulders. We both laughed setting the table. When Mum returned, we feasted on succulent roast beef wrapped inside of crispy, golden-brown pastry surrounded by thick gravy made from the drippings, a side of roasted potatoes, and a mix of steamed carrots, and cabbage. There was also a gravy boat added in case someone wanted extra. We ate, laughed, and became more acquainted with Bridgette.

"Do you girls have room for Skye's favorite dessert?" Mum asked, smiling. "Indeed!" I shouted out.

"I believe I can make room for dessert."

Bridgette chimed in.

"Good!"

Mum exclaimed, excusing herself from the table to retrieve it.

"By the way… what is your favorite dessert, Skye?" Bridgette asked, looking lovingly at me.

"Why…it's sticky. Toffee. Pudding sweetheart, what else would it be?" I said seductively, biting my bottom lip.

"Mph." was all Bridgette could muster as she licked her lips slowly.

"Here we are!" Mum called out, interrupting our flirting session. "I'm sorry, honey! But I ran out of brandy and had to use bourbon instead.

"Oh! That's perfectly alright Mum, I'm thankful you took the time to prepare it for me." I scoffed down a spoonful of it and belted out "Mm!" with my eyes closed, savoring the moment.

"Umm mmm! Anne, you out did yourself, this is delectable. I think this might be the best one I've had thus far!" Bridgette complimented her.

"Oh, stop it!" She waved her hand and blushed.

When we were through with lunch, we helped Mum clear the table and clean the kitchen while singing along to one of my favorite songs as a teenager. the Culture Clubs *"Do you really want to hurt me."* Afterward, we retired to the living space for about thirty minutes, during which time Mum gossiped about the day's church events. Finally, we gave Mum farewell hugs and kisses. Bridgette thanked her for her hospitality then followed me out toward the truck. "Sweetheart, you're welcome to come back any time." Mum yelled softly at Bridgette as she watched us smiling from the doorway.

On the ride back to Liverpool… Bridgette grew silent, staring off into space again.

"Is everything all right, sweetheart?" I intermittently glanced over at her as we approached the winding road.

"Yes, Hun." she responded, clearing her throat. "I'll be fine, just thinking is all." She smiled at me and then bowed her head.

"Okay love. I'm here if you wanna talk about anything. Anything at all."

The silence remained so I decided to play Steely Dan's greatest hits CD.

"I wish I didn't have to go home." Bridgette finally broke the silence but continued to stare out the window.

I was at a loss for words, I reached over and took her hand empathetically.

"I adore your sweet emotions." she said. I could feel her watching me drive. I raised her hand to my mouth, and kissed it gently, all while keeping my eyes on the road.

We arrived in Liverpool two hours later. "Would you like me to take you to the Inn to pick up your things? It's not far from here." I asked her, stopping at the fork in the road. "Yes! I told them I'd pick up my things tomorrow, but why wait, right?"

I took a left and within fifteen minutes, was entering the Inn's parking lot.

"Need help with your things, love?" I asked as I turned off the ignition.

"Sure… I'd like that." Her voice was melancholic as she descended the truck.

In the Inn, we took the elevator to the fifth floor and walked to room 522, where Bridgette looked through her tote for the card key. "Got it!" she exclaimed with relief before placing the card key on the wireless doorknob.

"Oh, wow, this is lovely." I crooned, looking around the yellow and black room. "I didn't expect the room to look like this."

Bridgette closed the door and locked it behind her, then took my hand and led me to the king-sized bed with its black velvet tufted headboard; and the finest gold-colored fitted sheets encasing the mattress. She laid me down on the bed and began kissing me passionately, placing her leg gently across my belly.

"I've been craving this *all day*" I slowly rolled Bridgette over and returned the favor. "Didn't you promise them you would pick up your things tomorrow?"

I asked, looking down at her tenderly.

"Yes." she whispered, reaching up to touch my hair.

"Why don't we stay here tonight?" I said unbuttoning her pants, not waiting for an answer.

"I like your place better, but; why the hell not?" she said, kissing my teeth because I was smiling widely.

Then she playfully rolled me onto my back quickly and straddling me, while unbuttoning *my* pants now. "Oh! You wanna play rough huh?" I teased, reaching up and tickling her. She was laughing hysterically and trying so hard to get away, she almost fell to the floor. "Whoops!" I called out, catching her by the shirt.

"Whew, that was close!" she said, stealing a quick kiss and then asking… "Would you like a nightcap love?"

"Absolutely! I don't have to drive anymore tonight so… yes!" I returned her kiss before letting her go to the mini bar.

"Hmm, there's only gin and vodka here. Pick your poison, love."

She smiled. "It doesn't matter sweetheart, surprise me."

Bridgette concocted a simple gin and tonic for herself and a vodka and soda for me, then she brought over the drinks which we gulped down, removed our clothes, and jumped into the bed.

"I'm really enjoying myself with you Skye." She said before laying in my arms.

"I'm enjoying myself too, sweetheart."

"Do you mind if I turned out the lights and closed the drapes?" she asked.

"Not at all."

Bridgette hurried out of bed, turned off the lights and closed the gold brocade drapes, quickly returning to my arms. "Do you mind if we didn't have sex tonight, Skye? I'm a bit tired." I don't mind sweetheart. I kissed her on the forehead appreciating her sincerity. We kissed and cuddled throughout the night before ultimately falling asleep, back-to-back.

Knock, knock, knock.

"HOUSEKEEPING!" A gentleman's voice yelled out from beyond the door. "NO, THANK YOU!" Bridgette yelled back, her voice raspy and dry. "What a way to wake up, huh?"

I said, rubbing my eyes, not fully awake yet.

"Sorry about that love, what time is it anyway?" she asked, rhetorically, looking around for a clock.

"Time to get up apparently." I responded dryly, yawning, and getting out of bed. I walked to the bathroom to relieve myself and take a shower.

After my shower, I found Bridgette in her underwear and her luggage by the door. "Wow! You didn't waste any time, did you sweetheart?" I teased.

"Nope!" Bridgette chuckled, her finger lightly tapping my nose as she passed me on her way to the bathroom. Fifteen minutes later… "All done!" she shouted, coming out of the bathroom fully dressed. She grabbed her tote, put on her jacket, and met me at the door. We both took a suitcase and rolled it down the corridor towards the elevators and down to the lobby.

"Good morning, I'm checking out of room 522." she told the front desk gentleman as she handed him the card keys.

"Good morning, very well. Did you enjoy your stay?" he asked her, looking up from the computer.

"I did indeed."

She said winking at me and making me blush on my way out the door.

"Very well then, you're all set. We hope to see you again, have a good day." he said, handing Bridgette the receipt.

"Thank you!" She said softly, quickly waving goodbye and meeting me at the truck where I had already put the luggage in the tray.

She got in and we drove out of the parking lot. "I'm hungry, but I don't want anything heavy." she said, rubbing her belly and grimacing. "You're in luck my sweet, I know just the place!" I told her, making a right turn at the corner.

Moments later, I pulled up to the Tabak Café. I parked in front and fed the meter before we went inside.

As soon as we took our seats, I ordered eggs Benedict, roasted ham with an espresso, and Bridgette ordered the eggs Florentine with mushrooms and spinach alongside an Americano with cream. We savored our delicious breakfast; I paid the bill and tipped the waiter then drove back to my place. While Bridgette put her luggage in her bedroom, I decided to reschedule my appointments to the following week so I could focus on her.

"That was easy." I said, smiling after hanging up the telephone and watching Bridgette go through my music collection.

"What would you like to do now Bridge?"

"Take a guess!" Bridgette yelled then took off running upstairs.

"I don't mind if I do!" I ran after her.

The week that followed was nothing short of a whirlwind romance. We took tango lessons at a nearby dance studio, ate delicious BBQ dishes on the rooftop of a social club, and took a trip to the Liverpool Empire Theater to watch a hilarious comedy where Bridgette was constantly grabbing my hand when the lights dimmed.

On Saturday morning, we enjoyed a breakfast of porridge and fresh fruit out on the gazebo while admiring the sun's sparkling reflection on the lake. Afterward, we went back inside and sat on the sofa to watch an old black and white classic movie called *"Paris Blues"* starring Sydney Poitier and Diahann Carroll. I was seated between Bridgette's legs, and she was massaging my scalp with her dainty fingers. Every now and then, I would throw my head back for a kiss. It was dreamy- so dreamy, in fact, that we fell asleep. We woke up a couple of hours later, with the back of my head lying on Bridgett's belly, and Bridgette was lying on one of the sofa pillows, staring up at the ceiling.

"I'm so relaxed with you." I told her, sitting up slowly.

"I know. I feel the same way." she responded, scratching her head, and stretching out her legs.

"So, love, remember when I tried to ask you a question at my mum's before you had to call the inn?"

"Mm-hmm."

"Well… I wanted to ask you if we could continue seeing one another. Like, in a relationship." My nerves were on pins and needles while I waited for her response.

"Oh wow, I didn't expect you to ask *that*." she chuckled apprehensively.

After a moment of silence, she asked, "Can we talk about this some other time?"

"Of course, sweetheart." I reached out for her hand and kissed it. "Of course." I repeated. "Okay, now that that's out of the way, did you by chance, pack any evening wear?" I asked as I stood on my two feet.

"I did!" "Where are we going!" She grinned.

"Well, since this is our last day together, I would like to have a lovely dinner at one of my favorite restaurants. It's an elegant and romantic place."

"My lady, I would love to have a romantic dinner with you tonight, and I have the perfect dress for it actually." Bridgette slipped off the sofa, regained her balance and curtsied jokingly again.

"Terrific! Let's go and get dressed then, shall we?" I took her hand, and we made our way upstairs, neither of us letting go. Once we arrived at the top landing, we kissed and went our separate ways.

Half an hour later… Bridgette yelled softly into my room while holding on to the door frame…" I'll meet you downstairs, beautiful."

"Okay! I'll be down in five minutes! I yelled back from the bathroom.

Bridgette walked downstairs but was too anxious to sit, so she stood by the sofa instead. Moments later…I descended the stairs wearing a little black dress with a black motorcycle jacket, red patent leather stilettos, and a matching clutch. My lips were lathered with a dark red matte shade, and my curls were tight and full of luster.

"Wow, Skye, you look like a movie star." Bridgette whispered in awe, unable to take her eyes off me.

"What, this old thing?" I teased, turning around slowly

so Bridgette could take it all in. "Indeed!" she said, fanning herself and panting playfully.

"You're one to talk. Look at you…; you're beautiful, love!" I exclaimed.

"Who me?" Bridgette teased, pointing at herself, and showing off her figure in her rose gold sequined cocktail dress. A pair of nude pumps, nude lipstick, and a rose gold sequined purse to match. Bridgette walked over to me and kissed me gently. "Shall we go?"

"Yes indeed, after you, my love." I opened the door for her and locked it behind me.

We both got in the truck and drove forty-five minutes to Kloss Maggiore, one of the most romantic French restaurants in Covent Garden, where the valet whistled at us as I handed over the keys. We were both flattered and smiling as we walked into the restaurant. "Reservations for two." I told the hostess at the podium, who called the general manager over to show us to our seats. I reserved a table next to the fireplace, which was the best of four rooms with white tablecloths, a bar, and faux Italian white lilies hanging from the ceiling.

"This is breathtaking, Skye." she said softly looking around in utter awe. "Thank you" Bridgette told the general manager as he pulled out her chair. "And thank you, Skye." She repeated, looking at mc lovingly. "For what, sweetheart?"

"For being such a magnificent person."

"Aww, love." It's my pleasure." I felt the urge to lean in for a kiss, but in that instant, the waiter showed up with the wine list and starter menus.

"Thank you." we repeated in unison, smiling at each other.

Bridgette opened the wine list while I opened the starter menu. Moments later…. The sommelier came over and took Bridgette's order for Alsace, a sweet, French white wine he poured tableside.

In contrast, I ordered sparkling mineral water with a slice of lime.

I opted for the warmed spiced parsnip soup with toasted walnuts, the red wine braised beef cheek, and Jerusalem artichokes with English black truffles for my main course. Whereas Bridgette ordered a starter of scallops, smoked mussels, shitake, and leek chowder; and for her main course, she ordered Scottish roasted hake fish with shaved fennel, orange, and saffron kalamansi sauce. We initially ate silently because the food was so divine, often looking at each other endearingly. The ambiance, the surrounding patron's conversation, the clinking of glasses toasting, and the classical piano music in the background all added to the majesty of the moment. This was the perfect culmination of my week-long romance with Bridgette, but most especially on our last night together. Henri Salvador's, "*Chambre Avec Vue*," began playing in the background as Bridgette ate her last bite of hake. She swayed her head to the music while picking up her wine and taking intermittent sips. I reached my hand across the table, took her hand, and smiled. "I haven't been this happy in a long time.

Who would've thought I'd run into you at the pub that night?"

"Life is unpredictable, and sometime, in the best way possible." she said, looking at me lovingly. I maintained my grip on her hand, just listening to her. I had already expressed my feelings and didn't want to push the idea of an ongoing romance, so I sat silently, admiring her.

We finished dinner and ordered dessert to share, a wild honey and vanilla Crème Brulé. We cracked the shell together before feeding it to each other and teasing as we licked the caramelized sugar slowly off our lips. We sat there enjoying each other's company while looking at the crackling fire and playing "footsie" until the waiter approached us with the bill.

"Oh! Thank you." I reached out for it. "I guess that's our cue" I joked. I paid the check, and the valet brought the truck around and opened the door for Bridgette, insisting I wait for him to come around to the driver's side to open mine. He came around, opened my door, and refused my tip. "I think the two of you are very beautiful, so this is my gift." He bowed his head and backed away. "Aww, thank you!" we yelled out the window as I pulled off. I reached over and took Bridgette's hand, rubbing it against my cheek and then holding it on my lap the entire forty-five-minute drive back home as we listened to Queen Latifah's rendition of Phoebe Snow's *"Poetry Man."*

Once at the house, we kicked off our shoes and unzipped each other's dresses as we made our way upstairs.

"Come take a bath with me." I said, reaching out my hand.

Bridgette took it without saying a word. "Wait a

minute, sweetheart, let me put my dress in my suitcase; you run the water, and I'll be right back." She winked, running to the bedroom.

"I thought you would appreciate some bubbles tonight." I said as Bridgette walked into the bathroom wearing nothing but her birthday suit, just as I blew the suds from my hands at her. "I do, indeed!" Bridgette laughed. "What a large tub!" I reached out to assist her, then she submerged her body into the water. "Ahh… this feels nice," Bridgette floated over to me, removing my wet hair from my face before kissing my forehead, then she traced her kiss to my lips, while a small amount of sudsy water fell onto the bathroom floor. We were so consumed by the heat of the moment that we didn't notice it.

"You make me feel…." I began to say, but Bridgette shushed me by kissing me. "Wow." I whispered, my eyes closing slowly as Bridgette turned around and snuggled between my legs. I wrapped my arms around her and closed my eyes briefly. Then I lowered my head and planted gentle kisses on the side of her neck.

"Mm, that feels good, love." she whispered.

I continued kissing her while softly moaning, and running my hands across her breasts, pinching her nipples, causing her to pant rapidly and bite her bottom lip as the sensation ran through her.

"Love…" She whispered.

"Yes, Sweetheart?" I replied in between kisses.

"Can we take this to dry land?" she asked, her breaths becoming deeper with each rise and fall of her chest.

"Umm-hmm." I replied, still kissing, and pinching her

nipples until she delicately grasped my fingers.

"Wash my back, love." she said moving forward, reaching for the bath sponge hanging from the free-standing faucet knob and handing it to me.

I lathered the bath sponge with the lemon verbena body wash I had on the wooden stool near the tub and slowly washed her back, then the rest of her body. "Turn around, sweetheart." I told her before using some lemon sugar scrub on her feet. "All done."

"Yes! It's my turn." Bridgette belted out.

"Turn around, love." she told me sweetly, getting on her knees. She began washing my back while I held my hair up.

"Let me help you out, sweetheart; I don't want you to miss a spot."

I teased, looking over my shoulder and winking before I bent over to allow her between my legs.

"Oh, my god." she said seductively as she washed between my legs, simultaneously squeezing out the sponge over my golden humps.

I was moaning the entire time. I turned around, took the sponge from her, letting it fall into the water, and tongue kissed her slowly. We used the detachable shower head to rinse our bodies, then got out of the tub and dried each other off. We walked into the bedroom, got in bed, and made love, slowly and purposefully, crying out in ecstasy; each of us panting from exhaustion when we were done, then falling fast asleep.

The next morning…. I kissed Bridgette on her cheek, careful not to wake her before I drove to my favorite bakery and picked up two flaky short-crust pastries topped with almonds and whipped cream, classically known as Bakewell Tarts, in addition to two large lattes. When I returned to the house, Bridgette was descending the stairs, wearing my robe.

"Oh! You're up! Good morning, love." I said, smiling and walking over to the dining table.

"Good morning beautiful, where are you coming from?" she asked pleasantly.

"I figured we'd have something classic and sweet this morning." I told her, removing the tarts from the bag and the lattes from the coffee holder.

"Yummy!" she responded, picking up the latte, sitting down and having a sip. "Delicious! Thanks, love."

"You're most welcome, sweetheart, and you look wonderful in that robe." I commented, grinning and handing Bridgette her tart.

"I woke up, and you were gone, so I needed your arms wrapped around me until you returned." she told me, blushing and biting into her tart. I sat down, and we enjoyed our tart, looking out the window at nothing specific. "I meant to ask you this earlier, sweetheart; what time does your train leave?" I asked, wiping whipped cream from the corners of her mouth.

"Three o'clock," she responded somberly, taking her last tart bite.

I paid close attention to her tone and body language as the conversation continued but kept my comments to myself. "It's eleven thirty now, and driving to the station takes about forty minutes, so we'll leave early to avoid traffic delays." I stared at her as she stared out of the window. "Let's cuddle and listen to music before we leave, if that's all right?" she said, turning from the window.

"Of course, sweetheart."

We left our empty latte cups on the dining table and moved to the sofa. "What would you like to listen to, sweetheart?" I asked her.

"I don't care, love, pick anything." Bridgette was looking sadder by the second.

I walked over to the music player and chose Stevie Wonder's greatest hits, with *"Love's in Need of Love Today"* being the first song.

We sat in each other's arms, listening to the music until I softly kissed her on her cheek and told her it was time to leave. Reluctantly, Bridgette went upstairs, dressed, and then I helped her bring her luggage to the truck before proceeding to the highway to take her to the train station.

This time, Bridgette initiated the handholding as I kept my eye on the road. I was very pleased with her display of affection. We arrived at the station at 2 pm, giving us plenty of time to say goodbye.

"I had the best time ever!" I told her, gently taking her hand for one last time. She smiled softly and repeated it. We sat at a table in the coffee shop chatting until we heard, "ALL ABOARD!" from the train conductor who pulled the train whistle at 2:30.

Bridgette hugged me tightly before kissing me softly. "Goodbye, sweetheart." I said softly while returning to her embrace. I took her hand and squeezed it gently before letting it go slowly as I backed away, blowing her air kisses as she boarded the train. She tried to return every one of them. "Call me." I gestured, putting my hand to my ear; Bridgette gestured that she would with a nod, looking at me through the train window. I stood on the platform until I could no longer see her, shaking my head as I slowly walked back to my truck because I was missing her already.

Later that evening…. she called me when she reached home, and we laughed and reminisced about our week together. Yet, after that phone call, I heard nothing. I called her, but she never answered. I occasionally became misty-eyed, asking myself questions daily like... "Did I say something wrong the last time we spoke?" "I thought she enjoyed being with me," and "What's really going on?"

Luckily, my schedule picked up greatly the next couple of weeks, and I found myself increasingly distracted without the luxury of spare time to think about Bridgette or our time together. One day, the phone rang. I deliberately took my time to answer because I was caught up with my sessions and a little down in the dumps. "Hello?" I answered with a deep sigh, plopping myself on the sofa.

"Skye. It's me, Bridgette."

I nearly dropped the phone. The last person I expected to hear from was Bridgette.

"Hello, Bridgette. How are you?" I asked, clearing my throat, not knowing if I should be mad or elated at hearing from her after all this time. All sorts of thoughts were going through my mind at this point.

"Skye, please forgive me for disappearing from you so

abruptly. You see, I was selling my marital home because I couldn't handle all the memories I shared with my husband here, and to my surprise, I had a buyer the day after my return."

The smile on my face was so wide and beautiful it made me blush, seeing my reflection in my new wall mirror. Bridgette's heart skipped a beat because she couldn't tell if I was happy or upset.

"Skye are you there, love?" she asked nervously.

"Yes, sweetheart, I'm here. I want too always be here for you.

I understand that things happen, love, but never disappear on me like that again, please." "I understand, love. I apologize. If you forgive me, I promise I'll never do that again." "Do you pinky swear?" I asked her playfully.

"I pinky swear." she responded, smiling from ear to ear. "But now I need something from you, okay?"

"Okay. What is it, sweetheart?" I responded anxiously.

"I need you to be patient with me."

"I've never been with a woman before; hell, I've never thought about being with one. But you, I want someone like you to love me, Skye. You fascinate me. You brought out a strange change in me, and I love it! I didn't believe I had space in my heart for anyone else."

"I can't explain this feeling, sweetheart."

"Aww, baby." I interjected softly, my hand across my heart.

"When I think of us, it brings me insurmountable joy, and I want to kiss and touch you. I'm honored to share sweet emotions and ecstasy with you, Skye." So..." she said in a childlike tone. "You wanna be my girlfriend?" Bridgette squeezed her eyes shut and crossed her fingers.

"What!" I yelled, my hand on my head. "Hell, yeah, I want to be your girlfriend!" I screamed, and we both started laughing. "I got a girlfriend! I got a girlfriend." I crooned, slowly dancing around in a circle, and then bumping my shin on the sofa's base. "She said yes.

She said yes!" Bridgette sang.

"Now, I need something from you." "Anything, love." She chuckled.

"When are you going to invite me to your new flat so we can christen it?" I asked seductively.

"I thought you'd never ask." Bridgette replied, returning the seduction. "I moved to Birmingham in an amazing one-bedroom flat with the most incredible views and within walking distance of downtown; I can't wait for you to see it!"

"You live in *Birmingham*! Say no more, sweetheart; give me the address. I'll forward my calls when I arrive."

"Yay!" Bridgette yelled out.

"Okay. Wait, wait, wait! I have to get a pen! Hold on, my love!" I yelled cheerfully, kissing into the phone before dropping it and running to retrieve a pen and pad. "Okay, I'm back, sweetheart." I said, breathing heavily into the phone while Bridgette chuckled at me. "Okay, I live in the Allegro apartments, 46 The Priory Queensway, Birmingham B5 6FS, 3rd floor.

"Oh, my darling... I cannot wait to see you again!" Bridgette exclaimed as she held the phone snugly to her ear with both hands.

"Neither can I, sweetheart, neither can I. I'll be there in approximately two hours."

"Okay, love… I'll see you soon. she said, kissing at me through the phone. I hung up the receiver slowly.

"Is this real…? I *have* a *whole girlfriend*!? *Who would've thought that!*" I whispered, holding my cheek in disbelief of my newfound love. I couldn't help but scream "Yes! Repeatedly at the top of my lungs before running upstairs to pack my bags, my curls dancing along the way.

The Sugar Cookie

Monique is a twenty-nine-year-old feminine, aggressive, brown-skinned lesbian of average build with voluptuous breasts that fit a D cup and thick shoulder-length hair that she keeps in a protective style of cornrows braided toward the back of her head. She likes to date casually and hasn't been in a serious relationship for five years. She vowed to steer clear of commitment after her ex-girlfriend broke her heart by leaving her for a man. Monique has the luxury of living off the trust fund her mother left her. Yet her passion for television prompted her decision to attend college and major in advertising marketing, landing a job with a major advertising company soon after graduation. She loves kids but hasn't decided if she wants to be a mother. She is known for sporting the occasional French-manicured nails and wearing a designer gold link necklace with a matching bracelet, diamond stud earrings, and a gold band ring on every other finger, including her thumbs.

Wanda is a tall thirty-three-year-old, brown-skinned lesbian with an athletic build, washboard abs (that she likes to show off at every opportunity), and pencil-thin legs who coaches the University of Maryland's women's basketball team. Enduring a childless life of singledom for far too long, she's in search of a God-fearing, sport-loving girlfriend, and she is willing to wait for her for as long as it takes.

Kendra is a thick-haired, strawberry-blonde, White lesbian of twenty-eight years who's the spitting image of the teenage Alicia Silverstone. She likes to dance and work out to maintain her toned body. She has an average build and moderate-sized breasts, a plump derriere, and well-defined legs, and she works as a disc jockey for a local radio station in her hometown. She is currently single, has no children, and is often attracted to women of African-American descent, no matter how they identify.

Keisha is a thirty-two-year-old petite, brown-skinned lesbian who stands five feet tall. Three years ago, she gave birth to twin girls, Alana and Donna, via in vitro fertilization with her ex-girlfriend. She has large breasts, a modest derriere, and a little muffin top to accompany them. She's currently single and works as a personal administrative assistant to the vice president of a large life insurance company. She's avoiding the dating scene until her children are of school age. Her ex-girlfriend has a fiancé with whom she gets along well, and they all play a positive role in the children's lives.

Denise is a Black, light-skinned lesbian with hourglass curves, thick thighs, and calves. She is known for always wearing high heels and clothes that hug her body too tightly. Her signature features are scarlet, red lipstick, and long curved fingernails. She's single, has neither children nor the desire to give birth to them, and has worked as a court stenographer for the last eight years.

All these ladies met at the grand opening of the Lesbian club The Sugar Cookie two years ago (except Kendra) and have remained friends since then.

The vanilla honeys are out tonight! Monique cheered, pointing at the women on the VIP line going into the club.

"Ain't that nothing? They must have a celebrity White DJ tonight or something, I guess," Keisha responded dryly.

"I'm not gonna lie, though. A few of them are kinda *fine*." Wanda teased, letting out a whistle.

"Give me a break! Don't they have their own club to go to? Shit, we can't have anything of our own. Damn shame! I bet all of them ain't even lesbians." Denise belted out, rolling her eyes.

"Well, that's not stopping me from talking to that blonde if I see her when we get inside. I know that!" Monique said, glaring at the crowd and grabbing her chin with confidence.

"You're just a hoe," Keisha said, making them all laugh hysterically.

"Whatever! Besides, God didn't put all these ladies out here, so I could only play with one of them!" Monique smiled sinisterly.

Keisha started fanning her off while the others shook their heads at her comment.

"You think like a man," Wanda finally said while rummaging through her purse for her wallet ID.

"Yeah, whatever works." Monique responded

shamelessly, hunching her shoulders and chuckling.

"All I know is I gotta use the bathroom..." Denise chimed in as they approached the entry door.

"Well, I hope you can hold it because you know those lines are *hella* long. And I take it you don't remember that there's only one toilet in each bathroom?" Keisha asked.

FOR REAL! the others shouted in unison, including the women behind them. They all burst out laughing together. Once inside.... Denise joined the line to one of the bathrooms, and just as Keisha predicted, they were both hella long.

"Oh, hell yeah! That's my jam! "*Mr. Lover Man*, Shabba!" Monique shouted as she whined her body to the bar, Keisha and Wanda directly behind her.

"Hey! How can I help you?" the female bartender greeted them, leaning forward to hear Monique better.

"Hey! Let me get a rum and coke, please." Monique shouted over the counter.

"Are you guys together?" She gestured with her index finger at Keisha and Wanda.

"Oh! Yes. Yes, we are," Monique answered, turning around quickly. "Hey Keisha! What you drinking?"

"Oh, umm... Let me get a wine spritzer."

"A what? Monique shouted, her hand cupping her ear so she could hear better.

"A wine SPRITZER!" Keisha repeated.

"Oh, my God, she wants a wine spritzer. This isn't the country club, honey." Monique shook her head, chuckling. "Wanda, what are you drinking?

"I don't know. Get me what you're drinking?" She

popped a mint in her mouth and winded her hips to the beat.

Monique turned to the bartender and said, "Okay, let me get two rum and cokes and a wine spritzer!"

"No problem." The bartender began mixing their drinks.

"Hey, what about me?" Denise asked, walking quickly over to them.

"Oh! What do you want? Hurry up! It's getting crowded over here."

"Okay, hold up, dang," Denise replied with a slight attitude. "Let me have a gin and tonic."

"A gin and tonic!" They all shouted with bug-eyed expressions.

"That's an old man's drink, girl!" Monique teased, yet turned around and told the bartender anyway. Monique handed them their drinks as the bartender handed them to her.

Afterward, they all walked toward the dance floor. *"Your body can't lie to me!"* Denise and Wanda sang out with Shabba Ranks and Maxi Priest, whining their bodies to the dance floor, Keisha and Monique following their lead. When the song stopped, they all walked near the wall to get out of the way of the other dancers.

"Hey!" Keisha tapped Monique on her arm to get her attention.

"Yeah, what's up?" Monique bent down so her ear was closer to Keisha's mouth.

"There are two floors here, right?"

"Nah, it's three floors." Monique sipped her drink

through the straw while scanning the room for the blonde.

"Oh wow! How did I forget that?" "What type of music do they play upstairs again?" She tapped Monique's arm again, this time in earshot of Denise and Wanda as they gathered closer.

"You still got mommy brain, huh?" Monique asked, chuckling. "Okay, so… as you can hear, this floor (pointing to the floor) is reggae and R&B. I believe the second floor is still house music, and the third is techno, soft rock, and pop music."

"Oh! Now I see why Blondie and her gang are here, then." Denise yelled out to Wanda, and they both giggled notoriously while Wanda held up her hand, waiting for Denise to give her a high five. "You don't have a bit of sense."

Wanda giggled and then took a sip of her drink.

Monique pretended not to hear them but secretly smiled and shook her head. She was set on having fun and didn't bother entertaining Denise's comment. *"Show Me Love"* by Robin S started playing, calling everyone back to the dance floor. They sang along and danced until they broke out in a sweat. A masculine-presenting, brown-skinned woman walked up to Denise and started dancing on her from behind, causing Denise to turn around and dance with her face to face. She was pretty. Her auburn-black, ombre locs rested on her shoulders, and her diamond nose ring looked good on her. The scent of Egyptian musk and the naturally occurring pheromones in the sweat emanating from inside her red button-down shirt intoxicated Denise, drawing her closer. Her dark denim jeans fit her body just right, and her masculine loafers were worn in the ultimate feminine way. She was a bundle of beautiful contradictions. But Denise knew how she identified. "What's your name, sweetheart?" She leaned in to ask Denise.

"Denise. she answered, blushing. "What's yours?

"My name is Tracey."

"Nice to meet you, Tracey." Denise was smiling wide, pretending to look around for her friends.

"So, are you single, Denise?" Her smile was half-cocked.

"Yes, I am." She continued to dance casually, still smiling. "Wait a minute… (she stopped dancing) Are *you* single?" Denise looked at her seriously as she waited for a response. "Yup, I sure am." Tracey's smile broadened, and then she licked her lips.

The record stopped, so they left the dance floor to talk, but… Gyptian's record *"Hold You"* began to play, calling them back to the dance floor. Tracey put her arm around Denise's waist as they whined, their bodies close together, forgetting that others were on the dance floor until the record finished playing. Tracey pulled a handkerchief from her jeans' back pocket, wiped the sweat from her forehead, and then tied some of her locs in a knot on top of her head before dabbing Denise's.

"Ooh! Thank you!" Denise said, frowning as she quickly removed Tracey's hand. She backed up slowly, instantly regretting it out of fear that she embarrassed her. *I hope she still asks me out later,* she thought to herself.

"Sorry… I didn't mean to invade your space like that.

Would you like a refill on your drink?" Tracey pointed at her empty cup.

Before Denise could respond, Keisha tapped her shoulder and said, "Denise, we're going to check out the scene upstairs."

"Okay." Denise responded bluntly and turned her attention back to Tracey. "Yes, please! But I'd like water instead." She handed Tracey the empty cup and then fanned herself with both hands to cool off.

"Okay, I'll be right back. Don't go anywhere!" Tracey winked and hurried to the bar.

"Oh, trust me...I ain't going nowhere," Denise thought sarcastically.

The others had just stepped onto the second floor when the DJ began yelling through the microphone. "All right, everybody! Today is Kendra's birthday! Come on! Let's say happy birthday to Kendra!"

HAPPY BIRTHDAY, KENDRA! everyone shouted out in unison.

Afterward, the DJ blasted a siren horn and slid on *"In da Club"* by 50 Cent. Everybody in the VIP section started cheering as Kendra danced out onto the dance floor, her posse following suit.

"Oh shit!" Monique mumbled, placing her empty cup on a table before turning to Wanda and saying… "See? Her name ain't blondie."

Wanda hunched her shoulders, then smiled coyly and chugged her drink.

Monique went back to observing Kendra, who was smooth with her moves, perfecting the latest dance trends, including the LA crip walk, throwing up her hands, and everything!

"Hell yeah! I'm for sure hollering at her tonight!" Monique rubbed her hands together and danced onto the dance floor with Wanda and Keisha in tow just as Remy Ma's *"Conceited"* was remixed in. Monique danced closer to the VIP section, watching Kendra's every move. She noticed one of her friends lift her champagne glass in a toast while a giant birthday cake was brought over with sparklers lighting it up.

Kendra was smiling ear to ear and momentarily turned her head toward the dance floor to catch Monique staring at her. A girl from her posse distracted her by pretending she would smash a piece of cake in her face until Kendra raised her hands and gestured her not to, so she was fed a bite of cake instead.

Monique couldn't take her eyes off Kendra, hoping to catch her gaze again, which she did. Monique jumped at the opportunity and gestured for her to come to the dance floor as Donell Jones' song *"U Know What's Up"* began to play. Kendra nodded and made her way through the crowd to the dance floor, where they danced together. Monique was thrilled because she yearned to have a much-wanted conversation with her.

"I thought this was the house music floor!" Kendra shouted over the music, keeping up with Monique.

"I know, right?" Monique shouted back. "Maybe the DJ got confused when she played 50 Cent's birthday tribute to you?" she said, hunching her shoulders playfully while keeping on the beat.

"Oh my God, you're right!" Kendra shouted, laughing hysterically.

Moments later… *"Follow Me"* by Aly Us began to play, causing an uproar of cheering as everyone ran to the dance floor. Monique and Kendra roared excitedly and upped their pace, dancing up a sweat.

Meanwhile, Denise was salivating as Tracey handed over her icy cold water….

"So, who did you come here with tonight, Sweetheart?" Tracey asked but was interrupted by another female greeting her as she strolled by. "Hey!

What's up, Candy?" She responded to the woman. The woman turned her head and repeated what she said.

"What's that? I can't understand you." She yelled out before the next record dropped. Tracey turned to Denise and said…" Excuse me, sweetheart. I can't hear her. I'll be right back. Don't go anywhere, okay?" She squeezed Denise's hand softly.

Denise nodded dutifully as Tracey jogged over to the other woman. Denise began drinking the ice-cold water and then patted her cheeks with the moist paper napkin wrapped around it while whining her body to Wayne Wonders' hit *"Turn Me On."* "Hey, would you like to dance? A beautiful woman asked, walking toward her and extending her hand. "No, thank you. I need to rest for a minute. Maybe the next song." Denise responded pleasantly.

"Okay. No problem. Maybe next time, sweetheart." She said before walking off.

"I am *not* attracted to women who look like me. What

are we gonna do? Swap lipstick shades?" she mumbled sarcastically, raising one of her eyebrows as she sipped more water.

A few minutes later, Tracey returned, glad to see Denise standing in the same spot. "Hey, sweetheart, thanks for waiting for me."

"I told you I would, right?" Denise grinned back at her.

'Yes, you did. Yes, you did," Tracey repeated, smiling softly.

"You have some pretty teeth." Denise told her.

"Aww, I do. Thank you, baby." She blushed. "Yeah… so," Tracey continued, clapping her hands together once.

"That young lady was my friend Candice. But we call her Candy for short. She wanted to know if I was still going to the diner for breakfast after we left the club… which I am." "Oh! Okay. What diner are you guys going to?" Denise put the water bottle up to her mouth, looking at her. "We're going to Mable's; I love her grits and house-smoked sausage! Mm!" she said, rubbing her belly and shaking her head just thinking about it. "It's about two blocks over."

"Oh! Maybe my friends would like to go; imma ask them when they come back downstairs."

"Good! That's what I was going to ask you before Candy interrupted me." Denise grabbed Tracey's hand and led her to the dance floor, where they grooved to a classic *"You Make Me Feel"* (*Mighty Real*). By Sylvester.

"I like the way you dance, Denise!" "Oh, yeah… Denise asked slyly, dropping it low to the intro.

"Yes, ma'am, I sure do." Tracey's said lustfully, licking her lips. She put her arms around Denise's waist as soon as she stood up, then eased her leg between her thighs as they danced rhythmically to the beat.

Afterward, they dabbed off their sweat and headed upstairs to look for Denise's friends since they hadn't returned. Denise immediately spotted Monique relaxing in the VIP section with Kendra, laughing and drinking. "I guess she found the blonde she was looking for." she mumbled, shaking her head while looking for the others.

"What did you say?" Tracey asked, furrowing her brows.

"Oh, nothing, honey. I was talking to myself." Denise reassured her. "Oh! There they are!" she shouted, grabbing Tracey's hand and hurrying to the bar next to another restroom.

"Hey, girl!" Wanda shouted at Denise as she retrieved her drink from the bartender. "Who's your friend?"

"Wanda! This is Tracey." Denise glanced at her warmly, then pointed at her friends consecutively and said, "These are my friends Wanda and Keisha!"

"How Y'all doing?" Tracey asked, shaking both of their hands.

"Nice to meet you." they said in unison.

"Would you like to dance?" Tracey asked Keisha, extending her hand out to her.

"Sure, why not?" She handed her drink over to Denise.

"She seems nice." Wanda commented, sipping her drink and tapping her foot to the beat of Barbara Tucker's *"Beautiful People."*

"Yeah, well… I hope so because I'm tired of hooking up with duds, girl. It seems like they're all the same, looking for a free ride and shit." "Hmph." She sighed deeply while rolling her eyes, then took a sip of Keisha's drink and watched them dance to *"I'll House You"* by the Jungle Brothers. Moments later, they both glided to the dance floor, and Denise handed Keisha back her drink. Two hours and a few dances later….

"LAST CALL FOR ALCOHOL! YOU AIN'T GOTTA GO HOME, BUT YOU GOTS TO GET THE HELL OUTTA HERE!" the DJ shouted over the microphone. "Let's go out with a bang, ladies!" The DJ slid on Crystal Waters' *"Gypsy Woman"* (*She's Homeless*), and everyone cheered, dancing and singing out the chorus.

Monique spotted her friends, then walked over with Kendra and introduced her. Everyone greeted her pleasantly, except for Denise, who just stood there placidly.

"So, is everybody going to Mable's for breakfast?" Tracey asked, looking at each of them. Monique didn't hesitate.

"Yes!" Kendra turned to Monique and said, "I know where it is; I'll meet you there. Let me double-check what else my friends have planned first."

"That's cool. Let's exchange numbers, just in case."

Kendra gave Monique her number and then walked back to the VIP section, where her friends were patiently waiting for her. "Are you guys ready?" Monique asked as she walked toward the staircase. Everyone, including Tracey, followed her. They all used the bathroom before leaving the club and walked together toward Mable's.

"Why do we have to walk, though?" Denise cried out, pouting.

"Denise, driving makes no sense because it's only two blocks away. Besides, we're not gonna find parking anyway." Monique responded, looking puzzled. "My feet hurt." Denise stopped in her tracks.

"You know what? I'll drive, sweetheart. Tracey chuckled. "You guys go ahead, and we'll meet up with you. Come on, babe." She grabbed Denise's hand and walked to the corner to get her silver Corolla. "I have a question for you." Tracey said while opening the car door for Denise. "Thank you."

"Yes, what do you want to ask me?" Denise plopped down on the passenger's seat.

"Why do you ladies always wear shoes you know will hurt your feet by the end of the night? I mean, you look good and everything, but… I'm just saying." she chuckled as she backed out of the parking space and drove off.

"Beauty is pain, baby." Denise winked. "Just kidding. I mean, well… because I didn't break these in yet, and they go with my outfit!" Denise removed her shoes and moaned slightly while rubbing her left foot.

"Okay, have it your way." Tracey said, hunching her shoulders and chuckling.

They pulled up to the restaurant, and luckily for Denise, Tracey's car was small enough to fit between the two cars already parked there. "Thank the lord!" Denise cried out, putting her shoes back on while Tracey opened her passenger door and waited to help her out of it.

Monique contemplated waiting for Kendra outside, then decided against it since she might not even show up. Also, Monique didn't want to seem too eager- even though she secretly was. She brushed off the thought and sat down with her friends at the first of three communal tables with a few vacant seats left toward the end. Monique saved a seat for Kendra next to her just in case she could make it.

As they looked over their menus, Keisha noticed Kendra and her friends enter the restaurant. "There goes your little friend." Keisha said, softly kicking Monique's foot under the table.

Monique looked up and was ecstatic! "Kendra!" she yelled as she stood up and gestured for her to come over and sit next to her. She noticed one of Kendra's girlfriends' telling her, "Go ahead, birthday girl," Kendra nodded in gratitude, making her way over to Monique's table without pausing.

"I'm so happy you made it!" Monique smiled like a Cheshire cat, and Wanda chuckled at her behavior. Monique pretended not to hear her while pulling out Kendra's chair. Kendra sat down smiling, placing her pink quilted purse on her lap and the chain around the back of the chair.

The group ordered practically everything on the menu except for the ice cream. Lisa Stansfield's *"All Around the World"* played in the background as patrons chatted noisily and laughed at full volume; waiters were running around and sweating as they removed empty plates, picked up fallen cutlery, and took additional orders. Forks were hitting the plates, and spoons were stirring in coffee cups rapidly. It was a beautiful and typical lesbian after-the-club breakfast morning.

"You wanna step outside for a minute after we're done

eating?" Monique asked Kendra.

Kendra nodded enthusiastically. A half-hour later, Monique gestured to the entrance with her head. They both got up, walked out, and sat on the iron bench beside the restaurant.

"Now that I have you all to myself, Miss Kendra." Monique teased, smacking her tongue on the roof of her mouth playfully.

"Where are you from?"

"I'm from New Hampshire!" she laughed flirtatiously, lacing her lips with ChapStick. "How about you?" "Where are you from?"

Monique fell silent, mesmerized as she gazed at Kendra's green eyes.

"Your eyes are gorgeous," she told her. Kendra blushed.

"I'm from here, Maryland." "Who do you know that lives out here?"

Monique cleared her throat and looked away briefly to avoid stuttering.

"My sister and my adopted "cousin," Kendra said, chuckling.

"Your *adopted cousin*?" Well, I never heard that term before. I take it they're not a blood relative?" Monique squinted her eyes and shook her head for emphasis.

"No, she's not. She went to college with my sister. My family fell in love with her, so we kept her!" They both burst out laughing.

"Okay, y'all kept her. That's a good one, okay." Monique chuckled, then paused. "I want to get to know you better. Are you planning on going home soon?"

"No, I'll be here for the duration of the summer. I want to get to know you, too." Kendra said, gazing into Monique's eyes this time.

"Cool!" Monique exclaimed, trying to maintain her cool, although she felt butterflies. "By the way, I meant to ask you… Where did you learn to dance like that?" she asked with a puzzled look yet impressed.

"Believe it or not, from Videos."

"For real! Videos? You're lying." Monique shook her head in disbelief.

"No, really! Kendra exclaimed, laughing. "I have a knack for learning dances quickly. I've been doing it since I was a kid."

"That's so cool." Monique smiled. "Do you like to go to the movies and stuff like that?"

"I love movies!" Kendra responded cheerfully. "Especially scary movies. I sneak my snacks in, too, because I don't want to miss ANYTHING!" she giggled.

"Oh shit…, I better take you somewhere else because I can't fuck with scary movies, sweetheart." Monique's tone was serious.

"I like *all* movies… we can go to *any other kind of* movie." Kendra stroked Monique's arm emphatically.

"Okay, I'll choose a movie and pick you up tomorrow so we can go and see it… deal?"

"Deal!" Kendra responded, relieved and smiling.

"I think you're pretty, by the way."

"Thank you. I think you're pretty, too."

They stared at each other intensely until the diner's

door opened and hit the wall, startling them as the crowd's commotion grew closer.

"Hey, you guys!" One of the girls in Kendra's group yelled out.

"Hey, Sarah. Sarah is my sister."

Kendra said as she stood up and turned to Monique.

"Nice to meet you, Sarah." She stood and reached out her hand.

"Likewise!" Sarah said, smiling pleasantly, and shook her hand. "Are you ready, Kendra? It's getting late." Sarah asked, removing her vehicle keys from her purse. "Yes. I'm ready." Then she kissed Monique lightly on the cheek. "Call me." she said, looking back intermittently as she and her friends walked to their vehicle.

"Good night, and happy birthday again. I'll call you later, baby!" Monique softly yelled, grinning.

Kendra blushed, quickly waving.

Moments later, Monique's friends were walking over to her. "Baby! Give me a break!" Denise sucked her teeth, rolling her eyes.

"Concentrate on what you got going on, miss thing." Monique said sarcastically, looking at Denise, then glanced at Tracey, who was waiting for Denise to write down her number. Monique began walking back toward the club to retrieve her car. "Y'all coming?" She turned to the others, causing Keisha and Wanda to pick up the pace.

Tracey took Denise's number from her hand and held it firmly. "Why are you giving your friend such a hard time, huh?" she asked, moving closer.

"You really think I'm giving her a hard time?" Denise

replied with an innocent look on her face.

"Yeah, sweety, it seems like it, but… I'ma mind my business." she chuckled, shaking her head slowly.

"I'm *not* giving her a hard time." Denise lowered her head. "Anyway, she knows what I mean!" She kicked a bottle top into the street, then looked up and smiled at Tracey.

"All right, enough about them. Let's talk about you and me." Tracey seductively moistened her lips with her tongue. "I enjoyed dancing with you tonight, and I'd like to take you out to dinner one night if that's possible."

"Of course, you can take me to dinner, handsome." Denise said, relieved that Tracey wanted to ask her out even after all the drama.

"Yes!" Tracey cheered, making a victorious fist. "Let me drive you back to the club because I know your feet are still hurting." she teased, opening the passenger side door.

"You're a real one!"

Denise said as she sat in the car. Tracey located Monique and dropped Denise off parallel to the side of her car, opening a piece of "Freshen-up" gum and asking Denise for a kiss as she got out.

"Sure." Denise said softly, closing the door and limping to the other side of the car to lean in the driver's window. She kissed Tracey and slipped in a Lil tongue action, almost taking her gum. "Your mouth tastes good." Denise smirked and backed up, licking the gum's sugar off her lips.

"Mm, Tracey said seductively, looking at Denise with lustful eyes. "I like that tongue, by the way." She said, chewing her gum slowly.

"If you play your cards right, there's more where that came from." Denise winked.

"I happen to play cards very well, baby. I'll talk to you later." Tracey winked back, half-smiling and slowly driving off.

"Later, smooches!" Denise said sweetly, looking over her shoulder before limping onto the sidewalk and getting in the back seat of Monique's burgundy Camry.

"Hey Keisha?" Monique called, pulling off. "What time is Karen dropping off the kids in the morning?"

"She's not." Keisha sighed peacefully. "The girls are staying with her until Tuesday. I have the *entire* weekend to myself for a change." She closed her eyes and sank further into the front seat.

"Lucky You!" Monique chirped.

She dropped Keisha home first, then Wanda, and lastly, Denise since her townhouse was a block from hers.

When they were finally alone…, Denise grew irritable again and asked… "Are you seriously going to date that girl Monique?"

"I mean…Yeah! Why not?" Monique responded, giggling oddly at her and looking perplexed.

"What's so funny?" Denise sucked her teeth.

"Denise, you're tripping." Monique made a right at the corner.

"Hallelujah!" she called out as she pulled up to Denise's house. Denise got out and slammed the door.

"Hey! Why'd you slam my door like that?" Monique yelled out the car window with a furrow in her brow.

"You know why!" Denise turned her head and yelled back as she limped up the brick stairs barefoot to her front porch.

"That's why your feet hurt!" she chuckled. "Soak those little piggies and get some sleep while you're at it!" Monique teased, burning rubber and beeping the horn repeatedly.

Denise turned her head and stuck her tongue out, but Monique was already at the end of her street.

"That woman is seriously tripping." Monique mumbled to herself as she waited at the stop light, Kendra crossing her mind, bringing a smile to her face.

The following afternoon… Monique was awakened by the noise of a car backing up next door, which caused her to cover her ears with her pillow before rolling out of bed, annoyed. "Ugg! That's what I get for living in the front," she shouted, throwing down her pillow and walking into the bathroom. She loaded her toothbrush with toothpaste, stepped into the shower, and turned the water on, quickly jumping when the cold water hit her skin. "I'm up now, shit!" she mumbled to herself, shivering and peeing. Then she dried off and sprayed on after-shower oil, put on pajama pants and a tee shirt, skipped to her newly renovated kitchen, and made herself a BLT with a glass of white grape juice. She sat down at the breakfast counter and noticed her wallet. "Maybe I put Kendra's number in here." she thought, opening it up to look inside. "Here we go!" She roared, shoving the last bite of BLT into her mouth and slapping the counter with excitement. She put her dishes in the sink and lifted her leg to pass gas before walking to her bedroom, falling backward on the bed and dialing Kendra's number on her new Nokia cellphone.

"Hello?" A woman's voice on the other line answered after the third ring.

"Hello, this is Monique. Is Kendra available?"

"Yes, she is. Hey there, Monique; it's Sarah, Kendra's sister!"

"Oh! Hey Sarah, how are you?"

"I'm great!"

"Oh! Here's Kendra. Will I speak with you some other time?" she asked.

"I...guess." Monique said with a confused tone of voice. She took the phone from her ear and looked at it before she started chuckling, quickly returning it.

"It's Monique." Sarah said as she passed the phone to Kendra.

"Hey!" Kendra chirped.

"Hey yourself!" Monique grinned. "You still want to go with me to the movies… right?" "Yes! Of course!" Kendra wrapped the telephone cord loosely around the fingers of her free hand, placing one of her bare feet on the other, grinning.

"Cool!" "Okay, wait… where are you staying again?" she asked, sitting in bed.

"I'm in Towson."

"Nice! I live in North Potomac, so I'm not that far from you. Give me your address, sweetie."

"Do you have a pen on you?"

"Yup, I'm looking inside my nightstand drawer right now." She grimaced, reaching for the pen. "Okay, I got it;

give me the address, sweetie."

"It's 8-4-0-0 Pleasant Plains Road.

"I'm familiar with the area, so I'll be there after four, okay? The traffic shouldn't be that bad right now."

"All right, I can't wait!" Kendra exclaimed, hanging up the phone and running to find something nice to wear before showering.

"Yes!" Monique said, folding up her phone and throwing it on the bed. She undressed and rummaged through her closet to find something casual but nice to wear for her date. She opted for loose-fitting Khaki cargo pants and a black tank top underneath a tan button-down shirt with black chucks. Then she doused herself with some baby powder fragrance body oil. She drove to the cleaners to retrieve her work attire, hung it on the hook in the back of the car before going to the gas station to fill the tank, and then headed toward the highway to Towson to pick up Kendra.

"It's three-thirty now," she mumbled, looking at the time on the dashboard. "I should get there by four-thirty, give or take…" She fiddled with the radio dial till she landed on *"Hey ya"*! by Outcast. "Aye! That's my jam!" After singing along for a while, she took out her phone and called Kendra again, suddenly remembering she had forgotten to tell her something.

"Hello." Kendra answered.

"Hey, sweetie. It's me, Monique."

"I know it's you." Kendra giggled.

"Cool, so Listen. I meant to tell you not to worry about bringing snacks with you today. I got this."

"Oh, but I was going to pack enough for the both of us!" Kendra said, perplexed and hunching her shoulders.

"Aww, that's nice, sweetie, but let me worry about the snacks today, okay?"

"Okay, that's fine." Kendra was still confused.

"Besides, it's a dine-in theater sweetie."

"Oh wow! I've always wanted to go to one of those theaters! They don't have theaters like this where I'm from!"

"Wow, really. I thought they had those everywhere." Monique chuckled.

"No, they don't! I'm so excited!"

"I'm excited for you, sweetie." Monique grinned. "I'll see you shortly, baby. Wear something cute for me, okay?" Monique winked as if Kendra could see her.

"I will." Kendra blushed, then hung up the phone quickly to take the rollers out of her hair.

Forty-five minutes later…. The Camry slowly crept down Pleasant Plains Road as Monique looked for Kendra's house number. "7987, 7990, 8400… "What the hell!" she exclaimed, scratching her head in bewilderment. "Well…. *This* is the address she gave me. She looked at the address again to make sure, then she parked in front of the mint-green-colored house with the white window shutters and a picket fence and honked her horn twice. *Beep, Beep.*

Kendra opened the door and came out running wearing metallic pink metal-framed sunglasses, a light pink and baby blue plaid short set with a white Cami underneath, a pair of low-top pink chucks, and a white quilted leather purse hanging from her shoulder. She walked up to the passenger side door and opened it.

"You look very nice, Kendra." Monique was checking her out from head to toe.

"Thank you! You look nice, too." Kendra said, getting in and smiling. She placed her purse on her lap, adjusted her seat, and then flipped her hair out of the way to put on her seatbelt.

"Mm… your hair smells good, too." Monique told her, sniffing the air.

Kendra blushed.

"Are you ready, sweetie?" Monique asked her, putting the car in drive.

"Ready!" Kendra responded, reaching over to run her hands across

Monique's cornrowed hair. "I really do like your hair." Monique looked over at her and smiled as she drove off to the Dine-In IPIC theater in Bethesda for the 6:40 showing of *Kill Bill*. They arrived at the massive movie theater's parking lot at 5:30, giving them ample time to order food before the coming attractions started. Monique could only find a parking spot in the back of the lot. "Damn!" she said, hitting the steering wheel with both hands. "This movie better be worth it because this is gonna be a long ass walk." She turned off the ignition. "Hey…" she called out before unlocking the doors. "I can look for something closer if you don't wanna walk." She secretly hoped Kendra wouldn't mind because the chances of finding anything closer were slim to none.

"Oh! No, I don't mind walking." Kendra unfastened her seatbelt.

"Thank you, God!" Monique mumbled, looking up at the sky and then unlocking the doors.

They both got out, and Monique re-locked the doors and turned on the car's alarm. When they neared the entryway, Kendra jogged ahead and held the door open for Monique. "After you." She said, smiling.

"Thank you!" Monique exclaimed, walking through with Kendra directly on her heels.

Monique ordered an artisan flatbread pepperoni pizza at the concession stand, a medium extra butter popcorn with a large orange soda, and a pack of Twizzlers. Kendra ordered chicken tenders and French fries with a side of fried macaroni balls, a small popcorn with extra butter, and a large diet Cola before walking into the theater and taking their assigned seats. When the attendants arrived with their food, they barely had room to put their drinks in the cup holders because people were seated elbow to elbow, so they put them on the floor beside them instead.

During the movie, there was a lot of gasping, followed by *oohs* and *ahhs*. When the movie ended, everyone stood up, cheering and yelling, "ENCORE! ENCORE"!

"They have to make a Kill Bill 2! That movie was awesome!" Kendra exclaimed as they left the theater. "Thank you, Monique."

"Aww, you're welcome, sweetie." Monique looked over at Kendra with an endearing little grin. "It *was* awesome; I'm sure a Kill Bill 2 will happen. They can't leave us hanging like that!" She chuckled. "Hold on, sweetie." Monique said, gently grabbing Kendra's arm. "I think we should use the bathroom before we go; what do you think?"

"Good idea!" Kendra replied, following Monique as she turned around and walked back toward the ladies' room.

"Why is the ladies' room line always so damn long?" Monique asked rhetorically in frustration.

"I have an idea. Follow me." Kendra told her quietly, grabbing Monique's hand and leading her down two doors to the men's room.

"Are you serious?" Monique whispered.

"Hell yeah! I do this all the time." Kendra chuckled. "I'll go first, and you look out for me, and then you can go, okay?"

"Okay. Monique agreed, hunching her shoulders while she stood outside the bathroom until it was her turn. "It's clean inside there, too! I'ma do this from now on!" Monique laughed as she exited the men's room while drying her hands with a paper towel. "Look over there," Monique pointed at a lady in line. See that lady in the white jeans?" "Yeah." That woman has been in the same spot since we left!"

"Which is precisely why I go to the men's room!" Kendra said, both bursting into sneaky laughter. When they got to the exit, Monique rushed over and quickly pushed the door open, making Kendra blush.

"I'm glad you enjoyed the movie, Kendra." Monique said as they walked toward the car.

"I really did." Kendra smiled, looking at Monique as she placed her sunglasses on her head.

"So, what do you want to do now?" Monique asked,

pulling her keys from her pocket and remotely opening the car door.

"Let's go to your place." Kendra grinned, opening the passenger side door.

"Sounds like a plan, sweetie. I hate when people park out of the doggone lines!" Monique commented, squeezing herself onto the driver's side. She turned on the ignition and eased out of the parking space.

"Where did you say you lived again?" Kendra asked, looking into her purse for her Chapstick.

"Montgomery County… It's in north Potomac." When Monique turned on the radio, *"Beautiful"* by Snoop Dogg feat. Pharrell Williams was playing.

"I love this song!" Kendra cheered, singing along.

As soon as Monique stopped at the red light, she turned to Kendra and said…

"You're beautiful." Then the light turned green, and Monique drove off. Kendra blushed but continued to sing the chorus while Monique jumped in and rapped with Snoop.

Half an hour later, Monique pulled up to her townhouse at 12415 Potomac Hunt Road.

"Wow! This is your place?" Kendra asked in awe.

"Yes, it is, sweetie." Monique chuckled, unlocking Kendra's door.

They walked up to the arched black front door with its gold mail slot, gold hardware, and black rubber welcome mat. To the right was a red planter box with a lighted topiary tree. "Would you like something to drink?" Monique asked her once they were inside the apartment.

She threw her wallet and keys on the breakfast counter and waited for Kendra to respond.

"What cha got?" Kendra responded cheerfully. "I like your place. Did you recently move in or something?" she asked, marveling at the surroundings while removing her purse from her shoulder and wrapping the chain loosely around her hand.

"Thanks, baby." "And no, I didn't recently move in; I just take good care of my things. She chuckled, walking to the kitchen sink to wash her hands.

"I see." Kendra replied.

"To answer your question, I have some white grape juice, aloe vera, orange juice, and water. Which one would you like, sweetie?" Monique asked, drying off her hands and opening the refrigerator.

"I'll have some water for now, please." Kendra sat on the black leather sofa and put her purse down.

"Would you like some ice with that?" Monique asked as she removed a drinking glass from the dishwasher.

"Sure." Kendra gazed at her reflection on the wall of mirrors across from the sofa, then took a brush out of her purse and brushed her hair.

"Here you go." Monique said, handing her the water and getting comfortable beside her. "So, tell me. Do you work?" Monique asked, now resting her back up against the arm of the sofa.

"Yes, I do! I work as a disc jockey at a local radio station in my hometown." Kendra placed the brush back into her purse.

"Oh! For real! That doesn't surprise me, though."

Monique said, grinning.

"Oh yeah! Why's that?" Kendra asked her, taking a drink of water.

"Because you have a lot of rhythm, baby." Monique laughed.

"Yeah, I do, don't I? Kendra winked.

There was a moment of silence….

"Do you know what the best part of the movie was for me?" Kendra broke the ice, setting her glass of water down on the clear acrylic end table.

"Aht aht. What part?" Monique asked curiously while folding her arms in front of her with a sly smile.

"This part!" Kendra jumped up and raced to the kitchen, positioning herself in a karate stance.

"Oh! That was the best part for me, too! Let's do this!" Monique said, getting up and joining her.

They re-enacted the fight scene between Vivica Fox and Uma Thurman, wrestling on the kitchen floor, not realizing this playful act was a form of foreplay. They were both turned on and on the floor.

Monique grabbed Kendra by the hair and kissed her aggressively, and Kendra started tugging on Monique's shirt with the hopes of ripping it off her.

"Whoa… hold up, baby," Monique said abruptly, letting go of Kendra's hair while gently removing her hands from her shirt. "I just bought this shirt, baby." She was serious but soft.

"Oh, I'm sorry." Kendra grew a little embarrassed.

"No worries, sweetie." She gave her a peck on the lips as they stood up. Then she removed her shirt and placed it on the chair at the breakfast counter before resuming her hands' position in Kendra's hair. Kendra removed her suit jacket as they kissed, then her shorts. Monique guided her backward toward the bedroom, pushing her gently down on the bed and removing her thong with her teeth, making Kendra pant in anticipation. Then she began sniffing the inside of Kendra's thighs to the top of her hairless box, then kissed her hairless lips while unbuttoning her pants and letting them drop to the floor. She shoved her head between Kendra's legs as her hands spread them farther apart, putting her hairless lips together and sucking on them. Then she opened them with her tongue and devoured her clit. "Damn, girl." She paused…" It's like velvet down here, and your clit is so fuckin fat and pink." "Shit." she whispered. She pressed her lips against her clit and motorboated it rapidly before she resumed sucking on it. Then she reached up to squeeze Kendra's breast through her Cami, making her nipples harden as she pinched at them. "Take that shirt off." Monique ordered, pausing to wait. Kendra rapidly removed her Cami and bra, then pushed Monique's head back between her legs. Kendra moaned a lot but wasn't much of a talker. Monique figured she'd get her out of that at some point, so she didn't ask her any questions. She put her hand inside the panties under her boxers and started moving her clit back and forth at the same pace she was sucking on Kendra's clit. Both of their squooshy sounds of wetness were music to her ears. "Fuck, baby!" Monique moaned, moving her clit back and forth faster as Kendra ran her fingers up and down the parts that separated her braids when she climaxed, arching her back and causing Monique to squeeze her eyes shut each time she squirted. Afterward, Monique slowly crawled to the head of the bed. "Whew!" she said, laying on her back and dropping her head on the pillow in complete satisfaction.

Kendra flipped her hair back and slid over to Monique's side. "That felt so good." she whispered into Monique's ear, kissing it, then tracing Monique's sideburn with the tip of her finger as her chin rested on Monique's shoulder.

"Yes, it was, and you taste good too, baby."

Kendra threw her leg across Monique's thigh and her arm across her chest before resting her head on Monique's shoulder while Monique ran her nails up and down Kendra's forearm before turning her head and kissing her forehead.

"I'm hungry for food now, sweetie." Monique sat up while Kendra tried to maintain her position. "What about you?"

Kendra lifted her head and looked at Monique, perplexed.

"Mm, mm, girl…Your eyes are so fucking pretty." Monique shook her head slowly in admiration, oblivious to Kendra's facial expression.

Kendra smiled back and poked her lips out for a kiss.

Monique kissed her, gently biting her bottom lip in between. "Let's order some food, sweetie."

"Sure, babe, *let's order some food.*" Kendra responded sarcastically, sliding her arm off Monique's chest and leaning back onto her pillow but leaving her thigh across Monique's thigh.

"Good!" She tapped Kendra's thigh, gesturing that she had to get up, to which Kendra slowly budged. "What about Italian?" Monique yelled out on her way to the kitchen to retrieve the menus from her "junk" drawer.

"Yeah! Italian sounds good." Kendra yelled back, slightly annoyed. "Why do I always whine up with the "touch-me, not girl?" Kendra mumbled, burying her face in the pillow.

Seconds later, Monique returned to the bedroom and hopped on the bed, opening the menu so they could both observe. "You all right, sweetie?" Monique asked in a concerned tone after noticing Kendra's facial expressions.

"Yeah, I'm all right." Kendra forced a smile. She placed her hair behind her ears and sat up, moving closer to Monique to view the menu.

"Cool." Monique said bluntly, not reading into her body language. "Okay now, let's see… hmm. I think I'll have the *penne alla vodka* and chicken parmesan." Monique said, patting her braids.

"Ooh… that sounds tasty!" Kendra commented. "I'm gonna try the lasagna and a Caesar salad with garlic bread."

"Every order comes with garlic bread, baby…, unless you want extra."

"No, that's good enough." "I'll buy a large sparkling Italian soda if that's okay with you, sweetie."

"I've never had an Italian soda, but I'll try it." Kendra hunched her shoulders.

"Okay." Monique responded, picking up the phone to dial the restaurant while walking toward the living room.

"Do you want anything else, sweetie, before I call them?"

"No." Kendra slid off the bed to go into the bathroom as Monique placed their food order and returned to the bedroom, meeting Kendra in bed, where they cuddled and waited for the food to arrive.

"Monique?" she called out softly but seriously as she sat up, her back against the headboard.

"Yes, sweetie." Monique leaned over the side of the bed to look for her socks.

"I like women. I like smelling, kissing, and tasting them, amongst other things."

"Well… I would hope so!" Monique interjected jokingly.

"I'm being serious, Monique." Kendra's facial expression was serious.

"Okay. I hear you." Monique located her socks and put them on.

"I don't understand how two women can make love, but only one gets to touch." Kendra looked at Monique seriously while picking at the sheet.

"I hear you, sweetie." Monique repeated lightheartedly before looking at her phone.

"Can you look at me, honey?" Kendra asked softly while gently touching her arm.

Monique turned to her and listened attentively.

"I want to make love to you, too, Monique." Kendra told her as the back of her hand touched Monique's face tenderly.

Monique nodded like she was pretending to understand.

"When was the last time you were in a relationship, Monique?"

"Five years ago." Monique informed her, appearing a bit saddened by the realization of it.

"Oh, I see," Kendra said, backing off slightly. "Did she hurt you, honey?' Kendra's voice was sincere.

"Yeah, she did," Monique said matter-of-factly, looking down.

"Okay, I understand now. But… look at me, honey," Kendra said softly, picking up Monique's chin. "I promise I can make you feel as good as you made me feel if you give me a chance." Kendra was wearing a devilish grin.

"Your ass betta be glad you're cute!" Monique giggled, teasing her just as the doorbell rang. "Oh shit! That was fast!" She hopped off the bed to answer the door.

Kendra slapped her thighs and rolled her eyes to the ceiling, falling back on the bed. She recognized that her message didn't get through to Monique, but she was nothing if not persistent. "I'll get you one day, my pretty," she mumbled, re-enacting the voice of the wicked witch of the West before rolling off the bed.

Monique tipped the delivery man and brought the food to the breakfast counter, where Kendra was already seated.

"That smells heavenly," Kendra said as Monique took the labeled food out of the bag and handed it to her.

"And it tastes as good as it smells, too!" Monique assured her. "The last time I ordered this food, it was pretty good!" She opened her pasta dish and then stabbed a forkful of pasta.

"Oh, wow! Hah, hah…it's hot!" Kendra belted out,

holding her mouth open to cool the food down.

"They're not stingy with the cheese, either." Monique commented, chuckling at Kendra's response to the heat as she cut into her chicken parmesan. Then she got up to retrieve wine glasses from the dishwasher for the sparkling Italian soda. "Do you want to listen to some music, sweetie?" Monique asked, chewing on a piece of garlic bread.

"Sure!" Kendra responded, putting the Cardini dressing on her Caesar salad.

Monique turned the CD player on, choosing John Mayer's CD and playing *"Your Body Is a Wonderland."* She slowly danced to the breakfast counter while Kendra swayed her head to the music, raising her fork and waving it in the air as she sang out the chorus. "I bet your body is a wonderland." Kendra winked at her.

"I hear you, sweetie." Monique blushed.

Minutes later, *"Daughters"* began to play. "This is a wonderful song; my listeners always request it." Kendra said.

"I can see why!" Monique swayed her head to the music, moving her pasta around the aluminum plate. "I'm stuffed!" she said, resting her back against the chair before sitting up and replacing the lid on her food.

"Me too!" Kendra commented, pretending to gag with a piece of lettuce hanging out the side of her mouth.

"You are so nasty." Monique teased, laughing at her. "Let's go in the bedroom and watch television."

"Yeah, I like the sound of that!" Kendra said eagerly.

Monique went into the bathroom to wash her hands

and brush her teeth while Kendra used the toilet.

Afterward, they got back into bed and under the sheets with Kendra lying in Monique's arms and her head resting on her chest. Monique was channel-surfing with one of her legs dangling out of the sheet. Eventually, she decided to watch CSI. Yet, within forty-five minutes, CSI began watching *them*.

Kendra woke up first and began kissing Monique softly on her lips. She glided her hands gently over Monique's breasts, causing her nipples to harden. Then she outlined them with the tip of her fingers and licked her lips with a strong desire to place each of the nipples into her mouth. She was excited, observing Monique squirming and softly moaning as her touch transformed her nipples. She tried to lift Monique's tank top to unhook her bra, but it was as if it was hard-wired.

Monique opened her eyes to find Kendra staring up at her. "If you wanted to suck my titties, sweetie, all you had to do was ask," Monique teased, sitting up, and removing her top, to unhook her bra.

"Wow, your breasts are so pretty," Kendra whispered. She took one of Monique's nipples into her mouth and nibbled on it while firmly squeezing the other breast. She suddenly stopped and kissed her before resuming, sucking both nipples aggressively. Her breathing became heavier while Monique moaned and squirmed, grabbing Kendra's hair.

Monique gently pulled Kendra's head back and put her hands between her legs. Then she thrust her body against Kendra's, causing her to fall back completely while mounting her and kissing her aggressively. "You want some more Lovin, baby?" Monique whispered before sucking her way between Kendra's legs.

"Yes!" Kendra cried out softly, realizing she couldn't have her way with Monique, so she decided to let Monique have her way with her again.

In the heat of the moment, Monique looked up from between Kendra's legs and asked her eagerly, "Can I get my strap, baby?"

"Can I eat your pussy?" Kendra asked, looking down at Monique seductively.

Monique smiled coyly before returning her attention to the space between Kendra's legs to suck on her some more. Kendra's lips parted slightly as she gasped with each climax while running her fingers between the parts of Monique's braids. When their lovemaking ended, Kendra rolled over onto her belly while Monique got up to get a glass of water. "Want something to drink?" she asked Kendra, still panting heavily.

Kendra didn't respond. So, she got the water, sat on the sofa, and thought about Kendra's question. *"Would I let her do the same thing to me? hmm,"* she asked herself. She finished her water, placed the glass in the sink, went back into the bedroom, and plopped herself on the bed playfully. But Kendra didn't budge. Monique eased her way up to Kendra. "Sweetie…" She pecked her cheek. "Oh, sweetie…." Monique whispered in her ear while stroking the middle of her back.

"Hmm?" Kendra softly moaned, with a few strands of her hair covering her face.

"Are you ready to go?" Monique nibbled on her earlobe.

Kendra's eyes popped open, and she turned around slowly to face Monique, who was smiling pleasantly.

"Are you about ready to go, baby?" Monique repeated.

"Well… I thought I was staying the night with you." Kendra responded in a surprised tone with a perplexing look on her face.

"Oh! I didn't even think of that, sweetie." Monique looked just as perplexed. "Besides," she continued, jumping to her knees and pecking Kendra's lips quickly before getting out of bed. "Wanda needs me to drive her to the auto mechanic in the morning so she can pick up her car on my way to work. Remember, baby…" she paused, picking up her bra and tank top. "You're on vacation, not me, boo." she chuckled.

"Oh, but it's after midnight, so I figured…" Kendra's voice was gloomy as she glanced at the digital clock, blinking her eyes rapidly.

Monique was at a loss for words and just listened to her.

Kendra slid off the bed and picked up her panties and clothes off the floor before slowly walking toward the bathroom.

"Wait a minute, wait a minute." Monique said softly, walking over to her and wrapping her arms around her tenderly, her face practically buried in Kendra's hair. "Maybe we can set up a sleepover before you leave Towson." Monique said sincerely, turning her around to look into her eyes directly.

"Yeah, that sounds good, but what time do you have to

be at work?" Kendra asked, almost whispering, removing the hair that covered her sad eyes as she puckered her lips for a kiss.

"Shit, girl. You fine as hell!" Monique said seductively while she shook her head before kissing Kendra all over her lips and neck. "I have to be in at 10. Let me get you home before my ass calls out tomorrow!" She chuckled. She grabbed the rest of her clothes and put them on while walking quickly to the kitchen to put away her leftovers.

Kendra put on her clothes and went to use the bathroom, leaving the door open. She wanted to ensure she heard Monique in case she changed her mind.

"You wanna take your leftovers with you, baby?" Monique shouted out from the kitchen.

"Sure! I forgot all about that." Kendra yelled back.

Monique bagged up Kendra's food and retrieved her keys while Kendra grabbed her purse from the sofa before they left.

"Would you mind if I turned on the radio, honey?" Kendra asked once they were in the car.

"Nah, sweetie, go for it." Monique smiled and sprayed the wiper fluid to clean the window shield.

Ludacris' *Stand Up* was on, and Kendra shrieked, "Oh! This is my song!"

"Hell yeah! Turn it up!" Monique cheered, pumping the breaks with the chorus.

They screamed, *"Just like that!"* in unison, Kendra dancing in her seat.

Monique grinned widely, and when the song ended, she placed her hand on Kendra's thigh and said… "Hey, sweetie?" "There's a Hip-Hop class on Thursday nights at this dance studio called Slow Motion in Gaithersburg that I wanted to check out; you wanna go with me?" Monique was secretly hoping she would say yes.

"Sure! You know I love Hip-Hop!" Kendra responded with a broad grin.

"Cool." Monique smiled, grabbing Kendra's hand and rubbing the top of it with her thumb.

"Do you mind if I ask my girls to come? You can invite your sister and your "adopted cousin" if you want to." Monique said, letting go of her hand to air quote while winking her right eye playfully.

"Sweet! The more, the merrier!" Kendra responded cheerfully as they pulled up to her sister's home. "I had a wonderful time with you today, Monique." Kendra looked at her affectionately.

"I did, too, baby." Monique grabbed Kendra's hand tenderly and planted a kiss.

"Call me tomorrow." Kendra said softly, opening the car door.

"Will do, sweetie." Monique air-kissed her and waited until she was safely inside before pulling off. She took a quick shower and brushed her teeth when she returned home. Out of the corner of her eye, she noticed Kendra's thong sitting on top of her clothes in the hamper while she was drying off. "No, she didn't!" Monique said out loud, laughing and shaking her head as she reached for the lotion. Afterward, she went into the kitchen to make herself a cup of tea with honey, grabbed a paper towel, and went into the bedroom. She removed the toenail clipper from her nightstand drawer, then got on the bed, put the paper towel under her left foot, and began clipping her toenails. She debated whether to call Kendra to let her know she made it home. But, after clipping her last pinky toenail, she decided to call it a night and go to sleep.

The following morning…the clock alarm went off, causing Monique to grunt each time before she pressed the snooze button. After the last snooze, she forcibly threw the sheet off her and shot out of bed. She used the bathroom and got dressed for work. She wore her favorite sky-blue pinstripe button-down shirt, navy-blue flair-leg trousers, blue argyle socks, and black loafers. Then she put on her jewelry, sprayed on her favorite cologne, and hurried to the kitchen, where she grabbed a disposable cup with a lid and made herself another cup of hot tea, this time with lemon and three sugars. She picked up her wallet and keys and headed to Rockville to get Wanda. *Beep, beep, beep*!

"Where is she? I'm gonna be late." Monique mumbled agitatedly, glancing at her wristwatch and looking out the passenger side window for Wanda.

A few minutes later, she noticed Wanda hurry out of her front door with a bagel in her mouth, her keys, and a coffee thermos in one hand and her purse in the other.

"Whew! Good morning sunshine, sorry I'm late." Wanda air-kissed Monique as she plopped down in her seat and closed the door.

She placed her thermos in the cup holder, sighed deeply, and quickly took a bite from her bagel.

"Women!" Monique teased, shaking her head as she pulled off.

"What?" Wanda said jokingly and chewing loudly. She had a "cat who swallowed the canary" look on her face, knowing fully what Monique was referring to.

Monique and Wanda laughed it off and talked briefly until they arrived at the auto mechanic. "Thank you, baby!" Wanda said as she hurried out of the car. Monique waved goodbye, beeped once, and continued her twenty-minute journey to work in Germantown. At the office, Monique called Keisha during her lunch break to see how she was doing but, within five minutes, was interrupted by another phone call coming in. "Hold a minute, Keish, my vanilla babe is on the other line."

"Oh! Excuse me. You two are still talking, huh? Girl, call me back later. I'll be here." Keisha chuckled and hung up the phone.

"Anyway." Monique mumbled sarcastically before clicking over.

"Hello, baby." Monique smiled.

"Hey!" Kendra said excitedly.

"I was hoping you'd call me to let me know you were home." She said softly, pausing for a response.

"I'm sorry, sweetheart, the time got away from me. So, what's up, beautiful?" Monique was interrupted by her co-worker. "Wait a minute, baby, hold that thought." She covered the mouthpiece and responded to her co worker, returning to the phone moments later. "Shit!" She whispered. "Hey, sweetie," "I have to go to a meeting. Can I call you back later?"

"Of course! Wait, before you go, quick question."

"Yeah, babe." Monique said, taking a writing pen from

her desk drawer and placing it in her shirt pocket.

"What kind of work do you do?"

"Oh! I'm an ad exec, baby."

"Oh wow!" Kendra replied in an impressed tone.

"Monique!" A male voice called out.

"Coming!" She said, getting up from her desk. "I gotta call you back, baby." she whispered, hanging up abruptly.

"All righty then." Kendra said playfully, hanging up the phone and then yelling at her sister, Sarah… "You want pizza"?

"Hell yeah! And make sure to get one with extra mushrooms and green peppers!" Sarah yelled back at her from her bedroom.

"Okay!" Kendra looked in the fridge to ensure there was enough to drink before calling in their order.

Later that evening, Monique was sitting at her breakfast counter looking over a few drawings for a project campaign when the phone rang, startling her. "Hello!" she said, picking up the phone quickly and knocking a marker on the floor.

"Hey! What's up?"

"This you, Denise?" Monique asked, picking up the marker and returning to her seat at the breakfast counter.

"Yes, it's me. What are you doing?"

"I'm working on this campaign project for work. It's not due for another two weeks, but you know me, I like to play. So, I gotta get this work out of the way before that." She said to her, giggling.

"I know what you mean, girl." "So, you talk to Blondie?"

"*First* of all, her name is Kendra. Say it with me, Ken…dra," Monique continued playfully.

"All right, *Kendra* then," Denise enunciated. "Did you speak to her?"

"I sure did!" Monique answered, turning the pages of the sketches she was brainstorming on.

"Did you take her out yet?"

"Yup. We went to the movies to see *Kill Bill,* and that shit was good, too!"

"Mph. That's good." Denise responded disinterestedly.

Monique noticed her attitude and quickly rolled her eyes but did not respond. "What about you and that female who drove you to the diner?" Monique sighed, dropping the marker on the stack of papers.

"We're supposed to be going to dinner on Thursday."

"Cool. Her name is Tracey, right?"

Monique asked, raising her left brow as she sat back in the chair. "Yes, her name is Tracey."

"Oh yeah, before I forget." she said suddenly, sitting straight up. "I wanted to see if y'all would like to go to a Hip-Hop class on Thursday, then we can have dinner afterward."

"Well… I don't know about any Hip-Hop classes, but I can do dinner. What restaurant do you plan on going to?"

"There's a Greek restaurant I wanted to try."

"Oh! That's different. I'm down, but let me ask Tracey if she wants to go; then I'll get back to you, okay?"

"Okay, Cool! Imma call Keisha and Wanda before I turn in for the night, boo." Monique chuckled.

"All right, girl. Talk to you later." Denise said.

"All right, cool." Monique hung up the phone and got back to work.

Meanwhile, Keisha was at home on the phone with her co-parent Karen. "How are my babies doing?"

"They're fine. When did they develop this hearty appetite, though?"

"Their appetite seems regular to me." Keisha shrugged her shoulders. "Well, I've never seen them eat like this!" Karen emphasized while laughing and cleaning off their high chairs. "The girls are growing up so fast, right?"

"Yes, they are. I can't believe there are almost four!"

"Where did the time go?" Karen continued. "I know, right? Where are they? I want to speak to them." Keisha said anxiously, listening out for their sweet baby voices in the background.

"It's past seven, and they had a busy day. They're in bed now, Keisha."

"Oh, I can understand that." Keisha said in a disappointed tone.

"Don't worry. They'll be home soon enough. Listen… Cicely and I wanted to keep them for the rest of the week if that's all right with you." Karen asked, crossing her fingers as she waited for Keisha's answer.

"They're your children too… and I could use a break so they can stay the rest of the week with you guys."

"Yay! But just so you know, I'm taking them to visit Cicely's parents… if you don't mind."

Keisha felt a bit sad, but she didn't let on. "Like I said before, Karen, they're your children too. And Cicely is going to be their stepmother soon. Plus, I like her. The more positive people the babies have in their lives, the better." She smiled.

"Thank you, Keisha." Karen said softly. "I'll call you tomorrow after they wake up so you can speak to them, okay?"

"Okay. That sounds good." Keisha responded just as her phone beeped, alerting her there was someone on the other line. "I'll talk to you tomorrow. Good night, Karen." She hung up and looked at the phone to see who was calling. Karen held onto the receiver in deep thought. "Hey, big head!" Keisha teased Monique when she clicked over.

"Hey!" Monique responded. "I know I'm taking a chance asking you this, but do you wanna go to a Hip-Hop class and dinner on Thursday?" She figured Keisha might say no because of the kids.

"You're in luck, my friend. It just so happens that Karen will have the kids for the rest of the week, so count me in!" Plus, I gotta lose this baby weight anyway." she said, chuckling and grabbing her midsection.

"You mean toddler weight, don't you? Those girls are three years old, woman!" Monique joked, giggling.

"Ha, ha-ha." Keisha smiled. "I'm going to shower then; I'm getting in bed and watching *The Wire*. Call me tomorrow and give me the address and the time."

"Oh, shit, I forgot that came on tonight, but I'm too tired; I won't be able to pay attention anyway, girl." Monique let out a yawn. "Remember that health-food store I took you to once in Gaithersburg?"

"Umm, hmm, I remember."

"The dance studio is right next to it. It's called *Slow Motion.*"

"Oh, okay, what time should I meet up with you? Wait, it's not just us, right?"

"Nah, all of us are going, even though I didn't ask Wanda yet. I'm pretty sure she's gonna say yes because… why wouldn't she?" Monique laughed.

"Right." Keisha chuckled. "What time should I meet you?" Keisha repeated.

"Six o'clock."

"Okay, I'll see you Thursday at Six o'clock."

"Cool. I'll reach out to Wanda either tonight or tomorrow. Monique yawned again. "I'll Talk to you later. Good night, Keish"

"All right, good night, boo."

They both hung up the phone. Monique stacked the papers neatly on the breakfast counter before brewing some tea, then jumped into the shower just when her phone rang. "Damn it!" She paused… "Nah. I'll call them back when I'm done." After her shower, she made her tea, carried it back to her bedroom, and glanced at the phone. It was Kendra. She got under the sheets, turned on the television, and called Kendra back. "Hey! Sweetheart." Monique huffed as she adjusted her twisted nightshirt.

"Hey! yourself!" Kendra responded cheerfully. "What are you doing?"

"Talking to you." Monique chuckled.

I know that silly." Kendra laughed.

"I was working on a project for work earlier, and it wore me out, so I took a shower, hopped into bed, and then called you, baby." Monique smiled.

"Aww." "It's pretty early... did you at least eat something?"

"I didn't get much rest, as you know." Monique chuckled. And I'm still full of that big lunch I ate this afternoon. The company I'm working on the ad for had lunch catered for us today." Monique said before yawning.

"That must've been nice. What did you guys have?"

"We had roast beef smothered in mushroom gravy, mashed potatoes, corn on the cob, green salad, and lots of desserts." she said, yawning again.

"That was a heavy lunch, but it sounds delectable! I only had pizza today, Kendra laughed. "So, do you have enough energy to talk. Kendra asked, lying on the bed.

"Yeah, that's cool. what would you like to talk about, sweetheart?"

"Well, I know we should've had this conversation *before* we slept together, she laughed. But since we already put the cart before the horse, I'd like to have that conversation now." Kendra smiled.

"Okay... you're freaking me out now." Monique said, quickly removing her nightshirt.

"No! it's nothing serious, honey." Kendra laughed, rolling over on her back and crossing her right leg over her left knee.

"Hold on, sweetie; I have to charge my phone. I'll call you back on my house phone, okay?"

"Okay. But hurry back!" Kendra told her playfully before hanging up. Kendra picked up the phone before the first ring went through. "Hello?" she said quickly.

"Oh, wow, I didn't even hear the phone ring." Monique giggled.

"So… I want to know a little more about you. You know, like…, how you grew up, your childhood; stuff like that." Kendra said, anxiously waiting to hear Monique's story.

"Hmmm. Where do I start? Let's see," Monique said, gathering her thoughts and taking one leg out from under the sheet. "Okay. Here it goes. I grew up in Mississippi on a farm with my mother and father. My dad sold it, and we moved to Maryland when I was seven. I was the only child that survived out of my mother's seven pregnancies, so, you know, I was spoiled." She laughed.

"Oh wow!" Kendra said in an impressive tone.

"Unfortunately, my mom died two years ago from cervical cancer. Monique fell silent.

"Oh, no! I'm sorry, Monique."

"Yeah, thanks, it's okay sweetie," she replied, clearing her throat, and taking a deep breath.

"Is your dad still alive?"

"Yes, he is. We haven't talked as much as we used to though, and it breaks my heart because I thought we were closer." Monique shook her head thinking about it.

"Do you mind if I ask you why?" Kendra asked cautiously.

"No, I don't mind at all. My mom set up a trust fund for me. Well, in other words, she had another life insurance policy my pops didn't know anything about, and she basically named me the only beneficiary."

"Oh, wow! That had to be tough when he found out,

huh?" Kendra said rhetorically. "Let me see if I have this straight. Your mom left you a trust fund, and you still went to college? Monique, wow. That's impressive."

"Thanks, sweetie. You and Keisha are the only people I told the story to about my dad by the way." she said, looking up at the ceiling. "But yeah, I always wanted to go to college, and thanks to my mom, I didn't have to take out any loans.

"That's awesome! Monique and thanks for sharing that part of your life with me." Kendra smiled sincerely. "What college did you go to?" she asked, waiting to be impressed some more.

"I went to Morgan State University and received my master's degree in business marketing."

"That's one of the first HBCUs, right?" "Holy shit! What do you know about HBCUs?" Monique asked in an impressive but shocked tone of voice.

"I know a little something about them." Kendra responded, blushing.

"Now miss lady… what about you? Tell me more about you." Monique said, taking a sip of her lukewarm tea.

"Well, my life isn't as impressive as yours, but here it goes." She chuckled.

"I'll be the judge of that." Monique retorted.

"Okay, I was born and raised in New England, also with my parents who are still together by the way"

"Cool. You still live with your parents Kendra?" Monique asked, spilling her tea as she placed the cup back on the nightstand.

"Good God, no! I can't live with my parents, they're

way too uptight!" she laughed, shaking her head rapidly.

"Oh, for real?" Monique chuckled. Keep going sweetie."

"I have one sister, Sarah, who you have already met and one brother, Johnathan. Johnathan is only sixteen, so he still lives with my parents. But he's a momma's boy and will most likely never move out." Kendra laughed.

"Cool." Monique responded, chuckling slightly.

"I went to the University of Vermont, majoring in journalism. In my junior year, I landed an internship at the radio station I'm currently employed at. Ultimately, I want to have my own television show like Oprah. She's so smart." Kendra said, her voice trailing off. "Wow! I thought you said your story wasn't impressive, sweetie."

"Well… Kendra responded shyly."

"It is impressive though! You set a goal for yourself and everything girl, you should be proud of that!" Monique said honestly. "I can see it now, "The Kendra Show" Monique gestured with jazz hands.

"Thank you, Monique, that's sweet." Kendra said bashfully.

"You can do it, baby; believe in yourself. Quick question though."

"Sure."

"Have you ever dated Black women before?"

"Black women are pretty much the only women I date."

"Hmm," Monique replied with a huge smile on her face. "Oh! No wonder you know about the HBCUs! "I get it now," Monique teased, making Kendra burst out into laughter.

"Am I the only White woman you've dated?" Kendra asked curiously.

"Yup, you're the first one beautiful."

"Thank, you." she blushed.

"So, how do you like it so far?" Kendra asked, twirling the telephone cord around her fingers while smiling.

"Well… I'm picking you up on Thursday, right?" Monique asked with a sly smile.

"Right!" Kendra replied cheerfully. "I'm glad we got to know more about each other." Her tone was sincere.

"Me too, sweetie." Monique said yawning. "Ooh! Excuse me.

"No problem, babe. I won't keep you any longer. I know you have to work in the morning… so, I'll talk to you tomorrow, okay?"

"Okay, sweetie. Goodnight, sweet dreams." Monique said yawning again.

"Sweet dreams," Kendra repeated.

They both hung up at the same time.

Thursday afternoon, Monique was on the highway in route to Kendra's house and waiting for a return call from Wanda. She left a message on Wanda's voicemail with the location and time she should meet them at the studio. Monique knew how busy Wanda can be with coaching games and wouldn't be surprised if she showed up without calling at all. Monique turned up the radio as "*Say Yes*" by Floetry played, her mind drifting to, her last sexual encounter with Kendra. She was anxious to see her again.

Twenty minutes or so later, Monique pulled up to Kendra's sister's house and got out of the car, unzipping her black and white windbreaker track suit jacket. As she walked up to the front porch to ring the doorbell her phone started buzzing.

"Hello?"

"Hey sunshine! It's me, Wanda."

Monique smiled widely.

"I got your message. Unfortunately, I can't make it to the Hip-Hop class, but I can make it for dinner."

"Oh! Okay, cool." Monique gave Wanda the address to the Greek restaurant.

"I've always wanted to know how stuffed grape leaves tasted. I'll see you later, honey. Bye-bye."

"Cool. See you later." Monique smiled and hung up the phone and then proceeded to the front door and rang the bell.

"Hey there Monique!" Sarah said pleasantly, opening the door, and stepping back.

"Come in, Kendra will be with you in a minute. Have a seat, please. Would you like something cold to drink?" she asked, closing the door.

"Nah. I'm good, but thanks."

Monique sat down in the green recliner chair while Sarah sat on the sofa to continue watching a new episode of *The Price Is Right*. Monique was yelling out prices at the television set along with Sarah by the time Kendra appeared from the back also wearing a track suit.

"Ahh… great minds think alike, I see." Monique said as she stood up to greet Kendra.

"That grey looks good on you, sweetie."

Kendra giggled and then walked over to give Monique

a hug, ending it with a kiss on the lips, making Monique blush.

"Are you ready to go, baby?" Monique asked her, her arm around Kendra's waist.

"I am." Kendra led the way to the front door as Monique bit her bottom lip and looked at Kendra's butt while she followed her.

"You guys have fun!" Sarah yelled out, waving goodbye, her eyes glued to the television. "One dollar! One dollar!" she screamed.

Once they both were by the car, Monique opened the passenger door for Kendra, and hurried to the driver's side. "I took the day off tomorrow by the way." Monique grinned.

"So, does that mean…."

Monique put up two fingers stopping her mid-sentence, and Kendra got the message and just smiled. "Are your friends meeting us there?" Kendra asked.

"Well, Keisha is, but Denise and Wanda weren't interested in taking the Hip-Hop classes, so they're gonna meet us at the restaurant."

"Okay. Hmm… what type of restaurant are we going to afterward?" Kendra asked curiously.

"Greek. You ever had Greek food before baby?" Monique asked, watching Kendra's facial expressions.

"Nope! This will be my first Greek food experience."

"Cool." Monique smiled as she joined Kendra in bopping her head to *"Bump Bump, Bump"* by B2K and P. Diddy.

Not long after, they arrived at their destination, and it

was no longer a Hip-Hop studio but an axe throwing venue instead. Monique looked over at Kendra perplexed. "Who knew?"

Kendra burst out laughing, then she looked over at Monique endearingly and said… "I don't care what we do, just as long as we do it together."

Monique paused. "That's so sweet, sweetie." She puckered up her lips and Kendra kissed them. "Come on baby, let's go inside."

As soon as they entered, Kendra noticed Keisha seated at the front entry first, and tapped Monique on the arm. "Look who's here." She smiled. Keisha spotted them.

"Hey boo!" she called out.

"Hey!" Monique replied, reaching out to hug her while Kendra waved hello nervously.

"Hey Kendra!" Keisha leaned in to hug her as well., then she turned to Monique and asked, "Are Denise and Wanda coming?"

"Nah, they weren't interested but, they're going to meet us at the restaurant. "Okay, that's good. But when did they change the venue to axe throwing?" Keisha asked, looking puzzled. "Hell, if I know!"

They all burst out laughing then Kendra stepped away to look around.

"Yawl wearing matching outfits already?" she asked, softly chuckling before Monique could answer.

"Nah. It's just a coincidence." Monique laughed.

"Yeah, okay." Keisha smirked.

Minutes later, Kendra walked over to them with a male instructor in tow. "And we're off!" Monique teased, causing them all to laugh, including the instructor.

Afterward, they all followed him to their section of the studio, where he explained the importance of throwing the axe so that the blade faces the target before releasing it. Even though they all verbalized they understood, the instructor waited for a return demonstration from the newbies before confidentially leaving them to assist the other guest that was waiting at the front desk.

"Alright, baby, you can go first," Monique told Kendra who picked up an axe confidently and hit the target on her first try. "Bullseye!" Monique cheered.

"Good job Kendra!" Keisha cheered.

"Alright, Keisha, your turn." Monique encouraged.

Keisha threw it but, it bounced back. "Oh shit! That must be a rubber axe or something, how did *that* happen?" she asked rhetorically. "Okay, Mo, it's your turn." Both she and Kendra cheered her on.

"You got this honey!" Kendra cheered.

Monique turned around and gave her a wink before throwing her axe. "Aww, man!" Monique cried. "Close but no damn cigar."

"You'll hit it next time!" Kendra rubbed her back lovingly.

Two hours passed, and Monique's phone rang, interrupting their game. "Hey, it's me Denise. Me and Tracey are at the restaurant, where are you guys?"

"Oh, hey, Denise. We're down the street. We'll be there in a few minutes."

Monique hung up the phone and told the girls.

"Is Wanda there with them?" Keisha asked, putting

down her axe, and picking up her purse.

"Nah. It's just Denise and Tracey." Monique grabbed Kendra's hand and they all left the venue and walked down the street toward the restaurant.

As soon as Monique made her way through the door…" Hey girl!" Denise shouted, walking over to her, and giving her a hug and a kiss on the cheek. Keisha and Kendra were directly behind her.

She hugged and kissed Keisha too, but only waved hello to Kendra. Tracey raised an eyebrow at her behavior but didn't make mention of it. Everyone noticed how Denise singled Kendra out, but Monique just shook her head and supportively grabbed Kendra's hand before walking over to the hostess and asking for a party-sized table, never letting go of Kendra's hand. Within minutes, they were escorted to a large table where Keisha and Denise ordered cocktails.

"Everybody agrees to wait for Wanda before we order dinner, right?" Monique asked.

"Right." They all said in unison. "You alright baby?" Monique whispered in Kendra's ear.

"Yes!" Kendra responded cheerfully, but she was blinking rapidly, and trying to appear unbothered by Denise's behavior.

Monique knew Denise's behavior bothered her and squeezed her hand tenderly. Ten minutes later, Wanda came in singing, "Hey yawl!" following right behind her was an unfamiliar female.

"Hey sunshine!" She said to Monique who stood up to greet her. "I'm glad you could make it." Monique said elatedly, quickly hugging her and then looking over and saying hello to her guest.

Afterward, Wanda placed her hand gently on Kendra's shoulder before bending down to say hello and give her a peck on the cheek. Kendra placed her hand on top of hers as she repeated her sentiments.

"What's up, sugar!" Keisha belted out after taking a sip of her drink.

"Hey boo!" Denise shouted, waving at her from the other side of the table.

"How you doin'?" Tracey chimed in.

"Hey, everybody… this is my friend Millicent. Millicent, this is everybody," Wanda finally said, waving her hand across the table and making everyone laugh.

"Hey guys." Millicent responded, innocently.

Wanda pulled out her chair, and she sat down eagerly. They all chatted and looked over their individual menus, deciding to start off with a few appetizers for everyone to share since neither of them have eaten Greek food before. They started with Tzatziki, Fava Santorini, and Saganaki, all served with fresh pita bread. For the entrées, Kendra and Monique ordered the marinated grilled lamb chops with oven browned potatoes and vegetables.

"I'm gonna order the Halibut filet with sauteed spinach, grape tomatoes, capers, olives and spring onions." Denise said.

"Now that sounds good, make it two orders please." Tracey commented to the waiter who was taking down the order at the end of the table.

Keisha ordered the eggplant stuffed with aromatic

ground beef, topped with bechamel sauce and chicken breast. Wanda ordered a shrimp salad, with a side of Dolma (grape leaves) and her guest Millicent was a vegan, so, she also ordered Dolma and a Spanakopita (fine layers of phyllo dough topped with fresh spinach and feta cheese). Everyone was enjoying their food and sharing laughter with the traditional Greek music playing in the background.

After dinner they all thanked Monique for introducing them to Greek cuisine and said their goodbyes with hugs and kisses.

"You wanna come home with me or would you like me to take you home?" Monique asked Kendra as she unlocked her car remotely.

"Is that a trick question, Monique?" Kendra asked her, chuckling nervously and playing with the zipper on her track suit jacket.

"Well… you know. I had to be sure. I didn't want to play myself" Monique smiled hunching her shoulders playfully. She knew with one-hundred percent certainty that Kendra wanted to be in her bed tonight, and she wanted her in it.

When they got to her house, Monique said… "I set out a fresh towel and wash cloth if you want to take a shower baby."

"Oh!" Kendra said, turning around rapidly. "You had every intention of bringing me home with you, didn't you?" Kendra exclaimed shaking her finger at Monique and poking her on the arm playfully.

"Ouch!" Monique exaggerated, rubbing the area with a

frown, and pretending to be hurt. "Oh, stop it!"

Kendra chuckled, removing her track suit as she walked over to the sofa. "I took a shower earlier babe, but thanks."

"Okay, suit yourself." Monique dropped her keys on the breakfast counter and sauntered to the bedroom taking off her tracksuit along the way and then carefully removed her jewelry. On her way to the bathroom, she caught a glimpse of Kendra drinking water on the sofa with her braless nipples peeking through her white tee-shirt, her matching bikinis bottoms, and white ankle socks. "Damn!" Monique mumbled, going into the bathroom, and getting in the shower. Moments later, she heard a knock on the bathroom door. "Come in, sweetie."

Kendra walked in completely naked and slowly opened the shower door. "Would you like some company?" she asked seductively.

"Oh my God!" Monique whispered softly, squeezing the soap out of the cloth.

Kendra moved in closer and asked Monique for the soap. Monique handed it to her in what seemed to be slow motion. Kendra ran the wet sudsy bar across Monique's breast down to her stomach before getting on her knees to wash her legs, and every inch of her. She motioned Monique to turn around and licked her way up the back of Monique legs, making them quiver with every lick. Monique moaned and bit her bottom lip, her palms against the wall while the shower water beat down on her plastic shower cap.

"I thought you took a shower already?" Monique

whispered, turning her head to get a glimpse of Kendra who was now licking her back.

"Can't a girl change her mind?" Kendra responded, her eyes closed as her lips left a trail of kisses up Monique's spine soft and slow.

"You're so fucking sexy." Monique said to her, turning around carefully and looking at Kendra's blue mascara running down from her beautiful green eyes and smudging her lovely face. Monique lifted Kendra up slowly, pressing her back against the tiled shower wall as they kissed tenderly. "Wait, baby." Monique paused, letting Kendra down slowly. "Let's get out of here before we bust our asses' baby…, this ain't the movies." she smirked licking her lips and making Kendra laugh. Kendra took the soap and wash cloth to clean between her legs before getting out and drying off, waiting patiently for Monique to do the same.

They softly tongue-kissed while Monique was drying off. Kendra abruptly stopped, dropped her towel, and ran out of the bathroom to the bedroom. Monique quickly dropped hers, and ran after her, swatting her ass before Kendra jumped on the bed giggling.

"I want you so bad, baby." Monique told her, looking down at her passionately, then pinching Kendra's left nipple and causing her lips to part as she grunted with pleasure encouraging Monique to pinch the right one. "You like that?" Monique whispered against her ear.

"Yes." Kendra answered softly then opened her legs and wrapped them around Monique's waist, pulling her down closer. "You wanna get your strap?"

"Fuck yes." Monique answered, lustfully.

"Okay, baby, go for it," Kendra told her, uncrossing her legs, lifting her hair, and removing one of the pillows.

"You sure you're ready for that, baby?" Monique asked her, licking her lips seductively.

"Yes, I'm ready." Kendra answered.

"Cool, baby, I'll be right back." Monique said, hurrying off to her hall closet and returning with several dildo's giving Kendra a choice of three colors and sizes.

"Wow!" Kendra said softly, widening her eyes and choosing the short, medium-width rainbow colored one. She helped Monique into her harness, then started a flow of lustful kisses. She thrusted her body backward onto the bed and opened her legs wide, inviting Monique to enter.

Monique climbed on the bed with her bottom lip in her mouth, holding the dildo carefully to prevent it from getting any lint from the sheet, then she got in between Kendra's legs and positioned herself for entry. She bent down and kissed Kendra again while placing her left hand on the headboard as her right hand guided the dildo into Kendra's opening. Kendra was a little dry, making it difficult for Monique to insert completely. "Wow, you're really tight, baby." Monique whispered. She removed the dildo and went down on Kendra, licking and then sucking her clit to moisten her before trying to enter her again.

Kendra gasped and began grinding her hips when Monique placed the tip of her tongue at her opening, circling it to tease her before coming back up to try again. Kendra, however, was still a bit dry inside. "I probably used too much vinegar this afternoon." Kendra chuckled bashfully, turning her face slightly. "Do you have any lube honey?"

"Yes, baby, I do. I'll be right back!" Monique told her, jumping off the bed holding the dildo in her hand as she hurried off to retrieve the lube from her medicine cabinet. She washed off the dildo and walked quickly back to the room. "Okay, baby, we should be good to go now." Monique smiled sinisterly while she squeezed the lube on the shaft of the dildo. She walked over to Kendra and said… rub it in baby.

Kendra obligingly got to her knees and let her eyes do the talking as she began rubbing in the lube, gripping it with both hands.

"Mm, mm, mm." was all Monique could say as she watched her before intermittently throwing her head back with a hand behind her neck, fully enjoying the moment. Kendra enjoyed watching her reaction. Monique reached out to caress Kendra's face and then leaned in to suck on her lips while simultaneously pinching her nipples, making Kendra gasp at the sweet pain. "Lay down baby and open your legs wide for me." Monique ordered her. Kendra obeyed but not before wiping the excess lube off her hands and putting it on her hairless box. "My god." Monique moaned, shaking her head slowly and stepping up on the bed. She guided the dildo once again, entering Kendra slowly with ease.

Kendra gasped and clung onto Monique's back while Monique tirelessly penetrated her. Both began to moan with each climax becoming greater than the last as beads of sweat fell from Monique's face onto Kendra. Kendra smeared the sweat around in ecstasy each time Monique placed her fist into the mattress for stability during the thrust. Kendra continued to moan out loud and Monique continued to drip sweat during her strokes, with Kendra sticking out her tongue to catch it, making Monique scream out in pleasure at the sight of it. "Oh, my God, baby… You're fucking fantastic…, you're fucking fantastic!" Kendra cried while her hands gripped Monique's ass, assisting her with the strokes, pulling Monique deeper inside her.

Monique's tempo began to slow down after she climaxed for the last time. Kendra squeezed her breasts together and offered her pink swollen nipples to Monique, who proceeded to suck on them slowly with her eyes closed, softly moaning, and then pulling out. Afterward, she laid her sweaty body on top of Kendra's one of Kendra's nipples still in her mouth, and one nostril pressed against Kendra's chest. They were both breathing heavily.

"Whew!" Monique commented, lifting her head before rolling off Kendra and loosening the harness, trying her best to give Kendra one last kiss. But she was too weak and instead dropped her hands to her side then softly snored.

Kendra looked over at Monique and smiled with satisfaction before removing her hair from her face, getting off the bed, and going into the bathroom to clean herself up. "Damn, that was good." Kendra mumbled, wiping herself and drying her hands before going back into the bedroom and laying down, Monique's snoring lullabying her to sleep.

The next morning, Monique woke up with cotton

mouth. She looked to the left side of the bed for Kendra. "Yuck!" she mumbled, smacking her lips together, frowning and getting up to clean out her mouth. Then she sauntered to the kitchen where Kendra was cracking eggs. "Good morning beautiful, I thought you left me." Monique teased, kissing Kendra on the nape of her neck.

"Good morning honey. "How do you like your eggs?" she asked, cheerfully.

"Do you know how to make eggs sunny side up?" Monique asked, one eyebrow raised.

"You bet I do. My dad loves his eggs sunny side up. "Cool." Monique winked, giving her two thumbs up. "Two sunny side eggs coming right up!" Kendra grinned.

Monique scanned the fridge for the cantaloupe she purchased the other day on her way home. "Do you like cantaloupe, baby?" she asked, taking it out and sniffing it.

"I love cantaloupe!" Kendra responded, sprinkling pepper on Monique's eggs. "I see you found your way around the kitchen." Monique smiled as she cut into the cantaloupe and scooped out the seeds.

"Well… your kitchen isn't that big, so, it was pretty easy finding my way around." She slid the eggs out of the pan onto a plate then handed it to Monique.

"These are perfect, thank you sweetie." Monique was already salivating.

'You're welcome, honey." Kendra replied, relieved that she didn't break the yolk as she walked with her plate of scrambled eggs to the breakfast counter to join Monique.

Monique placed three slices of cantaloupe on her plate. "How many slices do you want, sweetie?"

"Oh, I'll take three as well, thank you," Kendra replied, her mouth full of eggs. "They look and smell so fresh." Kendra lifted her plate to receive the cantaloupe. They ate their eggs and cantaloupe with one hand while holding hands with the other.

"Do you want to hang out today, sweetie?" Monique asked, letting go of Kendra's hand to push her last piece of egg onto her fork.

"Yes!" Kendra exclaimed, and then bit into her cantaloupe down to the rind.

"Cool." Monique responded, getting up to put her plate in the dishwasher, and gliding back, returning to kiss Kendra.

An hour later, they were dressed and out enjoying the afternoon at Nanjemoy Creek, where they took a guided scenic sailboat tour of the Potomac River, ending the excursion with a seafood dinner at *Captain John's Crab House* before Monique drove Kendra back to Towson.

Two weeks later, while they were in bed together, Kendra reminded Monique that she would be leaving the following Sunday.

Monique wasn't ready to let her go yet, but she understood. She cleared her throat and kissed Kendra on the forehead. "Listen, baby, Keisha always has an end- of- the- summer BBQ at her house, and I would love it if you came with me. It's on Saturday." Monique looked at her tenderly.

"Of course, I'll go with you, honey!" Kendra replied, scooting over, and laying on Monique's chest while running her fingers along the ridges of her tank top.

Suddenly, Monique sat up, rolled on top of Kendra, and began tickling her, causing Kendra to kick her feet up while begging Monique through her giggling to stop. Monique leaned back on her elbows in laughter before abruptly jumping off the bed and running into the living room and plopping on the sofa.

"Oh! You think you're getting away that easy?" Kendra yelled from the bedroom before hopping off the bed and running into the living room tackling Monique quickly and making her scream out "Mercy!" repeatedly. Kendra stopped and fell back on the sofa out of breath. "This was the best summer vacation I had in my whole life." Kendra told her lovingly.

"Cool… me too, baby." Monique said, taking a hold of Kendra's face in her hands, both exchanging tongues as they kissed each other tenderly.

The famous end- of- summer BBQ at Keisha's house was here! The music was a mixture of old school hip-hop and rhythm and blues with a touch of pop because Keisha knew Kendra was a DJ, and she wanted to show off her music game. Keisha was in her living room changing the diaper of one of the twins on the sofa when Monique and Kendra walked through the open front door.

"Hey, boo!" Monique shouted out to greet her.

"Your home is beautiful Keisha!" Kendra said softly enjoying the scenery. "Where would you like me to put the bottles of wine we brought for the party?"

"Aww, thank you, Kendra. But you didn't have to do that." Keisha put down her fussing toddler and tapped her pampered bottom before taking the bottles from her.

Meanwhile, Cicely was walking in through the back door, holding the other twin's hand. Cicely greeted everyone with a one- arm hug, and a cheerful hello. Keisha introduced her as Karen's fiancé, causing Kendra to look quickly over at Monique with a surprised look while Keisha and Monique chuckled at her reaction.

"Come on, you, guys! Let's go outside with the rest of the folks and enjoy this BBQ!" Keisha said, backing out the door while holding the wine bottles in the air as she danced to the beat of Lil Kim's "*Magic Stick*" with Kendra and Monique dancing alongside her. "Come with me for a minute!" Keisha told Kendra, snatching her away from Monique after putting the bottles of wine in the ice tub. "I want to introduce you to my co-parent Karen." Keisha continued, while Kendra looked back at Monique with a surprised look yet again.

Monique knew why, but she chuckled and hunched her shoulders. Karen noticed the two approaching the table and removed the right sided headphone to hear what Keisha had to say. "I want to introduce you to Kendra, Monique's girlfriend," Keisha told Karen, while Kendra blushed at her new title.

"Oh! nice to meet you, Kendra." Karen told her, shaking her hand and smiling.

"Nice to meet you too," Kendra commented before Karen had to return to the turntable. Keisha stayed at the table talking to Karen, and Kendra danced her way back over to Monique who was piling BBQ and potato salad on her plate. "I'm so impressed with the way Keisha and Karen co-parent…"

"Yeah, they're great," Monique retorted while Kendra started fixing herself a plate.

"Oh, wow. Keisha forgot to put the raisins in the potato salad, huh?" Kendra asked.

Monique's fork paused at her lips in shock while Kendra started giggling at the look on her face.

"I was just kidding honey… I was just kidding." she repeated, eating a forkful.

"Gurl…I was about to say." Monique chuckled, shaking her head before she continued to eat while bopping her head to the music of Matchbox Twenty's "Unwell".

Just after that, Cicely came out of the house with the twins, who gravitated immediately toward Kendra and Monique. They both wiped their mouths and put their plates down and then picked up a twin and started playing with them.

"You mind holding them a little longer while I set up their highchairs?" Cicely asked them.

"No, It's cool!" Monique told her while Kendra was dancing with her toddler. When Cicely returned, they put the twins down and she walked them over by the deck to feed them.

They quickly kissed then picked up their plates and finished eating. After a brief intermission, Karen resumed her DJ session and played "21 questions" by 50cent. Monique took Kendra's hand and began singing and rapping the lyrics while looking at her, making Kendra blush while also two-stepping to the beat. They kissed again then mingled with the other guests.

"Let's bring the lovers to the yard with this old school favorite." Karen said on the microphone, softly sliding on Mariah Carey's *"Vision of Love"* while Cicely brought her over a plate of food.

"Can I have this dance?" Monique asked Kendra in a smooth voice, extending her hand out to her.

Kendra took her hand with delight, and they slow-danced, looking at one another lovingly with Kendra's hands gently placed on Monique's shoulders.

Out of the corner of Kendra's eye, she observed Denise and Tracey walking in. Denise waved reluctantly at her while Tracey walked over to the buffet table near the grill to fix herself a plate. Denise walked over toward them and tapped Monique on her back, then she quickly walked over to where Keisha was sitting.

"That woman is so fucking rude," Kendra thought, while she faked a smile.

Monique turned around to see who tapped her, gestured hello with her head then quickly returned her attention to Kendra just before the music stopped. She took Kendra's hand and walked over to the buffet table. They greeted Tracey then grabbed something cold to drink. Kendra grabbed a beer while Monique grabbed a soda.

Wanda came through the doors next, with her friend Millicent, all greeting each other with cheerful hellos. Kendra noticed the corn on the cob by the other grill and asked Monique if she wanted an ear because she couldn't take her eyes off it.

"Nah, baby. I'm good. Go help yourself."

Millicent interjected, smiling "I was looking at the corn

too. I'll walk with you."

Monique tapped Kendra on her bum as she walked away, causing her to act surprisingly shy. "So, are you and Wanda a couple?" Kendra asked Millicent at the grill, putting her beer down and getting herself a paper corn cob holder.

"Yeah, you can say that." Millicent blushed, putting a hefty pile of salad greens and radishes on her plate, while Kendra was slathering herb butter on her corn. "Do you live here in Maryland?" Millicent asked her, pouring honey mustard vinaigrette dressing over her salad.

"No, I live in New Hampshire," Kendra replied, biting into her corn as drops of butter fell onto her chin, down to the front of her navy blue and white tennis dress. "Oops!" she commented grabbing a napkin.

"Oh, I have family in Vermont," Millicent shared with her as they began walking back to where Monique and Wanda were standing.

The toddlers were running in and out of the sliding back door until one of them tripped on the sliding door track and busted her lip. Keisha and Cicely ran over immediately to help her. They took the twins inside and cleaned them up, with Cicely returning with the news that Keisha was putting them to bed. Monique went inside to use the bathroom and bumped into Denise on her way out. "Hey, you!" Monique said, reaching out an arm to hug her.

Denise hugged her back. "Can I ask you something?" Denise asked her in a serious tone.

"Of course. What's up?" Monique replied, smiling.

"Why are you still with that girl?" Denise asked,

seeming a bit agitated.

"Say what?" Monique asked, slightly frowning, and confused.

"I said, why are you still with that girl." Denise repeated.

"Whoa!" Monique commented. "Let's talk inside. Monique's tone was serious but pleasant.

Denise followed her into the hallway.

"Yo… what's your problem, Denise?" she asked her with a wrinkled brow. "Did Kendra do something to you I'm not aware of or something?" Monique relaxed her facial expression, but her shoulders were raised.

"No, but she exists," Denise responded, sucking her teeth.

"What the…Why are you tripping? for real Denise." Monique said, perplexed at her behavior.

"I'm not tripping. I'm just saying, you never been with a girl like her before… right?"

"What difference does that make, Denise? You're not gonna keep disrespecting my lady! I'm serious man. This shit ain't remotely cool. And *everybody* sees when you do it. You're not gonna keep disrespecting me and making her uncomfortable when we get together. for real." Monique continued, pacing, and gesticulating with her hands and trying to keep her voice down.

"What about me?" Denise asked her, moving toward her slowly and gently taking her arm to stop her from pacing, which confused Monique even more.

"What about you, Denise?" she asked her, her eyes widening as she took a step back to move away from her.

"Why you never ask me to be your lady, Monique?" Denise inched in closer. Monique had her back up against the wall at that point, and Denise leaned in and kissed Monique on the lips. Monique stood there in shock before quickly moving to the side. That didn't stop Denise from opening her heart up to her, expressing everything she kept pent up for the longest time.

Monique put a finger to her lips and said, "Hold on, baby." She closed her eyes briefly then opened them slowly. "*Why* haven't you ever said anything to me before Denise? Why *now*?" Her tone was soft.

"Because you were a player, Monique." Denise responded. "But when you saw Kendra, you just up and changed your mind, and it pissed me the fuck off." Denise backed away slowly. "I always had a thing for you, Monique. You had to know that." Denise looked into her eyes.

"Shit girl… I didn't have a clue." Monique said, patting her braids. "Listen, baby, I'm flattered and everything, believe me I am. But… I wish you would've said something to me before, I'm with Kendra now, sweetheart. And we're serious." She took Denise's hands gently and looked at her sincerely. "When I'm in a commented relationship, I don't step out baby."

"So, you don't find me attractive then?" Denise asked, looking sad.

"Come on now, I never said that Denise… stop it. You know your ass is fine." Monique chuckled then licked her lips, making a sly grin. "Besides, what about Tracey? Yawl be at it for a while, and she seems like a nice enough person."

"What about Tracey?" Denise responded dryly with one of her eyebrows raised. "Oh wow."

Monique was at a loss for words. "Listen, let's head back outside and enjoy ourselves, okay?" Monique smiled.

"Okay," Denise responded, walking side by side with Monique toward the backyard.

Suddenly, Monique stopped, grabbed Denise's arm gently, and looked directly into her eyes kindly. "Denise, baby. Please stop being disrespectful to Kendra, I really like her."

"I will Monique. I'm sorry, boo." Denise said sincerely with a smile. Once outside, they walked their separate ways to their loved ones. Karen finished the night off with the classic party song *"Before* I *Let You* Go." by Frankie Beverly and Maze. All the guests came together in the middle of the yard, dancing and singing out the lyrics.

Denise stepped away from Tracey and danced over to Kendra. She grabbed her hand and apologized for her behavior before hugging her and kissing her on the cheek. Kendra was shocked but smiled from ear-to-ear glancing over at Monique, who winked and continued to dance and sing, eventually reaching out for Kendra's hand. Wanda and Millicent were dancing on each other along with Karen and Cicely, while Keisha looked down at the crowd from her bedroom window, bopping her head to the music, in the hopes of not waking up the twins. All the guests did their fair share of cleaning up the backyard including turning off the grill and hosing down the pavers, while Karen and Cicely disassembled the DJ equipment and loaded it into their van.

Afterward, Kendra went inside to use the bathroom while Monique waited in the car for her, then she drove to her townhouse to continue their evening together.

"I want you to stay the night," Monique said softly, removing her clothes, and helping Kendra remove hers.

They didn't say another word – They just looked at each other. Monique walked into the bathroom and turned on the shower, getting in with Kendra directly behind her. They both washed their bodies, dried off, and snuggled into Monique's bed, still… a word was yet spoken. They tongue-kissed slowly with purpose, while Monique ran her hands through Kendra's damp hair, both breathing heavily into one another's mouth.

"Make love to me," Monique whispered, laying down, spreading her legs, and squeezing her breast upward to lick each of her nipples.

Kendra was pleasantly shocked, moaning at the sight of her. She climbed on top of Monique, taking over her breast, sucking her nipples hungrily. Monique squealed with delight, unable to keep her body from moving. She panted as her wet box dripped onto the sheets. Kendra nibbled her way down to Monique's neatly trimmed hairy box, glistening with moisture. She parted Monique's lips, exposing a large brown pearl that she began sucking on gently. Monique's body was out of control, making Kendra hold down her thighs to keep her calm. Monique continued to squeal and moan louder each time Kendra's mouth encircled her pulsating pearl while softly shouting…

"Oh, Shit!" repeatedly. Monique's final climax was so

hard, it had Kendra reminiscing about her dive off the deep end of a swimming pool. "Come here, baby." Monique called out, reaching for her.

Kendra took her hand as she crawled toward her slowly, softly kissing Monique's body on the way to her mouth.

"I…I love you, Kendra," Monique said, looking into her eyes unapologetically.

"I love you too, honey," Kendra replied.

They both hugged each other, as if it were the last time. The following morning, they ordered breakfast in and made love once again and took a shower together before Monique had to drive Kendra to her sister's house to pack for her evening flight to New Hampshire. They rode all the way to Sarah's house holding one another's hand. Monique kissed Kendra's hand at every red light until they pulled up to the house.

"I'm gonna miss the fuck out of you, baby," Monique told her, looking at her lovingly.

"Aww, honey," Kendra responded, rubbing Monique's cheek with the back of her hand. "I'm gonna miss the fuck out of you too."

Monique got out of the car, opened Kendra's door, and helped her out. They began tongue kissing passionately and slowly, as Monique pressed Kendra's back against the car door with her arms wrapped around Monique's neck.

"Cool," Monique said softly, looking down at her and smiling before letting her go.

Kendra walked to the front door, turning around often to blow kisses at her. Monique stared at her lovingly with tear mist in her eyes until Kendra was inside safely. She shook her sadness off and got back into the car, turned on the radio, and started jamming to *"Never Leave"* by Lumidee on her way back to Potomac.

Two years later… Wanda was a vegan and gave Millicent a promise ring on the day after they were both baptized at their new home church. Denise broke it off with Tracey because Tracey wasn't clingy enough for her, she wanted a woman to dote over her, and until she found this woman, she would date, and date often. The twins were in kindergarten, and Keisha made time for a special someone named Nicole, who was the nurse at the twins' primary care doctor's office; she was smitten with the three of them. Karen and Cicely were still together and are planning a destination wedding in Jamaica in February, one week after the jazz festival (because of the traditionally low airfares). They wanted all their guests to be able to attend.

On one of Monique's many trips to New Hampshire to visit Kendra, she made private dinner reservations for two on a balcony overlooking the grand landscape at one of New Hampshire's most romantic restaurants. Five minutes after being seated at the restaurant, the waiter arrived with their pre-ordered dinner of grilled Halibut, herb roasted chicken, dumplings with Acorn squash bisque and a roasted beet salad Monique ordered earlier. Afterward, they shared a slice of blue forest cake and toasted each other with their glass of white wine.

"I love you," Kendra told her softly.

Monique wiped her mouth with trembling hands, cleared her throat, pushed back her chair, and got down on one knee.

Kendra slapped both of her hands around her mouth in utter surprise as the tears filled her eyes.

Monique cleared her throat again and looked away to keep herself from crying and screwing up the proposal. "Sweetheart," Monique said, Kendra hands gripping both sides of her seat now.

"Yes?" Kendra replied, her voice shaking.

"I love you and I can't see myself with anybody else but you." She continued, her voice cracking. Monique opened the blue velvet box that housed an 18kt gold and platinum ring with a two-carat cushion cut Canary yellow diamond, surrounded by white diamond rounds. "Will you marry me, baby?" Monique asked nervously.

"Yes! Yes! Yes!" Kendra replied, screaming with joy and holding out her left hand for Monique to place the ring on her finger.

"Cool!" Monique said, a tear falling down her cheek as she grabbed Kendra. She lifted Kendra out of the chair with a tight hug before kissing her softly as onlookers cheered and congratulated them.

Kendra flashed her ring and thanked everyone as they walked out of the restaurant. Within the year… Monique relocated her job to New Hampshire, and Kendra got her own radio talk show. Keisha and Sarah, who were appointed as maids of honor, helped Kendra and Monique plan their lavish wedding at a spectacular mountain resort in Lincoln, New Hampshire. The twins were the ring bearers. Wanda, Millicent, Denise, and Kendra's adopted cousin Simone were the bridesmaids; and Kendra's brother, Johnathan and three male co-worker friends of Monique's were their escorts.

The wedding was held outdoors in a glorious chapel next to a stream with the splendor of nature at everyone's feet. Family and guests were ushered to their seats in white wooden chairs, where the backs were adorned with white tulle tied in a bow and marigolds tucked inside them. They watched the bridesmaids walk down the aisle, each wearing a one shoulder burnt orange satin gown arm in arm with the escorts in white tuxedos. The maids of honor followed, wearing marigold yellow strapless gowns, and stopping at Monique who was at the altar, wearing a white lace jumpsuit, trimmed in white satin with detachable train, as she waited for her bride, and her heart pounding with anxious delight. The pianist began to play the bridal march, and Monique's heart skipped a beat when she saw her gorgeous bride walking toward her with her arm in the cuff of her father's.

Kendra was wearing a matching white satin and lace bridal gown with a train she recently purchased; and a white lace trimmed veil handed down from her mother. Monique was so nervously happy she didn't recognize the special guest in the front row. When Kendra met her at the altar, they held hands and read aloud their personal vows to each other. Afterward, the officiate pronounced them married, and the crowd clapped wildly for them as they cried happy tears, sealing their marriage with a kiss before turning around and holding up their ring fingers in victory.

Suddenly, Monique gasped. She began crying profusely. She walked toward the distinguished gentleman in the front row, who was wearing a cream and tan colored three-piece suit and standing with Kendra's parents.

"DADDY!" Monique cried out.

"Nique, Nique!" Her father replied smiling and opening his arms to receive her. They hugged each other tightly while Monique whispered, "This has got to be the best day of my life!" Her eyes closed as she cried happy tears. Her father told her how proud he was of her and how much he loved her; while Keisha and Kendra winked and gave each other the thumbs up, happy with themselves for making this possible.

All sixty family and friends gathered in the beautifully decorated cocktail reception room that was filled with the colors of the wedding party. The guests admired the room while looking for their designated tables. Kendra and Monique walked with their fathers to the middle of the room and danced to *"Dance with My Father"* by Luther Vandross. All of them crying happy tears.

Afterward, Kendra and Monique were escorted to their brides' table by their fathers before they went to their table and joined the other guests to look over the outstanding cuisine menu. The photographer took pictures nonstop of everyone bringing in gifts and greeting the brides at their table or doing just about everything until it was time for the brides to take their special moment photos. They followed the photographer outside where they took several romantic pictures under tall fully bloomed green trees, on the lush green hills that portrayed the beauty of the cascading Smoky Mountains. They took their last set on the wooden bridge that crossed over the stream.

Once back inside, they sat down at their table and waited to be served their food. Everyone was given a choice of soup and salad, New England clam chowder with onion, potatoes, and bacon in a creamy broth, a field salad of mixed greens, grape tomatoes, red onion, cucumber, and carrots topped with white balsamic and herb vinaigrette. There was also an appetizer of either Philly steak and cheese dip, or crispy Brussel sprouts tossed with siracha ginger butter and sesame seeds. And finally for entrees, there was grilled black Angus beef ribeye with house-made beef butter, crispy smashed potatoes, sauteed green beans, and spicy vegetable stir fry.

After dinner, they cut the wedding cake and fed it to each other with the guests looking on in admiration, while the photographer captured the moment for them. The wedding came to a pleasant end with Keisha and Sarah securing the cake's top tier along with gathering the gifts for them, while Denise flirted with Simone. On their way out of the venue to their honeymoon, everyone threw lavender flower petals at them, encouraging them to stop and kiss each other once more. They took off running down the stairs hand-in-hand before jumping into their new white beamer and driving off into the sunset with five rainbow-colored tin cans hanging from the bumper.

Lavender on the Bayou

"This must be the hottest May I have ever felt! Louisiana was never this damn hot when I lived with Maw-Maw growing up," Marie said to herself aloud, twenty minutes after driving off the U.S. Route 190 from Texas into Lake Charles, Louisiana. The top of her brand-new, red candy-apple-colored Jeep was down as she drove into the circular driveway of the beige lime-plastered, two-story colonial home on the Bayou she recently inherited from her dearly departed grandmother Apolline. "I was too busy being a kid; I guess I didn't notice the heat." She chuckled, picking up her floppy straw hat from the passenger seat and tucking her Frizzy, prematurely greying, black hair inside.

She climbed out of the car, adjusted her black capri pants, and slammed the door. Then she removed her luggage from the back seat while looking at the second-floor wrap-around balcony, finally walking up the six neutral-colored paver stone steps leading to the spacious front porch. She set her luggage beside one of the two black rocking chairs to open the solid white French double doors.

Marie walked inside smiling as the fond childhood memories engulfed her senses. She couldn't help but inhale the faint aroma of lavender and vanilla that her grandmother tended to hand out and burn throughout the home, most likely thriving in her backyard garden still. "Hmm, her sweet labor of love," Marie mumbled, closing the front door behind her and placing her keys on the dehydrated sage leaves left in the abalone shell on the stone console table. She shook her head slowly, remembering her grandmother's voice.

Marie walked through the wide vestibule into the first parlor, leaving her luggage on the bare, lusterless walnut wood floors. In the entryway, she picked up a patchwork quilt thrown over the back of the mustard-colored Victorian easy chair that her grandmother would sit in while she sewed and retold stories of the old days when their family migrated from Hispaniola (modern-day Haiti) before making a home for themselves in Louisiana. Marie recalled this memory fondly as she held the fresh-smelling quilt to her nose with one hand, the other hand resting on the back of the easy chair.

She stared out into the distance and walked down memory lane when suddenly, she began to feel the intensity of the heat. "Whew! It's hot!" She quickly removed her hat and tossed it along with the quilt onto the easy chair as dust particles flew about. She pulled the chain on the vintage ceiling fan before turning on the bronze metal floor fan adjacent to the fireplace, where dusty family portraits lined the mantle above the cracked black marble fireplace hearth. She unbuttoned her white blouse, exposing her white lace bra, holding her bosom before the fan as the warm air from both blew on her sticky skin.

She closed her eyes, imagining cool air blowing on her. "Where in the heck is the central air thermostat, anyway?" As soon as she walked out of the parlor, she found the thermostat on the wall by the entryway's door frame, turning it on to a cool 63 degrees. She stood there momentarily, facing the vent above her to allow the cool air to blow directly on her face as loving memories of her grandmother played over in her mind. Apolline Baptiste was a devout Catholic Creole woman with a mixed heritage of African, French, and Native American descent. She was a delicate, red-skinned beauty standing at five-foot-seven inches with a tiny waist, soft petite hands, and waist-length, kinky-straight, silver hair she let hang freely. Her mouth was always curved into a smile, and her eyes were dark and soft yet fiery- when someone (especially Pawpaw) made her angry. She would raise her angelic voice and then smoke her "special" tobacco in her long-stem pipe- a habit she sustained well into her nineties. Perhaps that's why she always smiled.

Maw-Maw was a well-respected community member revered for healing folks and selling lavender syrup, oil, and vanilla powder to some of the local grocers. I can't say I knew Maw-Maw to do much else, really. The French called her a "Traiteur" (translated as treater or natural healer in English). She never accepted payments for her healing work but would accept the money if offered as a gift. She never married the man we knew as Pawpaw, who impregnated her with four female children. One of my aunts died of "crib death" when she was two months old, and I don't think Maw-Maw ever forgave Pawpaw for that since he was the only one at home with her when it happened.

We were taught to stay out of grown folks' business, and we did- unless we wanted a sore behind (which my brothers seemed to want more often than not). People say Maw-Maw was a plaçage because she was a kept woman of Creole descent. Pawpaw was a kind man- of not too many words, who provided for the family well, I must say. He stood at six-foot-four inches tall. He was handsome, extremely fair-skinned, with straight dark hair. He was hardly home, so I could understand why people got that idea. But no one dared ask Maw-Maw if this was true outright. Well…, at least I didn't. And when Pawpaw passed, the community came by in droves to pay their respects, leaving behind money, food, and gifts for her, none of which she needed. But if you ask me, they came by to be noisy. You should've seen them looking and whispering as they wandered around the house, but it was a spectacle when Maw-Maw died ten years later. They had a parade, and everyone wore tee shirts with her picture on them, dancing alongside and behind her casket, which was placed inside a carriage pulled by two white horses down to the cemetery. They sent Maw-Maw home in style- yes, indeed. I couldn't attend because my work had me so far away, and that broke my heart, but the rest of the family did, so they took pictures and videos and saved a shirt for me. In any case, I made it to the will reading.

My mother, Vivian, was an alcoholic and died at

seventy-two from Cirrhosis, two years after Maw-Maw. My aunts could be the next runners-up if they continue drinking like they did. They all developed an unhealthy liking for mint juleps on a count of Maw-Maw throwing "get-togethers" whenever Pawpaw came home (who encouraged them). Their being called "bastards" throughout middle school didn't help either. They graduated to straight bourbon and began sneaking boys into the house in no time. It was an easy liking to develop because Pawpaw always had plenty of that stuff around, and as soon as it was gone, Pawpaw replaced it-no questions asked. In other words, there was a never-ending supply of alcohol at Maw-Maw's house.

My brothers and cousins were the most irresponsible boys known to man! (Didn't listen to a word Vivian said). Not only were they lazy, but they also grew up to be stingy as hell! I'm not surprised that they're still single with no children! They couldn't be bothered with anything that had to do with spending their own money, so it was a no-brainer that Maw-Maw left me this beautiful old thing; she knew I'd take care of it. When the lawyer read the will, nobody was the least bit upset with me inheriting the house; they applauded. Thank God! Maw-Maw showered me with the most love because I was her only granddaughter, and apart from my height and body ratio, I favored her more in looks and attitude than my mother or aunts. Maw-Maw was also disappointed with their unhealthy relationship with alcohol and "jezebel" behaviors than she cared to show. Besides, they favored Pawpaw mostly, so it's no surprise they liked alcohol as much as he did.

Marie is six feet tall with broad shoulders, large hands, and a wide back. Still, a feminine face, flawless brown skin with red undertones, and elbow-length prematurely greying curly Black hair. Yet, despite her charming personality and good looks, her stature intimidated most women. She was never in a monogamous relationship with a woman, only choosing to engage in casual dating and the occasional flings with married ones. So, she went to trucking school, got her CDL license, and became a long-distance truck driver to keep her mind occupied with something other than women. She certainly did daydream about coming home to a beautiful woman and having a loving, peaceful, monogamous relationship with her, but so far, no such luck.

She didn't sweat it because she knew one of these days she would find Ms. Right. Until then, she would be her only lover because she was tired of having meaningless relations and one-night stands. "Shit!" Marie snapped her fingers. "That reminds me… I have to pick up some batteries for my new toy!" she chuckled, finally cool enough to move away from the air conditioner vent.

"This old house could use some sprucing up, that's for sure," she thought, looking around at the dated interior as she picked up her suitcases and slowly walked toward the staircase, reminiscing about the good times she and her brothers had running up and down them. "This house is just how I remember it- elegant but simple," she thought, setting her suitcases down again at the foot of the stairs to walk toward the kitchen. She pulled open the cobweb-designed pocket doors where fine China plates hung on the walls near the kitchen and dining room. French porcelain cups, saucers, and silver serving trays were housed in the mahogany buffet cabinet against the dining room wall where faded antique French country wallpaper hung. In contrast, some other walls had eggshell-white paint peeling off them. The vintage ivory provincial living room furniture was wrapped in hard yellowing plastic on a Persian-styled wool area rug; there was a Victorian floor lamp with its sun-faded ivory-beaded shade to the left and an identical table lamp to the right.

"And what would a home be without a high-polished ebony baby grand piano in the center of it all?" Marie mumbled, smiling nostalgically while playing *"chopsticks"* before returning to the staircase. "I can still feel you, Maw-Maw," she said aloud, looking up the stairs as if her 106-year-old grandmother would appear at any moment. She unconsciously ran two fingers across the intricately carved wood banister. She noticed the thick dust remnants on her fingertips and generously sneezed. "Looks like dusting is going to be my first task!" She climbed the tapestry-carpeted stairs, gently touching the family portraits lining the wall on her way up. Then she dropped her luggage at the door of her childhood room before entering her grandmother's large and beautifully decorated vintage bedroom to lie across her king-sized bed with the floral chenille bedspread, her white quilted bathrobe resting at the foot. "Mm," she whispered, taking a deep breath in. It smelled like a sweet cross between the lavender perfume she wore and a hint of that "special" tobacco she smoked.

Marie hugged one of the bed pillows tightly, curling up in the fetal position, tears of endearment welling in her eyes.

She sat on the bed and wiped her eyes before entering the ensuite to turn on the faucet in the tub to let the rust run; then, she took a quick shower in her grandmother's bathroom to wash the day off, subsequently, wrapping herself in a bath towel and retrieving her suitcase from the doorway. She opened the door and walked into her childhood room with her eyes darting from wall to wall as posters of her teenage crushes, Mariah Carey and Whitney Houston, still hung up there. Almost as if time remained suspended in the room, her ballerina jewelry box was still in the same position on top of the ivory-colored lace runner on the dresser, with a purple and green feathered Mardi Gras mask resting next to it and colorful beads with a purple boa hanging from the side of the standing mirror.

Marie placed her suitcase on the white queen-sized metal canopy bed with its sunflower bedding, smiling at all the memories while pulling out a soft pink, sleeveless chiffon blouse, white linen shorts, and flat white espadrille sandals to go into town for groceries to last the rest of the week- in addition to some fresh lemons to make her grandmother's famous lavender syrup-flavored lemonade. She loosely pinned up her hair, went downstairs, and looked in the pantry for the lavender syrup. Having always admired the cottage-core aesthetic since her youth, she adored the look of the lilac-tinted water with fresh lemon slices floating on top of the glass pitcher. She turned the copper oxidized knob on the distressed wood pantry door, which fell slightly off the hinges to one side.

"I guess this comes with the territory!" she said aloud, chuckling, as she walked inside and pulled on the light switch cord inside the cool brick-walled storage room to discover more than enough lavender syrup, jellies, and canned preserves to last her for a while. She took out one of the jars of syrup and placed it on the counter; then she opened the refrigerator door to peek inside, and surprisingly, it was clean and empty. Then she hurried to the front door, picking up her keys on her way out. She got into her Jeep and drove toward North Peter's Street in the French Quarters, passing *Angeline's* restaurant and deciding to have dinner before "Makin' groceries" (the way shopping for groceries is said in New Orleans). at the market. She parked the Jeep a block away, returned to the restaurant, and requested a table on the enclosed back patio, where she ordered two Louisiana crab cakes, southern fried Okra, and a plate of Louisiana crawfish Etouffee with steamed white rice. She washed it all down with one bloody Mary, a mint Julep, and a glass of water. When her belly was full, she sat there for a while, taking in the sights and sounds and watching couples displaying affection and smiling at the beauty of it, longing for a love of her own.

She left a generous tip for the waitress, then went to the register, paid her bill, and went about her day. The evening air was mild and refreshing, so the walk back to the vehicle was comforting. Marie grabbed a shopping cart as soon as she arrived at the crowded market. She picked up a whole chicken and the remaining ingredients to make a gumbo, pickles for frying, fresh lemons for the lemonade, and a pack of AA batteries for her new toy.

She put away the groceries back home, adjusted the thermostat, and bathed. Afterward, she climbed into her grandmother's comfy bed and fell asleep within minutes.

A big rig's horn blew the following afternoon, waking her up earlier than she planned to. "Shit!" she yelled, grabbing at her chest, her senses in disarray. When she glanced through the window, she yelped, "Oh wow! They're here a day early! They weren't supposed to be here until Wednesday!" She jumped out of bed and sported her grandmother's robe, rushing to the front door to let the movers in.

"Uh, good afternoon, ma'am! We have a delivery for a Miss… Marie," a stocky, built man said as he removed his cap and folded the invoice he was reading from.

"Yes, good afternoon. I'm Marie." she said, tightening her robe. "What time is it, by the way?" she asked him curiously.

"Oh, it's 12:15, ma'am," he replied.

"All right, you can start bringing the things in now. I wasn't expecting you guys until tomorrow," she said pleasantly, opening the door wider and removing strands of hair from her face.

"Sorry if this inconveniences you, ma'am, but we finished our previous load earlier than expected, so here we are!" He chuckled, extending his hands for emphasis.

"No, it's all right; I'm glad I was home, though!" She raised an eyebrow and pinned her hair while moving out of the way for the movers, giving them directions on where to place the small furniture and boxes.

The movers were finished in less than an hour and gave Marie her invoice receipt. She gave them a hefty tip, then closed and locked the door behind them, returning upstairs to wash her mouth and face. She brushed and re-pinned her hair, then came back downstairs to prepare herself something to eat, stopping at the buffet cabinet first to retrieve the glass pitcher to make her grandmother's favorite lemonade. In the kitchen… she turned the knob on the radio that sat on top of a green cloth-covered table adorned with a bowl of glass fruit. A sermon was taking place on the station it was previously tuned to, so she changed it, stopping at Aaron Neville's *"Tell it like it is."*

Ring…Ring… "Oh, lord, what did they leave behind?" Marie sighed, sucking her teeth and hurrying to the door. "Yes?!" she said irritably, yanking open the door. Immediately, she was bewitched by the smell of gardenia perfume coming from the statuesque woman whose back was facing her. The woman quickly turned to face Marie when she realized the door was open. "Oh! Hello." The woman smiled, holding a covered cast iron pot. "Hello yourself." She replied, unable to say much more. Marie was spellbound by her smooth, chocolate-colored skin, baby doll eyes, and deeply dimpled cheeks. "What a sight for sore eyes. She thought.

The sun shone like a spotlight over her dark, short, curly hair, giving it a navy blue hue. Her white cotton dress outlined her voluptuous body effortlessly, and when her dress strap fell off her right shoulder, Marie glanced at her modest, powdered bosom. "Whew! It's hot today, huh?" The woman giggled. "Hi, my name is Naomi. I knew

Apolline very well, and it broke my heart when she passed," she said sympathetically. Are you Marie?" she smiled.

"Why, yes! I'm Marie," she said excitedly, then widening the door and saying… "Come in, come in!" after being released from Naomi's hold.

"Oh, thank you!" Naomi said, entering the house. "Apolline spoke so highly of you when I visited. You're her granddaughter, the truck driver, correct?" Naomi asked, looking back at Marie while walking quickly toward the kitchen. Marie was on her heels. "I went to the funeral hoping to meet you, but Vivian told me you couldn't come. And I came by each day after that, hoping you'd be here. Then, I gave up. But on my way home from work last evening, something told me to drive by. I figured the car parked there must be yours, so I cooked you something to eat today because I knew one thing for sure." "What's that? Marie cleared her throat.

"There wasn't any food in this house worth eating!" Naomi laughed. "I made you a pot of my famous turkey jambalaya; Apolline loved it! I hope you like it, too." She took a long breath and placed the pot on the stove. Then she turned around, looking for a chair to sit in.

"Why, thank you. That was very thoughtful," Marie told her with a bashful smile. "So… you live around here, Naomi?" Marie asked with a lump in her throat while going to the dining table and pulling out a chair.

"Thank you," Naomi said, taking a seat. "Yes, I rent a house not far from here on Black Bayou Lake in Monroe. I only lived there three weeks before I met Apolline at the grocery store a few years ago. She was my only friend for a while and was so kind to me and full of wisdom. I couldn't believe it when she told me she was a hundred and three!" She continued with her eyes wide. "We talked for a good hour straight! Would you believe it?" she asked rhetorically, her eyes still widened, her hand now on her bosom as she laughed.

"Yeah, I could believe it," Marie responded, chuckling also. "You must be extraordinary because my Maw-Maw didn't keep company with many people."

"Now that's a *fact!*" Naomi agreed, snapping her fingers to solidify her point. "And not long after our talk, she told me to make a pass and sit with her sometime, and I certainly took her up on that offer. I made a pass the following day and practically every other day until she went home to rest." She smiled softly and hiked up her dress to get more comfortable.

Marie cleared her throat, unsure what to say, and returned to the kitchen to make the lemonade.

"Oooh! Are you making Apolline's famous lavender syrup lemonade?" she asked, licking her lips as she watched Marie roll the lemons on the counter to soften the cut.

"Why yes, I am!" Marie responded, smiling awkwardly.

"Mm. You don't mind sharing a glass of it with me, do you?" Naomi asked, grinning again.

"I don't mind at all!"

"Good! We can have it with the jambalaya then." She slapped her thighs joyfully, stood up, and walked to the buffet cabinet, where she took out two dinner plates.

Marie's eyes followed her the entire time; she was amazed at her familiarity with the house. She became aroused after noticing Naomi's dress caught between her butt cheeks as she placed the plates on the dining table. "Relax, Marie." She told herself.

Naomi casually pulled the dress from her cheeks and sat down, smiling at Marie.

"Ahem. I'm about ready to slice some green tomatoes to fry. I think it'll be great with the jambalaya." Marie told her, hoping she didn't look too suspicious.

"Sure! I love fried green tomatoes, and I can't wait!" Naomi responded delightedly before swaying her head to the sounds of George Benson's *"Berezin'."* "Oh, I see you like listening to WTIX, huh?" Naomi closed her eyes in between the rhythms.

"Yeah, I sure do. I love how they mix current music with the oldies." Marie chirped. "No other station can do it like 94.1 FM, honey!" Naomi chimed in.

"We play what we want and nothing else!" they both said, reciting the station's catchphrase in unison.

As they both laughed, Marie couldn't help but give Naomi the once-over. "My God, she's beautiful," Marie thought. "You know what?" Marie shouted out, redirecting her focus. "What?" Naomi answered gleefully.

"When I was about twelve, I called the station and won $100. I had to give it to Vivian, though." Marie chuckled, gazing off in remembrance with a sly smile.

"Really!" Naomi said, impressed with her story.

"Mm-hmm, but I only got through once!" Marie

responded, stirring ice into the lemonade pitcher and retrieving a glass to pour the lavender-tinged liquid into. Then, she graciously walked it over and handed the glass to Naomi.

"Ahh, this looks exactly like the lemonade Apolline made! Thank you, baby. Now, the proof is in the pudding! Let me taste it." Naomi continued, putting the glass to her lips and taking a swallow. "Oh yeah, baby, it tastes just like it posed too! Okay, nah. You passed this test and made your Maw-Maw proud!"

They both looked at each other and burst out in laughter again.

"I had no idea your Cajun accent could be so heavy." Marie commented, continuing to laugh at her.

It's not; I used to put it on thick like this to make Apolline laugh. I'm just being funny," Naomi continued, smiling at Marie.

Marie noticed how Naomi looked at her but shook it off and went into the kitchen to turn down the vegetable oil in the cast iron pan. Then she sliced and seasoned the tomatoes and dumped them into a batter of milk and eggs before coating them in yellow cornmeal and flour and frying them to a golden brown. Meanwhile, they were enjoying the music in silence.

"So, are you keeping this place or selling it?" Naomi asked, finally breaking the silence as she glanced at a wall of peeling paint.

"I'm not sure yet." Marie sighed deeply. She brought the pot of jambalaya and fried tomatoes to the table after changing the oil-soaked napkin underneath it and adding some cutlery. "Here we go." She pulled out her chair and said… "But I know I will fix up this place and modernize it. You know what I mean? The house has good bones and flawless architecture, don't you think?" Marie took a bite of the tomato.

"It certainly does." Naomi agreed, swallowing the last of her lemonade.

"It could definitely use some upgrades, but like… what?" Marie asked rhetorically, hunching her shoulders before eating a spoonful of the jambalaya. "Maybe I'd have to change out the old pipes and re-sand the floors. The HVAC and the furnace might need to be replaced, too. Everything else is just cosmetics, I hope."

"I wouldn't know where to begin! But it sure is a beautiful home." Naomi commented, scooping out more jambalaya from the pot and putting it on Marie's plate while she chewed a piece of fried tomato.

"Oh! Thank you, but I can do that." Marie told her, trying to take the spoon.

"Nonsense. I know you can, but I want to do it for you." Naomi smiled, flaunting her deep dimples before putting the spoon down.

"This is delicious, Naomi. I see why Maw-Maw loved this dish," Marie told her, swallowing another spoonful.

"Thank you! But I knew you would." Naomi teased, wrinkling her nose.

"Okay, now… Marie thought. "She's beautiful, *and* she can cook?! She better be careful, gone wind up getting herself in trouble." Marie chuckled to herself.

They continued to eat silently. Naomi picked up the

pitcher to refill their glasses. "Well…" she said, putting the pitcher down. "How long are you here for?" she smiled, cutting off a piece of tomato.

"Long story short, I'll be independent in a few months, so I took some time off to care for everything here before opening my own trucking company.

"Oh wow, that's fantastic, Marie! Congratulations girl! Apolline always spoke highly of you, and now I see why. She was so proud to call someone like you her granddaughter." Marie blushed.

As they took their last spoonful, Naomi got up from the table and said… "I'll wash the dishes for you and then be on my way." She grabbed some empty dishes and placed them in the sink.

"Oh, that's all right. And thanks for the food, Naomi. Hey, you don't have to leave yet, do you? Why don't you hang around and let's talk for a while? I was just getting to know you." Marie told her, secretly hoping she wanted to stay.

"I didn't want to bother you and wear out my welcome already," Naomi responded without turning around, pleased to receive Marie's invitation.

"Nonsense! I'm enjoying your company. Besides, I want to see why Maw-Maw was so obsessed with you," Marie teased.

"All right!" And don't ever thank me for food. I love to cook for people," Naomi responded in her best Cajun drawl, turning around and playfully crossing her eyes at Marie before returning to wash the dishes.

Marie laughed and watched Naomi's cheeks move

from side to side through her dress each time she rinsed a dish. All she could think of was getting in between them. "Damn, she's funny, too!" It's been too got damn long," she thought, shaking her head and removing the straight pins from her hair before clearing the remaining dishes from the table and pushing in the chairs.

"I can help you decorate or paint when the time comes if you want me to." Naomi offered her as she rinsed the last dish.

"I'd like that. The more help I get, the faster I can get it done." Marie placed the pot in the refrigerator while Naomi watched her.

"Take my number, and you give me yours before I forget," Naomi told her, drying her hands on the dish towel en route to the kitchen bathroom.

"Of course!" Marie responded, eagerly looking around the kitchen for a pen. "Girl… I wasn't letting you out of here before I got it!" Marie mumbled, chuckling to herself. Naomi entered the bathroom, leaving the door open, conveying a level of comfort Marie was unfamiliar with. Marie could not find a pen in the kitchen, so she searched the dining room and retrieved one from the buffet cabinet drawer while pretending it was commonplace for a guest to use the bathroom with the door wide open. Naomi wiped herself, flushed the toilet, washed her hands, and dried them on the hanging towel before coming out, grabbing the pen from Marie's hand and writing down her telephone number. Naomi's behavior enthralled Marie, and she couldn't wait to spend more time with her. They talked for a few more hours about their families, Naomi's job as vice principal of Ouachita Parish High School, and what Marie might want to do with the house. Eventually, Naomi decided it was time for her to leave, and she got up while exhaling residual laughter.

"It was so nice to meet you, and I'm glad you liked the food," Naomi told her as she walked toward the front door.

"Thank you for coming over, Naomi. It was nice to meet you, too." Marie secretly wished she didn't have to leave at all. "Maybe we can go to Harrison Avenue for dinner and drinks on Friday. I'm meeting with the contractor tomorrow; otherwise, I would ask to take you to dinner tomorrow." Marie smiled softly and held the door open for her.

"Sure, baby, Friday would be fine. Besides, it'll be the weekend, and I can stay with you longer." Naomi winked while gently tapping Marie's forearm, looking at her kindly with the sun setting behind her. "Marie…" Naomi called softly, tilting her head to one side, trying to understand where Marie's thoughts were. Is everything all right?

"Oh! excuse me," Marie lowered her eyes shyly. "I got lost in my thoughts and that beautiful sunset behind you." She pointed to the sky.

"It truly is beautiful." Naomi said after turning around and looking at it for a moment and then descending the stairs and taking her keys out of her purse. "Would you like me to call you when I get home?" she asked, looking up from the foot of the stairs, tossing her keys from hand to hand.

"Absolutely! I want to know you got home safely,

"baby." Marie said in her best Cajun drawl.

"Okay, I hear you!" Naomi laughed. "Goodnight." She smiled, waving goodbye as she hopped into her car and drove off.

Marie waved back and stood there watching her slowly turn into a diminishing black dot on the horizon. Then she sighed deeply and closed the door while her back lay against it, thinking about her afternoon with Naomi. She walked back into the dining room and turned off the lights. "Lord, have mercy! mmm mm mm!" She mumbled softly, going up the stairs and smiling at the thought of spending more time with Naomi. She suddenly remembered that she had left the batteries on the kitchen counter, so she returned to retrieve them, returning upstairs and placing them inside her new toy. She took off her panties and placed her toy's frequency on the medium setting. Then she lounged across her childhood bed and opened her legs, placing the toy's tip directly on her pearl. She imagined herself and Naomi naked in the lavender garden, kissing and touching each other as she got closer to the climax. "Oh, my god…" she moaned aloud softly, licking her lips as the images of making love to Naomi intensified, taking over her mind, causing her to call out Naomi's name as she orgasmed repeatedly. Marie let go of her new toy, allowing it to roll between her legs onto the bed. She was exhausted and lay there for a while before getting up to use the toilet.

She sat on the commode in the bathroom, but her legs went numb before she could relieve herself because her pelvic muscles were so contracted. She heard the phone ringing, wiped herself quickly, and then hurried to retrieve it, yanking it up. "Hello!" she said hastily.

"Hey, it's me, Naomi. I made it home, and I'm getting ready to jump in the shower," she told her, grunting as she removed her bra.

"Okay, good," Marie responded, secretly wishing she could shower with her. "Goodnight," Naomi said softly.

"Goodnight." Marie repeated, only hanging up once she heard the dial tone. She put two braids in her hair, showered, and went to bed, looking forward to meeting with the contractor tomorrow.

The following morning, Marie decided to go to *Café Du Monde* for a café au lait and beignets, one of her favorite pastimes when she visited New Orleans. When she returned, she went straight into her grandmother's backyard. She wanted to see if the garden was still thriving with its lavender and vanilla trees. And to her surprise, the lavender was teeming with life. The vanilla trees were all dried up, but the garden still had potential. She was flooded with a wave of positive emotions as she picked up the gardening shears hanging on the shed. She remembered helping her grandmother pick vanilla beans, pruning and cutting the lavender. "Isn't this something?" she mumbled, wiping away tears. "Everything looks so much bigger when you're a little person." She scratched her head and walked through the tall grasses to cut some of the visible flowering lavender. She cut a handful before returning inside for a vase, finally spotting one atop the refrigerator. She placed the lavender into it and set it in the center of the dining room table. "Might as well tidy up the house," she thought, putting on some music, which always seemed to make cleaning less of a chore. She was so exhausted when she was done that she plopped on the sofa and took a quick nap, only to be startled awake an hour later by the doorbell and a hard, repetitive knock.

"Oh, lord!" Marie exclaimed as she wiped the drool off her lip and hurried to answer the door. She opened the door to find an unfamiliar woman standing there… "Yes, can I help you?"

"Hello. I'm the contractor, Imogene. Are you Marie?" She asked.

"Yes, *you're* the contractor?" Marie asked with a pleasant smile. "I sure am!" The woman responded gleefully.

"You caught me by surprise!"

"I get that a lot." She chuckled, waiting to be invited in.

"Lake Charles is full of surprises these days! Nice to meet you; come in! Let me show you around."

As soon as Imogine walked in, she placed the blueprints under her arm on the dining table, then followed Marie around the house, listening attentively to the changes she wanted implemented. Once the walk-through was over, Imogine unrolled the blueprints and spread them across the table, breaking everything down to Marie and explaining what could be done. Marie verbalized that she understood.

"Where are my manners, by the way!? Would you like a glass of lemonade?"

Marie asked. "No, thank you. I have to get going. She said, tallying up some figures and giving them to Marie. Marie was shocked at how low under budget the bill was, so she decided to include further services like knocking down walls, checking the furnace, and refinishing the floors. "Can my crew and I start next Tuesday?"

"Absolutely!" "How long do you expect the project to take?"

"We should be done in about four weeks, give or take." She said as she rolled up the blueprints. "But you might want to book yourself into a hotel if you don't have any family you could stay with during the construction."

"Oh! I was planning to stay out of your guys' way upstairs," Marie said confusedly.

"I wish that could be, but I'll have to shut off the water and the central air. I don't mind you staying, but I'm pretty sure you'll be uncomfortable." Imogine chuckled, placing the blueprints under her arm.

"Oh yeah, without a doubt!" Marie grinned. "No worries, I'll get a room. I'm just so excited to get the work done this quickly!"

"Okay, then. I'll see you with my crew next Tuesday morning bright and early!" Imogine said with a smile, reaching out to shake her hand.

"Quick question."

"Sure, what is it?" Imogen responded, folding her arms in concern.

"Can you discard the old furniture for me?"

"Of course! And at no extra charge, deal?" Imogen smiled.

"Deal!" Marie replied, walking with her to the door. "By the way, how bright and early is bright and early?" Marie asked with a comically raised brow. Imogine chuckled.

"Is 7 a.m. too early for you?" Imogine asked, still chuckling at Marie's facial expression. "No, 7 a.m. is fine." Marie said pleasantly.

"All right, I'll see you then."

After they said their goodbyes, Marie continued to tidy up before she cooked the gumbo she had been craving since she arrived and then called the hotel to make reservations. She pondered calling Naomi. "Let's be daring." She whispered as she dialed her number nervously, leaving the rice on the stove to boil.

"Hey, you!" Naomi said when she answered the phone. "Whatcha doing?" She kicked off her heels and put away her briefcase in her office.

"I met with the contractor today."

"Oh, yeah, I remember. How did that go?"

"First off, the contractor was a female," Marie told her excitedly.

"Really… that's new."

"I thought so, too!" She told me that she gets many comments about it."

"I bet she does." Naomi replied dryly, walking into her bathroom, and wiping off her lipstick.

"She gave me a good price for everything, so… all you have to do is help me paint."

"Of course, I'll help you paint. That's great, Marie! When are they going to start the construction?" Naomi asked, taking off her work clothes now.

"Her crew will be here next Tuesday at 7 a.m., so I have to get a hotel for about four weeks."

"Oh, no! Why?" Naomi asked in a concerned voice.

"Because there won't be any running water or air conditioning at the house."

"Hmmm." Naomi mumbled, tapping her chin.

"What's that?" Marie asked, barely hearing her.

"Oh, it's nothing, just thinking aloud. "Are you buying new furniture as well? Or haven't you decided you're gonna stay yet?"

"No, I haven't decided yet." Marie replied.

Their phone calls became a daily ritual for the upcoming days, with quite a bit of flirtatious banter between them until, finally, Friday arrived. Marie couldn't wait to pick Naomi up for their evening dinner date. She drove to the lake house at 5039 Sweetwater Drive in Monroe to pick up Naomi, who came out of the house wearing a beautiful orange tropical print backless halter dress with white wedge sandals and carrying a white crochet pocketbook in the crook of her arm. Marie got out of her Jeep wearing a short-sleeved, linen, coral-colored button-up shirt and beige linen pants with brown leather thong sandals, her hair pulled up loosely in a ponytail.

"You look beautiful this evening, Naomi," she said as she opened the passenger side door for her.

"You look beautiful, too, Marie. And I love your hair like that." Naomi held up her dress to prevent it from getting stuck in the vehicle door; then, she plopped down in her seat. Marie hurried to the driver's side and drove them to one of the most popular restaurants on Harrison Ave called *Mondo's*, known for their healthy Mexican cuisine. "I hope you like Mexican food," Marie said as they pulled up to the restaurant.

"I do!" Naomi stayed seated, waiting for Marie to open her door.

When they were seated at their table, they ordered drinks to start. Marie ordered a virgin Caribbean Old Fashioned, and Naomi a Mondo Secret Recipe White Sangria. Soon after that, the waiter brought over their drinks.

"Cheers!" They clanked their glasses together before taking a sip.

"I have to be careful with this one," Naomi said, taking another sip.

"Why? Is It too strong for you?" Marie asked, her eyebrow raised.

"Just the opposite!" She swayed her index finger back and forth. "it's sweet. You know what they say about those sweet drinks, right?" Naomi smiled coyly.

Marie's interest was piqued. "What *do* they say?"

"They sneak up on you," Naomi whispered, playfully covering her mouth. "I don't want you thinking I'm easy." Naomi teased her, batting her eyes.

"Nah, I won't think you're easy… drink up! You're in good hands, baby." Marie chuckled. The waiter returned to their table. "Are you ladies ready to order food now?"

"Yes, I'd like to start with the blue corn cheese enchiladas," Marie told him.

"Oh! That sounds good, Marie!" And I'll try the blue corn tamales."

"All right, ladies, I'll return with your orders." He told them pleasantly before walking away to put the orders in.

"So, Marie, I met your whole family; they seem so sweet," Naomi told her, smiling and picking up her drink.

"Aww, thank you," Marie said, picking up hers.

"By the way, how is Vivian?"

"Oh!" Marie said, almost spilling her drink. "I thought you knew."

"Knew what?" Naomi asked her, looking puzzled.

"Vivian died two years ago, baby."

Naomi gasped. "I'm sorry, Marie."

Such is life, Naomi." Marie smiled softly and changed the subject. "You mentioned you're renting the house you stay in, right?"

"Um-hm, I do."

"Please, God, let this woman be single." Marie prayed to herself. "Are you single?" Marie asked, crossing her fingers underneath the table.

"VERY!" Naomi responded, rolling her eyes and taking another sip of her drink while the waiter walked over with their food.

"That's good to know." Marie breathed a sigh of relief. "So, it's safe to say you live alone, too… right?"

"Yes, ma'am. You're batting a thousand tonight, baby." Naomi chuckled, opening her tamales and taking up a forkful. "This is pretty good,"

"Mine is pretty good too!"

"I like the way your mouth moves when you're eating." Naomi winked at her. "Do you eat everything like that?" She continued looking Marie in the eyes while she chewed. "Ahem!" Marie gestured, clearing her throat. "Everything, like what?" Marie asked, placing her napkin on the table.

"Like it's the best thing you ever ate," Naomi answered in a sexy tone. "If I put something in my mouth, and I like it, you better believe I'm gonna eat it like it's the best thing I ever ate," she responded in the same sexy tone.

"Oh, boy!" Naomi smiled bashfully, her dimples taking center stage. "Is it hot, or is it just me?" Naomi asked, fanning herself.

"No, it's *us*, baby." Marie answered seductively, chuckling, causing Naomi to blush once more.

"Are you ladies ready to order your entrees now?" the waiter asked, interrupting their wordplay. "I'm ready." Marie said.

"Okay, what are you having?" he asked her patiently.

"I want to try your grilled citrus-marinated chicken. What does that come with?" she asked him, closing the menu. "That comes with Mexican rice, Mexican three bean, and three pepper salad."

"Okay, yes, I'll have that."

"Okay, and you miss? What should I get for you?" he asked pleasantly, turning to Naomi. "I'll have the grilled Tilapia bowl with chipotle avocado crema." she told him, closing her menu.

"Okay, no problem. I'll be back in like twenty minutes. Is that okay?" the waiter asked, picking up the menus.

"Yes, that's fine," they both said in unison as the waiter quickly walked away.

"Now look at us!" Marie raised her eyebrow as they both chuckled. Marie glanced at Naomi's almost empty glass and asked… "Would you like a refill?"

"Yes, I would." Naomi responded, raising her glass,

and drinking the last of it. Marie raised her hand to get the waiter's attention, ordering additional drinks for them.

"Do you have any children, Naomi?"

"Yes, I do. A son. His name is Calvin, and he'll be fifteen in a couple of months." Naomi smiled.

"Interesting." Marie commented, horrified by a thought… "Oh my God, not another straight woman! Why me, lord?"

"He lives with his dad in Nashville," Naomi said, interrupting Marie's negative thoughts. "We have a good relationship, although he doesn't call unless he needs something. You know how teenagers can be." Naomi chuckled. "How about you? Do you have kids?" Naomi asked, her fingers interlocked under her chin and her elbows resting on the table, waiting for Marie's answer.

"Hallelujah!" Marie screamed inside before answering her. "No! aht aht. No children." Marie shook her head for emphasis. "I never wanted children for some reason."

"Neither did I, but…" Naomi paused, hunching her shoulders and eating the last piece of her tamale. "Are you single?" Naomi asked nervously.

"Yes, I am." Marie smiled, leaning back from the table to let the waiter place down the plates. "So, you grew up in Nashville?" Marie asked, looking down at the plate.

"No, baby. I grew up in Kentucky and then came to Louisiana when I was in high school." Naomi grinned, digging into her food.

"Oh, that's interesting." Marie tasted her food.

They enjoyed each other's company until they were ready to leave. Afterward, they used the restroom and went to the Jeep, thoroughly satisfied that neither of them had anyone else to compete with nor answer to. Marie drove Naomi back to her home, all the while wishing she could spend more time with her.

"Thanks for taking me to dinner tonight, Marie." Naomi looked over at her and smiled softly. "I had a good time."

"The pleasure was all mine, baby." Marie squeezed Naomi's hand quickly while waiting for the car in front of her to turn left.

Twenty minutes into the drive…. Naomi softly says… "We didn't order dessert. I bought Hubig's pies on my way home today. Why don't you come in and have some with me." she said, looking at Marie.

"Oh, my God! I love Hubig's pie! What kind did you get, babe?"

"Let's see." Naomi giggled and was thrilled Marie wanted to come inside.

"I bought two peaches, one coconut, and two cherries." "Okay, I'll have a peach pie," Marie said as she pulled up to Naomi's house. She hurried to open the door for Naomi and followed her into her home.

"Make yourself comfortable, baby." Naomi told her, throwing her purse on the sofa while Marie closed and locked the door behind them.

"I like this open floor plan. How many bedrooms does it have?" Marie asked her, looking around for the bathroom.

"It has two bedrooms, but I use one as my closet because I have a ton of shoes, and the closets aren't big enough." Naomi chuckled, undoing one of her sandal straps.

"I bet you have a ton of clothes, too, huh?" Marie teased.

"I do!" Naomi responded, laughing as she kicked both sandals off. Then, she made her way to the kitchen to heat the pies.

"Where's your bathroom, babe?" Marie asked, continuing to look around.

"It's in my bedroom; it's a weird setup because it is and isn't. You'll see what I mean when you get to my bedroom. Go down the hall and turn to the right."

"Got it." Marie was delighted to be anywhere near Naomi's bedroom. The bathroom was inside the beginning of the bedroom, with a door separating the two. "This is weird." Marie thought, instantly admiring its cleanliness and the fancy towels hanging on the towel bar. When she was done, she walked back to where Naomi was and had a seat on the sofa. "I heated the pie, babe."

"Would you like a glass of white wine with it?" Naomi asked, placing the pies on the coffee table.

"No, I don't think that's a good idea." Marie chuckled while reaching for the pie.

"Why not, babe?"

"Because I have to drive home, baby." Marie looked perplexed.

"Why do you have to go home? Is someone waiting for you there?" Naomi asked seductively.

"Ahem…" Marie replied. "No, nobody is waiting for me." but internally, she was screaming, "HELL YEAH!"

"So… would you like a glass of wine with your pie, baby?" Naomi asked, smiling alluringly at her.

"Yes, I'd like a glass of white wine with my pie. Thank you." Marie smiled.

"Good! I was beginning to think you didn't like me." Naomi hurried to the kitchen to retrieve the chilled white wine from the fridge and two glasses from the mounted under-cabinet glass holder, pouring each of them a glass. "Here's to good health!" Naomi said, raising her glass.

"To good health!" Marie repeated, and they both took a sip.

"Tasty." Marie commented.

"Would you like to listen to some music?" Naomi asked before sitting down.

"Sure!" Marie replied, taking another sip of wine before placing her glass on the table. Naomi looked through her music collection and decided to play the Isley Brothers' *"For the Love of You."*

"Oh! That's a good one!" Marie shouted softly.

"I knew you'd like it." Naomi winked, smiling, and sitting beside her on the sofa. They ate the warm pies and finished the wine while they laughed and talked about random things. Suddenly, Naomi moved closer to Marie, leaning in and kissing her tenderly on the mouth, encouraging Marie to kiss her back.

"Is this why you wanted me to stay?" Marie whispered, pulling away slowly and looking Naomi in the eyes.

"You bet your ass, that's why." Naomi pulled Marie by the shirt toward her and kissed her again.

"My, my, my," Marie whispered, shaking her head

slowly. "Has anybody ever told you that you're a good kisser?" Marie asked, her eyes partially closed.

"Why, is that what you're gonna tell me?" Naomi asked her with a sly grin.

"It depends." Marie said with a half-cocked smile.

"It depends on what?" Naomi's eyes were dreamy.

"On… if anybody ever told you that." Marie chuckled softly.

"Well… Yes, I've been told I was a good kisser once before." "Well, I think you're the *best* kisser." Marie told her, running her hand over Naomi's hair while Naomi leaned her head into it, enjoying her touch.

"I would invite you to shower with me, but…." Naomi paused; her eyes lowered.

"But what, babe?"

"But… it's too damn small!" Naomi said, pretending to cry, causing them both to burst out in laughter.

"I DID NOT expect you to say that. "I tell you what." Marie said, still laughing. "You shower first; then I'll take mine, okay?"

"Okay, sounds good!" Naomi replied, getting up and taking the plate and wine glasses into the kitchen, beginning to wash them.

"Stop that!" Marie softly yelled at her, hurrying into the kitchen. "I'll do that; you take your shower, babe."

Naomi kissed her, then removed her earrings, placing them on the counter and hurrying off to shower. Marie dried off the plate and the wine glasses before returning to the sofa and continuing to listen to the music.

Twenty minutes later, Naomi finished her shower and

entered the living room barefoot, wearing a long, sheer black negligée and a matching robe. She smelled like the gardenia perfume she wore the first time Marie met her.

"Have mercy," Marie mumbled, standing up and complimenting Naomi on how beautiful she looked and how sweet she smelled.

"Thank you, baby," Naomi replied, blushing. "Did you need anything else out here?" she asked Marie softly.

"No, baby, I think I have everything I need." She winked. Naomi blushed again as she glided gracefully to the kitchen to turn off the lights and the music. Then she took Marie's hand and walked to her bedroom. "My turn," Marie smiled and headed to the shower. When she was done, she tiptoed out and softly called Naomi's name when she entered her bedroom.

"How do you feel?" Naomi asked her in a low voice, lying underneath the top sheet without her negligée. "I feel even better now," Marie said softly. "Drop your towel and come over here." She said with seductive eyes. Marie dropped her towel and sauntered over to the bed.

"You're positively stunning," Naomi commented.

"Thank you," Marie whispered, pulling back the sheet and getting into the bed. "Oh wow! I didn't realize you had a dock outside your bedroom; it's beautiful, baby." She looked out the double doors in astonishment at the bayou surrounding it.

"I know! I was lucky to get this place." Naomi replied, leaning over and kissing Marie's lips softly as Marie shut her eyes. "Open your eyes." She whispered, caressing the side of Marie's face.

Marie slowly opened her eyes and placed her hand on Naomi's cheek.

Naomi turned her head slightly to kiss Marie's hand tenderly. Marie was awestruck. "When was the last time you had a massage, baby?" she kissed her hand again.

"I never had a massage." Marie said softly, perplexed by her question. "Okay, baby, turn on your stomach; I'm gonna give you your first one." Naomi reached over and picked up the bottle of massage oil from her nightstand.

Marie turned onto her stomach while Naomi straddled her, warming the oil in her hands before massaging it into Marie's back. "Mm, hmm, that feels good." Marie moaned, balling up the pillow to lift her head.

"Good." Naomi said softly, becoming aroused as the oil touched her pearl while her body moved slightly back and forth on Marie's lower back.

Marie could feel the warmth of the oil, clueless to the fact that Naomi's juices were a part of it. The warmth of the oil, the weight of Naomi's body on hers, and the music of the crickets in the background imbued the scene with a dream-like quality. Suddenly… Naomi rolled off Marie and began pouring the oil all over her breasts. "It's my turn." Marie began massaging the oil on Naomi's breasts slowly with lustful eyes before leaning in and kissing her intensely. She pinched and held her nipples one by one, causing Naomi to quiver and gasp with pleasure. Marie held her bottom lip in her mouth as she watched Naomi's reactions before kissing her intensely again, then placing her hands gently around her neck.

Naomi opened her thighs slowly, and one of Marie's

thighs knelt between them while she kissed and licked Naomi's neck voraciously. Then she slid her fingers up and down her slippery pearl before sliding two fingers gently inside her.

Naomi grabbed Marie's wrist, thrusting her fingers into her faster and harder while they moaned aloud softly. "Oh, my God!" Naomi begged for more, breathing heavily into Marie's mouth.

Marie couldn't stop heaving as she felt the heat and sweetness of Naomi's breath on her. When she finally removed her fingers, she started sucking on them.

"Oh my god… "I love it," Naomi whispered, her baby doll eyes nearly closed.

Marie continued to lick her fingers while staring intently at Naomi before pushing her legs apart and thrusting her head between them. Naomi began to pant in anticipation while running her hands across her hair. Marie pushed back Naomi's lips to expose her pearl, which she sucked on gently yet hungrily, then repeatedly inserted her stiff tongue in and out of Naomi's canal. She held her voluptuous cheeks tightly and tasted the sweet drippings Naomi offered her. Naomi's high-pitched orgasmic screams caused Marie to follow suit, surrendering to the multiple orgasms that overtook her yet withholding her screams.

Naomi gently pushed Marie's head off when she couldn't stand it any longer, sweating and panting from exhaustion and satisfaction. Marie lay beside her, satisfied and fulfilled.

Moments later, Naomi retrieved the oil and returned

the favor. She massaged and pinched Marie's breasts, causing her to orgasm once more. "Ooh," Naomi said seductively. "You like that, huh?" She spread Marie's legs apart, getting between them and feasting on her like the pies they enjoyed earlier. She slowly released Marie's pearl at the dissension of her climax, surprisingly climaxing herself. Naomi stayed between Marie's thighs, kissing her soft skin as she ran her hand up and down her well-oiled legs while Marie gently rested her hand in Naomi's hair.

Moments later, a gentle snore was heard from Naomi. Marie snickered and nudged her gently as she slowly sat up. "Let's change the oily sheets before we call it a night, baby." "Oh wow! "You put me to sleep. Sorry about that," she chuckled softly.

"No need to apologize, baby. I'm glad I can wear you out." Marie teased, getting off the bed and picking up her towel to pat the oil off her skin. Naomi stole a kiss on her way to the linen closet, returning with clean sheets and a towel to pat her oil off. They changed the linen together and dropped their oily towels on the floor before snuggling into bed. They kissed tenderly while thanking one another for a lovely evening. They pulled up the sheet and spooned, with Marie's arm around Naomi's waist and her face buried in the back of her neck until they fell asleep.

The following morning, Naomi was the first to wake up. She looked over at Marie, who was sound asleep on her stomach. She smiled at the sight of her and kissed two of her fingers to place them lightly on her back. She slid out of bed, put her negligee and robe back on, and headed to the bathroom to freshen up before going into the kitchen to make breakfast, first taking out the folding tray tables and setting them in front of the sofa. She had purchased a freshly baked loaf of brioche bread the other day and decided to make French toast with it. So, she prepared the ingredients. She distributed the vanilla flavoring, the cinnamon, and the nutmeg in a bowl before slicing the bread. Then she took the eggs, whole milk, sweet, condensed milk, cream cheese, and leftover strawberries from the refrigerator. She put the strawberries in a separate bowl, removed the sugar canister from the baker's rack, and sprinkled three tablespoons on the strawberries to macerate them. "Syrup done." She said, smiling. Afterward, she took down her food processor to blend the creams for her homemade whipped cream.

"What am I missing?" she thought aloud. "Got it!" She placed a filter in the coffee maker and brewed a fresh pot of coffee.

Back in the bedroom… Marie was finally opening her eyes and looking over her shoulder, expecting to see Naomi lying there beside her. She figured she was in the kitchen cooking after smelling the butter cooking. Marie stretched her arms and legs out the width of the bed, smiling pleasantly before sitting up and looking at the beautiful scenery outdoors. She saw a shed in the distance next to a large Spanish moss-hanging Cypress tree that she couldn't spot the night before. "I hope Naomi has a boat in that!" She reminisced about fishing with her brothers. "Monroe's Bayou is famous for its bass, so I hope we go fishing one day." Marie thought, scratching her head as she got out of bed and went into the bathroom. Afterward, she joined Naomi in the kitchen.

"Good morning, beautiful!" Marie sang out bar-less and barefoot, wearing only her button-down shirt and hip-hugging underwear while brushing her hair back into a bun. "Good morning!" Naomi cheered, taking the last slice of French toast out of the pan. "Have a seat, baby. I hope you like French toast," Naomi said, air kissing her while pouring the sliced strawberries and syrup on Marie's French toast and then topping it with a dollop of whipped cream.

"Yes, ma'am, I do now!" Marie chuckled softly, moving the folding tray out of her way to sit on the sofa. "Good! You made coffee, too!" Marie continued, putting the brush on the sofa beside her and rubbing her palms together, delighted to have a cup.

Naomi walked to the sofa and handed Marie her plate while placing hers on the other folding tray.

"Mm, this is so pretty," Marie said, holding the plate to her nose.

"It's gonna taste even better." Naomi winked, walking to the coffeemaker to pour them a cup. "I have sugar and cream; how do you like yours, baby?"

"Dark and sweet like you, please." Marie sliced into her French toast, smiling from ear to ear. "I like this bread, too, baby. What's the name of it?" Marie asked, chewing with her mouth full.

Naomi walked back over with paper napkins, sat next to Marie, and licked the whipped cream off the corner of Marie's mouth before answering… "Brioche." The whole act seemed so casual that it was erotic, causing Marie to pause in awe.

"You're something else…; you know that?" Marie responded, licking the remaining sweetness off her lips.

"I know." Naomi responded, cutting into her French toast with her award-worthy dimpled smile as Marie shook her head admirably.

"What's on your agenda for today?" Marie asked her, sipping her coffee.

"I don't have any plans. Why?" Naomi asked, smearing her whipped cream on a piece of plain toast.

"Well, I have to go home and change my clothes first, but I wouldn't mind checking out the tour of Marie Laveau's house today and then a jazz cruise afterward."

"That sounds like fun!" Naomi said gleefully, her mouth full of toast.

Marie smiled at her reaction while finishing her coffee. "All right then, it's a date!" Marie said softly, raising her almost empty coffee cup to Naomi, who returned the gesture.

After breakfast, Naomi took a shower, and Marie cleaned the dishes before going into the bedroom to put on her clothes. She then returned to the living room and waited for Naomi.

"I'm ready, baby!" Naomi softly yelled twenty minutes later. She walked out of her bedroom wearing curve-hugging white denim capris, a black sequined racerback tank top, black patent leather open-toed flats with the matching pocketbook, and thin silver hoop earrings.

"You look lovely…*and* smelling as fresh as a daisy!" Marie commented, standing up with keys in hand, anxious to start their day.

"Thank you, baby." Naomi grabbed Marie's hand, kissing her softly before unlocking the door and then holding it open for Marie, who walked to the Jeep and opened the passenger side door, waiting patiently for Naomi. Next, they drove off with the top down, listening to Kool & The Gang's *"Summer Madness"* on their favorite radio station in the background. The drive was a whole vibe.

When they arrived at Marie's home, Marie escorted Naomi up the stairs and to the front door.

"I'm a little thirsty for some reason." Naomi commented.

Marie hurried into the kitchen and poured the last of the lavender-tinted lemonade while Naomi closed and locked the door.

"I see you were in the garden," Naomi commented cheerfully, walking into the dining room and seeing the lavender on the table before taking the glass of lemonade from Marie's hand. "Just what I needed... thank you, baby."

"You're most welcome. I miss picking them with Maw-Maw," she told her lovingly, lightly touching them.

Naomi tenderly placed her hand on the side of Marie's face before shooing her off to go and get dressed. Marie laughed, quickly kissing Naomi on the cheek before running up the stairs excitedly. Naomi waited patiently in the parlor for Marie while she finished her lemonade. She was back thirty minutes later with her hair slicked back tightly into a braided ponytail, sporting an all-white linen suit with a pair of black sandal flats and a black leather man purse thrown across her upper body.

"Wow! You look and smell…distinguished," Naomi commented, standing up and walking toward her.

"Distinguished? Ooh la la." Marie chuckled. "Thank you, baby." She leaned in for another kiss, and Naomi returned the kiss while playing with Marie's ponytail.

"Shall we go?" Marie asked with a grin as she was looking into her eyes.

"Yes, let's go before we… Never mind," Naomi said, taking hold of Marie's hand and walking toward the door as Marie softly laughed.

When they arrived at 628 Bourbon Street in the French Quarter, they joined the crowd before Marie Laveau's House of Voodoo for their guided tour. The group was led inside and given truths, facts, mysteries, and misconceptions about the most powerful Voodoo priestess in New Orleans- believed to influence the city to this day. They were able to make "Gri Gri" bags (pouches to carry for good luck) as souvenirs before ending the tour at ST. Louis Cemetery #1, where Marie Laveau was believed to be buried.

"Wow, she was Catholic and became a Voodoo priestess even with all those constraints of Catholicism!" Naomi said, bewildered.

"Yeah, I know, but with all the conflicting information about her, who knows what's true?" Marie replied sincerely, hunching her shoulders with her hands in her pockets as they walked to the pier to board the jazz cruise steamboat.

Once at the pier, they walked up the ramp, where they were directed to climb a flight of stairs to the second deck. Marie removed her wallet from her cross-body purse and paid for their tickets before they were escorted to a table. Feeling a little hungry, they hurried to the buffet table to avoid the crowd, filling their plates with red beans and rice, Cajun fried chicken, salad du jour, sweet tea, and white chocolate pudding for dessert. They feasted on these delicious foods as they sailed on the Mississippi River and watched the sunset through the deck's window while listening intently to the captain's tale of the route.

"Another beautiful evening," Naomi said, smiling lovingly at Marie. "Another beautiful evening, thanks to you." She winked, slurping on her sweet tea through a straw.

"My pleasure, baby." Marie responded sweetly. "Let's go out on the deck."

Naomi got up to follow her. They leaned on the rail, basking in the view before playfully dancing to the live band's rendition of Duke Ellington's *Jubilee Stomp*." They continued to laugh and dance to their hearts' content before the steamboat returned to the dock, and the passengers were informed that the cruise was complete.

"I don't know the last time I had so much fun!" Marie said, chuckling softly and gently gripping Naomi's hand while Naomi smiled lovingly at her.

"Are you coming home with me tonight?" Naomi asked, feeling hopeful as they approached Marie's car.

"I'd be happy too," Marie replied, kissing Naomi's hand and opening the Jeep's door for her. "Let me stop by the house and pick up a pair of jeans and a nightshirt or something, okay?"

"Of course, baby…, Yay!" Naomi whispered just as a burp slipped out. "Oops!" she said, pretending to be bashful while covering her mouth and showing off those dimples.

"No worries." Marie laughed. "Oh, I meant to ask you something earlier."

"Sure, what is it, baby?" Naomi asked curiously.

"Is there a boat in your shed?"

"Yup! A brand new one, sure is. "Wanna go fishing for bass tomorrow?" Naomi asked her.

"Yes! I sure do!" Marie exclaimed, taking the back roads home, eager to be in the comfort of Naomi's arms again.

"I'm glad you're happy about that baby. And guess what else?" Naomi asked.

"What, baby?" Marie was struggling to keep her eyes on the road.

"There's a fish cleaning station and a stove out back, so I'll fry it up after we catch some." "Yes!" Marie mumbled.

Minutes later, Marie pulled up to her home and hurried inside to gather her things while Naomi waited in the Jeep. When they finally returned to Naomi's home, they removed their clothes, washed their private parts, and gathered in the living room for a nightcap in their underwear before retiring to Naomi's bedroom.

"Are you ready to go to bed, Marie?" Naomi asked her.

"I am," Marie replied, handing her the empty wine glass.

"Leave that on the table baby, I'll wash it later." Naomi

took Marie's hand and led the way to the bedroom. They began kissing one another hungrily and sloppily, while stepping out of their panties. They continued kissing their way to the bed, sucking on each other's faces, and panting. Naomi entered one of her fingers into Marie's canal. "Oh… My…" was all Marie could muster.

Her mouth was slightly ajar, and Naomi took the opportunity to spit into it and then bite on Marie's bottom lip while continuing to penetrate her. Marie was practically convulsing under her touch.

"You. Make. Me. So. Fucking. *WET!*" Naomi grunted lustfully as she added in another finger.

"Damn…" Marie cried out, softly, moving her body to the pace of Naomi's fingers. "I love how uninhibited you are," Marie continued to whisper, pulling Naomi closer to her and they both slobbered on one another again.

Naomi slowly withdrew her fingers from Marie's canal and placed them into her mouth. "One good turn deserves another." Naomi was breathing heavily and winking at Marie, taking the time to lick each finger slowly.

"You're irresistible, girl… You know that?" Marie whispered to her, flipping Naomi over, pulling her breast out of her bra and putting one of her nipples into her mouth, sucking it aggressively, while placing her fingers inside her.

They both screamed out in ecstasy repeatedly, while grinding and "finger popping" each other. Finally, falling back on the bed, breathing heavily. Marie tried to lift her hand to caress Naomi's face, but she was too weak. Naomi noticed it and cracked a smile before they both fell asleep effortlessly. Hours later, Marie woke up to find Naomi still laying on her back. She covered her with the bed sheet before using the bathroom and returned to find her lying on her side now. She got back into bed, pulled the sheet up on herself, kissed Naomi softly on the cheek and fell back asleep.

The next afternoon, they went into town to buy green onions and fresh ears of corn to make hushpuppies with the fried bass. Once they were back at the house, Naomi left the groceries in the Jeep and asked Marie to help her retrieve the boat, rods, and tackle box from the shed.

"Gladly!" Marie exclaimed.

After the boat was successfully placed in the water, Naomi quickly kissed Marie and hurried to the Jeep for the groceries and ran into the kitchen to prepare the hushpuppy batter and homemade remoulade dipping sauce. Marie was out back on the deck threading the fishing line.

"All right, you ready, baby?" Naomi asked, walking through the bedroom door, and placing the batter on the table next to the deep fryer and cast-iron pan sitting on the burners.

"I'm more than ready baby! and that's a nice set up you got going on over there by the way." Marie commented, looking impressed but anxious to go fishing.

"Thank you!" Naomi sang to her as she set up the cleaning board and the radio to enjoy music when they returned with the fish. When she was done, Marie held out her hand to help her onto the boat. Once they were out on the Bayou, Marie exclaimed… "These fish are biting today, baby!" as she was reeling in her first catch. But the fish got tangled in the marsh's overgrown grass. She gallantly untangled it while Naomi watched her excitedly and waited for her catch.

It took them a good forty minutes to catch four medium-sized basses. Marie caught three, and Naomi caught one. After they docked the boat, Marie brought the fish over to the cleaning station, while Naomi tied the boat down. She was beaming with delight and proud of herself.

"You need me to do anything, baby?" Marie asked, washing her hands with the hose attached to the sink.

"No baby, you can relax for now." She took out the stainless-steel fish scaler and gutting knife, then turned on the radio, and they grooved to *"No Rhyme No Reason"* by George Duke while she de-scaled the fish.

"Hey, you," Marie said as she walked back over and held Naomi's chin.

Naomi put her descaling on pause when Marie kissed her.

"I'm grateful we met. I just thought you should know that." Marie smiled and then returned to her seat.

Naomi blushed, biting the corner of her lip seductively, then she resumed descaling the fish afterward, seasoning and scoring it, frying it whole to a golden brown. When the fish was done, she placed it in a food grade tin pail with a piece of brown paper bag to drain the excess grease off. Next, she tested the oil's heat in the deep fryer before dropping spoonfuls of hushpuppy batter into it. "Dinner's ready!" Naomi called out playfully while bringing the food over to the patio table and sitting across from Marie.

"That looks scrumptious!" Marie commented, licking her lips hungrily, making Naomi smile.

"Oh, shoot!" Naomi said, suddenly jumping up to go back into the house.

"What is it?" Marie asked.

"I forgot the napkins and the beer."

"I got it, baby. Sit down." Marie said, gently grabbing her arm to stop her. She jogged off and quickly returned with napkins, two ice cold beers and the homemade remoulade sauce Naomi left on the counter. "I'm so glad Maw-Maw met you down at that grocery store." Marie dipped a hushpuppy in the sauce before flopping down in her seat and stuffing it in her mouth. She shook her head happily with remoulade hanging from her chin.

"Aww, baby, me too!" Naomi squealed before wiping the remoulade from Marie's chin with her finger and putting it in her mouth.

"I'm really enjoying myself with you," Marie said with admiration in her eyes.

Naomi blushed while tearing off a piece of fish with her hands. "Are you staying with me tonight baby?" while "*I Like Dreamin'*" by Kenny Nolan was playing on the radio in the background.

"I wish I could stay, baby, but I have to pack. Don't you remember I have to leave the house on Tuesday because of the construction?"

"Yeah, I remember." Naomi looked down and took a small bite out of her hushpuppy. "What's the matter, baby?" Marie asked, moving to Naomi's side of the table.

"Well…, It just doesn't feel right… with you staying in

a hotel, especially that expensive hotel you chose! You're spending so much money as it is. Besides, Apolline was like family to me and would turn over in her grave if I didn't invite you to stay with me." "You know I would love to stay with you, baby," Marie told her, placing her hand on Naomi's thigh. "But I've already paid for a month's stay, and I believe it's nonrefundable."

"Oh, wow," Naomi said gloomily.

"Listen, I tell you what. How about you stay with me at the hotel and at the end of a week, I'll see if I can get a refund then stay with you until the house is completed?"

"For real?!" Naomi exclaimed, throwing the hushpuppy into her mouth, and chewing rapidly.

"Yes, for real." Marie giggled at her silliness.

Suddenly, Naomi threw her arms around Marie's neck and squealed with delight, shocking Marie.

Marie wrapped her arms around Naomi where she could, planting kisses on her neck. "Could you stop being so lovely? You're driving me crazy!" Marie said, gently squeezing her. "Go pack your bags, baby," Marie whispered in her ear before kissing her lips and breaking away to continue eating.

Naomi wiped her mouth, guzzled down her beer and ran into the house to pack her things. Marie watched her, overjoyed to finally have someone she dreamed about having a future with.

On Tuesday afternoon, Marie picked Naomi up from work, and they went to dinner at a popular restaurant in the quarter that had a live band.

"Are you ready to head to the hotel for check-in, baby?"

Marie asked empathetically after pushing her plate to the side.

"Whew!" Naomi responded covering her mouth as she belched. "Excuse me, baby. and yes, I'm ready to head to the hotel. I had a long day."

"I can see that, let me pay the check so I can get you into bed," Marie said, winking at her playfully.

"I'm going to the bathroom…; I'll be right back." Naomi smiled, her dimples on full display.

"I'll be ready so we can head out when you're done, baby." When Marie managed to flag down the waitress, she was informed that Naomi had already paid the bill. Marie gasped and then gave the waitress a large tip.

When Naomi returned to the table, she placed her hand gently on Marie's shoulder, indicating she was ready to leave.

Marie stood up smiling lovingly at her. "When did you pay the bill, baby?" she asked, on their way to the exit door.

"On my way to the bathroom." Naomi winked.

Marie was fortunate enough to find parking near the hotel's entrance, so she and Naomi easily took out their luggage and entered the hotel's massive lobby. They gazed in awe at its brown and beige checkered marbled floors and the giant grandfather clock near the reservation desk. The large crystal chandeliers endowed the lobby with a regal atmosphere.

Marie retrieved her room key, and asked… "Are you ready baby?"

"I read about this!" Naomi exclaimed, pointing to the hotel's famous carousel bar.

"They have a rooftop swimming pool too." Marie was smiling from ear to ear at Naomi's excitement.

"Come on, baby… the room is on the third floor." She hurried toward the elevator. "I wanted to take you for a drink tonight, but I know you're tired, so, maybe tomorrow we'll have dinner and drinks here instead of going out."

"Yeah, tomorrow would be better." Naomi loudly yawned.

"Wow!" they both uttered, putting down their luggage near the door once inside the beautifully decorated room. There was a king-sized bed, colorful botanical artwork on the wall above the headboard, and a beige tufted chaise lounge at the foot. Wide tan pinstriped walls, and floral blackout drapes hung from the windows. There was a cobalt blue dome chandelier, a huge mahogany armoire in the sleeping quarters, and a set of French doors connecting to the next room. Together they opened them and there was a sitting room decorated with the same pinstripe walls. This room, however, had a loveseat, a writing desk and a coffee table with a few literary works placed on it.

Marie returned to the main room and picked up her luggage from the front door and placed it near the armoire, then she pulled out the luggage stand for Naomi's.

"This room is gorgeous! You should have your contractor style your bedroom just like this!" Naomi said gleefully as she returned to the main room, removing her work clothes, then hurrying to the luxurious bathroom, which housed a two-basin green granite sink with gold faucets encased in dark wood furniture and a gold trimmed glass shower enclosure wide enough to accommodate them both. "Guess what, baby?" Naomi said, trotting out of the bathroom.

"What, baby?" Marie asked joyously, removing her clothes. "The shower is big enough for both of us!"

"Well… I'll wash your body if you wash mine. Come here, woman!" Marie teased running after Naomi who took off into the bathroom. They kissed, tickled, and washed one another's back before getting into bed in the nude. Naomi laid down on Marie's chest until she fell asleep. Marie kissed her on the forehead and turned on the television to watch the nightly news, only to wake up hours later to the alarm and the morning news. They both kissed each other a good morning and got dressed, grabbing breakfast in the hotel before Naomi was dropped off at work. Afterward, Marie went over to her house to see how the construction and the architectural details were coming along.

Later that afternoon, Marie picked Naomi up from work and went back to the hotel. They both washed the day off and made love before going downstairs to have dinner and drinks at the carousel bar. After dinner, they decided to go for a night swim on the rooftop. They spent the rest of the week in the hotel, living like tourists, until Marie checked out. Marie was unable to get a refund but was given a credit for the balance to use another time.

"At least I didn't lose the money!" she told the hotel clerk after thanking him and saying goodbye.

They played house at Naomi's for the next three weeks and a half, discovering with each passing day that they were compatible in almost every way possible, and the ways they weren't only enriched their romantic experience while respecting the differences.

One day, Imogene called and informed Marie that the construction was going to take a little longer because there was reconstruction that needed to be done due to the water pipes deterioration. And although Naomi was empathic with her, she felt intense joy at having Marie at her disposal. Marie expressed her concern about going over budget, so, Imogene compensated for the inconvenience by offering that her landscaper cleans up the back yard, reinforces the shed, and prunes the garden for her at no extra charge. "Thank you, Imogene!" Marie replied, surprised at her generosity. "How much longer do you suppose it'll take though?"

"It shouldn't be any longer than two-weeks." Imogene responded confidently.

"Well…" Marie said, letting out a deep sigh. "What choice do I have?" she chuckled, excited to see the outcome.

For the following two weeks, Naomi returned home from work cheerful every afternoon while playing the domesticated housewife of Marie's dreams. They took turns cooking and enjoyed eating the homecooked meals together in the evenings while making sweet soft love at night and taking turns falling asleep in the other's arms. One morning, after Naomi left for work, Imogene called Marie to inform her that the construction was complete and ready for her review. Marie couldn't reach the house fast enough. Once she arrived, she walked up the squeaky-clean staircase and porch and opened the front door. It was more divine than she ever imagined. The interior looked like it was ripped from the pages of an architectural magazine. Imogene gave her the open floor plan she desired with the baby grand piano taking center stage in the middle of the room, and two white columns with Corinthian capitals separating the living and dining space all sitting atop the beautifully refinished, polished mahogany floors. The fireplace was refaced in gray and white marble with a new set of black matte fireplace tools.

"Wow! You guys outdid yourselves!" Marie told Imogene, her mouth ajar.

"I'm so happy you like it, Marie!" Imogene responded blushing at the complement. "Come on, let me show you the kitchen," Imogene told her, leading the way.

"Oh, my gosh!" Marie said, stopping in her tracks while looking around the updated kitchen, which had modern stainless-steel appliances: a six-burner stove with warmer plate, a wall-mounted pot filler, and matching cooker hood. There was a white iridescent glass mosaic backsplash throughout and custom-made white shaker cabinets with silver door handles on the front and back walls. Marie stood there slowly shaking her head in utter amazement, her mouth still open.

"Let's go out back." Imogene told her, grinning at her reactions and opening the back door.

Marie stepped out and felt like a child again. "Maw-Maw," she said aloud softly as the tears welled up in her eyes. "You managed to take me back in time," Marie told Imogene as she looked at her innocently. All the garden's overgrowth was removed and cleared out, leaving the remaining lavender standing tall ready to multiply and bloom again. The shed was no longer tilting, and it was given a fresh coat of white paint trimmed in lavender. Marie gave Imogen a soft hug. "Thank you," Marie whispered, walking backward into the house. "You fixed the door!" Marie shouted, pointing at the storage closet, and pouting childishly in a show of happiness.

Imogene chuckled. "I did more than that!" she said, turning the polished copper doorknob on the resurfaced storage door.

Marie walked inside and tried pulling the cord to turn on the light, but the cord was removed and replaced by a light switch that was wired to a black, ceiling-mounted light fixture. The brick walls were cleaned and had floating cypress wood shelving anchored to them with the lavender syrup, jellies, and preserves jars cleaned and placed on top on them. This left Marie speechless, making Imogene's face hurt from smiling so much as she waited patiently to escort Marie upstairs to the primary bedroom.

"YOU GOT TO BE KIDDING ME!" Marie shouted! taking a step back and her hands gripping her hair. "I can't believe you did this!" She looked over at Imogene with wide eyes. "I can't wait to show Naomi, she's going to faint!"

"Well… I did my best to give you what you asked for." Imogene smiled, proud of herself. "Oh, my God, this is exceptional," Marie said as they entered the bathroom. She traced her fingers along the tan and gold etched marble floor to ceiling tiles before walking into the massive shower. She began admiring the polished gold rain and body shower heads. The other rooms were blank canvas apart from wainscoting, crown molding and wide baseboards. "I can't wait to show Naomi…, she's going to be thrilled when she sees this place." She thanked Imogene repeatedly.

"My pleasure, Marie truly."

They descended the staircase, and Marie showed Imogene to the door, being left alone to enjoy.

Later that afternoon, Naomi pulled up to her house. When she opened the front door and called out Marie's name, she was smacked in the face by the smell of the dirty rice and crispy crawfish beignets Marie cooked for dinner. "Yes!" she said, simultaneously kicking off her shoes, dropping her purse on the sofa to look for Marie, who was sitting out on the deck staring out onto the Bayou. "Hey, baby, is everything all right?" Naomi asked, walking out to greet her.

"Oh, hey, baby. Everything is fantastic! How was your day?" Marie responded as she got up to kiss her.

"It was a good day, but it's even better now," Naomi responded, planting another kiss on Marie's lips then showing off those dimples with a grin.

Marie took Naomi's hands and looked her directly in the eyes lovingly. "I want to ask you something, baby." Marie said softly.

"Sure baby, but can you ask me over dinner? I'm starved?"

They hurried into the house laughing. As Naomi proceeded to take off her work clothes, Maire went ahead and prepared their plates then set them on the table. A few minutes later, Naomi came and sat at the table in her bra and panties and dug into the dirty rice. "So, what did you want to ask me, baby?" she said, rapidly taking a bite of the crawfish beignet. "You are hungry, aren't you, baby?" Marie chuckled. "I really am," Naomi grinned.

"When is your lease up on this place?" Marie asked her seriously. She took a spoonful of dirty rice and placed it in her mouth as she waited for Naomi's response.

"Another three months. Why, baby?" Naomi asked, looking puzzled.

"Just curious is all," Marie responded, staring at her affectionately.

"All right, baby." Naomi licked her fingers and smiled. "Damn, this is good!" Naomi took a deep breath and started eating at a normal pace.

"Guess what, baby?" Marie asked, curbing her enthusiasm about the construction. "What?" Naomi responded, putting down her fork and listening attentively.

"The construction is finally completed," Marie told her, pretending not to be overly excited.

"Really! I'm so happy for you baby. When can we go and see it?" Naomi asked her excitedly.

"We can go after dinner if you want to." Marie pulled apart a beignet, withholding the fact that she'd seen it already.

"Aren't you excited, baby? Naomi asked perplexed by her attitude.

"Of course, I'm excited baby. Why you ask me that?" Marie asked her, grinning inside. "Nothing, I guess." She hunched her shoulders. "I just thought you'd be happier, baby because it's been a while." Naomi said, finishing her plate.

"I'm happy, baby. I just don't show it like you do, I guess." Marie responded, bursting at the seams as she held this secret.

After dinner, Naomi went and threw on a sundress, sprayed on perfume, and rubbed in some leave-in moisturizer cream on her curls while Maire cleared the table, washed the dishes, and cleaned the kitchen. They took Marie's Jeep and headed to the house.

"I'm so excited!" Naomi exclaimed, moving anxiously from side to side.

"Me too!" Marie giggled, turning the key in the lock, and opening the door. "Oh, my God! This is beautiful, Marie!" Naomi belted out, looking for Marie's reaction.

"I have a confession to make, baby."

"What is it?" Naomi asked in a shaky tone of voice.

"I've seen it already." Marie chuckled.

"No wonder you were so calm!" Naomi said, swatting Marie playfully on the arm, making Marie laugh.

Marie showed Naomi the restored garden, impressing her at every turn. "I have a big surprise for you upstairs, baby. But you have to close your eyes." Marie grabbed her hand and walked her upstairs. "Okay, baby…you can open your eyes now." Marie opened the bedroom door.

You got to be kidding me!" Naomi shouted. "This is exactly like the room in that pretty hotel we stayed in Marie!" She covered her mouth in disbelief.

"Yeah, I know. I reacted the same way when I first saw it. Come, let me show you the bathroom."

Naomi was amazed at everything she saw, but it

caused her to have mixed emotions. She was happy for Marie, but unhappy to see her go.

"Baby," Marie called out softly in one of the empty rooms.

"Yeah?" Naomi answered, looking melancholically at her.

"Remember when I asked you when your lease was up?"

"Yeah, I remember." Naomi answered, her eyes darting from side to side as she looked into Marie's.

"Well... I asked you because I've decided to stay, and I wanted to know if you would move in here with me and make this a home..." Marie asked sincerely, running her hand across Naomi's hair.

Naomi slapped her hand across her mouth, backed away and stared at Marie practically in tears. "You mean it?" Naomi asked softly, removing her hand.

"Of course, I mean it. You can't possibly think I would've recreated the hotel suite if it wasn't for you, do you?" Marie asked softly as she walked closer to Naomi and tongue-kissed her slowly. "Call the owner and let them know you'll be moving out by the end of the week," Marie told her tenderly.

"You want me to break the lease?" Naomi asked her.

"Yes, baby. I'll pay for the remaining months and help pack up your things. I don't want you to be stressed out or have to miss work, I got you, baby," Marie assured her, winking and kissing her again.

Naomi screamed out "I love you!" She held out her arms and whirled around joyously, causing Marie's love to blossom even more in that very moment.

One month later Naomi was completely moved in. In the summer that followed, Naomi's son Calvin spent some time with them. He spent most of his time with Marie while Naomi was at work, causing them to form a deep bond. Calvin went with Marie every afternoon to pick Naomi up from work, and sometimes she would let him drive. Occasionally, they would go out for dinner and engage in other activities, such as movies and sporting events. Even after Calvin returned to Nashville, he kept talking to Marie on the phone every day.

Naomi continued to decorate the home with little to no input from Marie because she was given the title "Woman of the House," while Marie got her trucking company in order. Five years later, Marie and Naomi tied the knot in a beautiful ceremony. Naomi retired from teaching and Marie's trucking company converted into a multi-million-dollar business with eight drivers in two locations- one, in Louisiana and another in Nashville (which Naomi's son manages). They ended up renting out Marie's inherited home because she just couldn't give it up and purchased a gated waterfront mansion in Shreveport Louisiana where they remain happy until this day.

Intermission - Peyton's Place

"Ahhh, listen to that saxophone blow…" Marlow thought, having an intimate solo dinner of steak, asparagus, and potatoes au gratin. She closed her eyes as she slowly chewed while the saxophone reminded her of a time when she had a love so sweet. She sat in the high-back black velvet seat at a three-seated table in a steel-blue silk slip dress, sporting 1ct black diamond stud earrings and a dainty silver wristwatch. She was on the rooftop of one of the swankiest jazz lounges in Phoenix, sipping on her second glass of white wine, allowing the music to make love to her soul. Her trance was interrupted when a male and female couple approached her table and pulled out the two empty seats. Marlow looked over at them and was transfixed by the woman's beauty, and she didn't care that her fascination was apparent. The woman's skin was the hue of a mature coconut shell, and her breasts were full and perky in her fitted indigo denim flair-legged halter jumpsuit. Her toes were painted a chalky white; she sported clear strapped sling-back high-heel sandals and a crystal-encrusted clutch, and her dark brown hair partially covered Her gold hoop earrings. Marlow could tell the woman had recently layer-cut and curl-bumped her hair, evidenced by the new salon hairspray smell in the air not there before the woman's arrival. She would know her hairdresser uses the same kind.

"Good evening." The woman said, smiling at her before she sat down. "These seats aren't taken, are they?"

"No, they're not." Marlow replied, placing her fork on the napkin beside her plate.

"My name is Kennedy, and this is my friend Mark." She stepped slightly to one side, giving Marlow a full view, while Mark smiled and waved pleasantly before they both took a seat.

"My name is Marlow." She responded, picking up her napkin, wiping her mouth, and staining it with her mocha lipstick.

The band began to play a rendition of Stanley Clarke and George Duke's "Sweet Baby." Kennedy softly tapped her neutral-colored stiletto nails on the table as she marveled at the band. Mark called the waiter over and ordered a bottle of champagne for the table. Marlow pushed her half-emptied plate away and began to snap her fingers and tap her foot to the music, watching the band until Kennedy lightly touched her arm, offering her a glass of the champagne and letting her know Mark bought it for the table.

"Oh, wow. Thank you." Marlow responded, raising her glass to Mark.

Mark acknowledged her gesture, and she smiled at Kennedy as she poured her champagne, then cheered her afterward. Kennedy inched closer to Marlow and asked her a question. "So, you came here alone?" Her voice was soft, her eyes seductive.

"I did." Marlow responded, looking at Kennedy with the same seductiveness as she tilted her head back, sipping her champagne.

"You're brave." Kennedy smiled coyly at her and then gulped her champagne.

"Brave?" Marlow asked, still holding her flute and pleasantly perplexed.

"It's gonna sound cliché, but I'll say it anyway." Kennedy laughs. "What's a pretty girl like you doing in a place like this?" she asked with a wink, causing Marlow to blush.

"Because I didn't have a date." Marlow smirked, drinking the last of her champagne. "Will you excuse me?" I have to use the ladies' room. She told her, picking up her silver satin purse.

"Of course." Kennedy replied, standing and moving her chair closer to the table to allow Marlow to get by as the band began to play their rendition of Bobbi Humphrey's *"Harlem River Drive."* "Thank you." Marlow blushed. Kennedy stared at Marlow walking away from the table, her tan skin glistening from the fragrant body glitter lotion she had applied, matching her silver beaded sandals as her silk dress clung to her body in all the right places; she moved methodically with her womanly glide across the rooftop, while the music posed as her theme song.

Five minutes later…. Kennedy whispered a few words to Mark, excused herself from the table, and went to join Marlow in the ladies' room. Once in the bathroom… Kennedy leaned against the terracotta tiled wall and waited for Marlow to exit the stall.

"Oh!" Marlow exclaimed after noticing Kennedy standing there.

Kennedy stood there smiling at her and pretending to view the images on her phone. Marlow washed her hands, holding her purse under her arm, then dried them under the hand dryer.

"Don't you have to use the bathroom?" Marlow asked her, giving her a once-over look.

"No, I'm good. I wanted to ask you a question."

"Sure, what's up?" Marlow asked her, looking in the mirror, reapplying her lipstick, and adjusting her dress.

"Have you ever been to the club downstairs?" Kennedy asked her with a sly grin.

"They have another club downstairs." Marlow asked her with a look of surprise on her face.

"Yes," she laughed devilishly. "It's called Peyton Place. Would you like to come with me? But it's only a good time if you're open-minded," she interjected before Marlow could answer.

"I'm a Pisces; I think I'm as open-minded as they come," Marlow chuckled softly.

"Oh! I'm a Scorpio, so we're good." Kennedy said seductively before winking at her. "Okay, so if you're ready to go, follow me." She told Marlow as they were walking out of the bathroom.

"Wait!" Marlow said, stopping suddenly. "What about Mark?"

"No, he can't come to this club, honey. It's only for couples, but more specifically for women who love women."

"Aren't you guys a couple?" Marlow asked, confused at her response.

"Mark is one of my closest friends. I didn't want to have dinner or drink alone tonight, so I asked him to accompany me as my designated driver. He'll be all right. Follow me." Kennedy told her cheerfully, walking out the bar's front door and down a flight of black iron stairs connected to the outside of the club leading to the basement where the club stood.

"Hey, ladies!' The woman at the door shouted out light-heartedly. "How can I help you this evening?" She said, standing behind a podium.

"Hey yourself!" Kennedy responded cheerfully. "I'm a lifetime member. My name is Kennedy Shade."

"Okay, let's have a look." The woman said, reaching inside the podium and pulling out a ledger.

"Okay, I see your name here, the woman said, returning the ledger. Welcome back, Ms. Shade." "It'll just be a twenty-dollar cover charge for your friend. But you're in luck; it's bald-headed beaver night! So, if ya got one, you get in free!" The woman turned to Marlow, her giggle becoming a smoker's cough.

"Well, it must be my lucky night because I just happened to have one." Marlow said, smirking and then biting her bottom lip.

"Well, show it, honey!" The woman told her, appearing to salivate in anticipation of seeing it.

Marlow looked around first before pulling up her dress, then moved the front of her G-string to the side and showed off her bald beaver, turning the woman and Kennedy on. Kennedy tipped the woman, who thanked her and stamped both hands, encouraging them to have a good time on their way into the purple-lit club as the heavy steel black door closed behind them. *"Slave for You"* by Britney Spears played throughout while women of all shapes, sizes, and complexions walked by, smiling at them, each scantily clad.

Kennedy gently grabbed Marlow's hand and asked… "Do you believe in one-night stands?" while observing Marlow's body language and facial expression before punching in the combination on the black and gold keypad to open the red door they stopped in front of.

Marlow answered her with a soft yet resounding "Yes," staring at her with seductive eyes before being led through the door onto black and white checkered floors; everything else in the room was red, including the lights. In contrast, soft jazz music flowed from the hidden speakers within. The linen on the king-sized bed was 1000-count red Egyptian cotton, and a modest selection of whips, handcuffs, dildos, and anal plugs were placed neatly about. They were (except the whips and handcuffs) all housed on wall-mounted shelves next to red crystal bowls filled to the rim with condoms and lubricants. "The interior designer certainly loves the color red," Marlow thought with a coy smile.

Kennedy closed the door, then threw her purse on the bed and began Kissing Marlow softly on the back of her neck before walking in front of her and doing the same on her collarbone, pulling down her dress straps to kiss her shoulders, causing Marlow to become weak in the knees. "You smell lovely," Kennedy whispered, breathing lightly on the left side of her neck. "I saw how you looked at me when I came to your table tonight." She continued breathing harder into Marlow's ear before sticking her tongue in it, causing Marlow to shiver and drop her purse to the floor before placing her hands lightly in Kennedy's hair, relishing the sensations.

Kennedy became silent and began sucking on Marlow's neck, moving to her face, kissing it softly, but brushing past her mouth purposefully. At the same time, Marlow was untying Kennedy's halter top, revealing her breasts adorned with black fur pasties. She stopped kissing Marlow to pull her dress over her head and removed her jumpsuit, both staring in awe at the other's beauty.

"Do you like it soft?" Kennedy asked as she walked Marlow backward, slowly toward the bed, simultaneously putting one hand loosely around her throat, causing her to gasp with pleasure and slowly closing her eyes. "Or do you like it rough?" Kennedy continued, spinning Marlow around quickly, placing her arms behind her back, pinning her hands together, and gently pushing her face down on the bed.

"Oh my god." Marlow mumbled, becoming moister because of Kennedy's assertive foreplay. "You're making my fantasy come true. You can do whatever you want to do." Marlow told her, turning her face slightly to unmuffle her words and moisten her lips.

Kennedy let go of Marlow's hands and gently bit her on her back down to her ass cheeks. Marlow's fingers gently grasped the bed sheets as she sighed with pleasure. Kennedy placed one of her hands between Marlow's legs to rub her significantly large clit, then she slid her thumb slowly into her moist canal and lifted her bottom toward her mouth, eventually removing her thumb to suck her from behind. Marlow's moans were out of control as she crawled toward the head of the bed, grabbing at the sheets, with Kennedy's thumb returning to its position even deeper inside her, penetrating her more rapidly. Marlow opened her legs and spread her cheeks wider because the alcohol she drank previously took away her inhibitions. Kennedy penetrated her faster and deeper, licking her backyard canal simultaneously until Marlow's screaming climax halted her as her body went limp.

"Turn on your back," Kennedy ordered as she slowly got off the bed to retrieve the spreader bar and the wedge pillow. She returned to the bed and gently placed Marlow's ankles in the padded cuffs of the spreader, keeping her legs apart. Then she assisted Marlow in turning to her stomach on top of the wedge pillow, which again hiked her cheeks, exposing her backyard canal. "Just a minute, baby, I forgot one more thing," Kennedy returned to the wall-mounted shelves, returning with an anal plug.

"Be gentle, Kennedy. I haven't done this in a while." Marlow told her.

"This hole has muscle memory, too, baby," Kennedy

chuckled. "But no worries, my beauty, I'll be gentle with you," Kennedy assured her as she doused the anal plug with lubricant while her hyper-salivating mouth almost made her drool. Kennedy started nibbling on Marlow's butt cheeks before slapping them, causing her to squirm and softly beg for more. Kennedy slowly introduced the plug into Marlow's backyard canal, causing her to fade in and out of consciousness from the overwhelming sensation of it. Kennedy put her hands between her legs and massaged her clit, moaning in ecstasy while looking at Marlow's reaction as she repeatedly orgasmed from both orifices, her flaccid arms down by her sides.

When Marlow got her bearings together, she reached back, grabbing Kennedy's wrist. "I've had enough baby."

Kennedy's body jerked as her last climax ran through her, causing her body to slump onto Marlow's, her heart beating rapidly. Her forehead and upper lip were overrun with perspiration as she unbuckled the straps around Marlow's ankles. She fell onto the right side of the bed as Marlow lay on the left and gently pushed the wedge pillow to the foot with her feet. After a little while, Kennedy sat at the edge of the bed, tapping the residual preparation off with the back of her hand while Marlow got off the bed and glided to the swing she observed in the corner.

"Mm, My favorite." Kennedy told her in a playful but naughty tone, watching her. "But I need a drink first." Kennedy continued, deeply sighing while combing her hair with her hands and walking over to the ice-filled water pitcher on the free-standing bar she had set up.

Marlow watched Kennedy's every move lustfully as

she gently ran her hands over the front of her body. "Can I have a glass of water too"? she asked, touching her throat seductively, then positioning herself to sit.

"Of course, you can, baby." Kennedy poured her glass after finishing hers. "Here you go, sweetheart." She said, bringing it over to her. "I need to use the bathroom before we continue unless…" she said, biting her bottom lip; "You're into golden showers." She laughed seriously and puckered her lips for a kiss.

"Muah." Marlow kissed her softly, touching Kennedy's face and telling her to use the bathroom. "She has no idea how freaky I am." Marlow thought to herself before chuckling aloud.

Kennedy exited the bathroom and walked over to the swing where Marlow stood patiently waiting to strap her in. Kennedy put one thigh at a time into the holster, exposing the cherry-colored clit of her baldheaded beaver and holding on to the ropes; at the same time, Marlow was stepping into a harness attached to a dildo, with a pair of nipple clamps between her teeth.

"I can't fucking wait!" Kennedy snarled softly, throwing her hair from her face and licking her lips with overwhelming anticipation.

Marlow walked over seductively and applied the nipple clamps to Kennedy's nipples while putting her tongue in and out of her mouth. As she did so, Kennedy hissed with pleasure. Marlow held on to the swing ropes and entered Kennedy's love box canal slowly but deeply, causing Kennedy to swing her body forward as she panted in pleasure. Marlow's thrusts became faster when she began to climax, causing Kennedy to howl as she climaxed with her, her eyes rolling into her head repeatedly, preventing her from uttering another sound, yet her juices were flowing excessively.

"Yes, baby, keep Cumming, keep Cumming!" Marlow shouted, slowing down and enjoying how Kennedy's eyes repositioned as the sweat flowed down her face.

"Please don't stop," Kennedy repeatedly mumbled as she slowly came too.

Marlow thrusted her hips into Kennedy's canal harder for the last time before she pulled out, grabbing the swing's ropes and tongue-kissing Kennedy aggressively.

Afterward, Kennedy laughed sinisterly, licking her lips before instructing Marlow to retrieve the anal beads from the peg wall behind her. "I don't need lube, baby," Kennedy told her just before Marlow stuck her hand into the red crystal bowl to retrieve some.

Marlow walked over, got in between Kennedy's thighs, and inserted one bead at a time into her backyard canal while tongue-kissing her until all the beads were inside, with the ring pull being the only visible one; at the same time, Kennedy grabbed her back in ecstasy.

"Now, go and get that vibrator wand from over there," Kennedy told her, pointing to it.

Marlow did as she was told and returned, turning it on and placing it on Kennedy's clit. Kennedy squirmed with pleasure, begging Marlow to pull out the beads slowly. Marlow gently grabbed the ring and began slowly pulling out the beads one by one as Kennedy started gasping for air, climaxing, and nearly fainting as the last bead was removed during her final and hardest climax. "Sweet Lord!" she shouted, trying to catch her breath. "I need help, baby; I'm weak." she told Marlow, chuckling softly, who was glad to assist her out of it. Kennedy held on to Marlow tightly as she wobbled to the bed while Marlow released herself from the harness.

They both lounged on the bed diagonally, closing their eyes. Fifteen minutes later…. Kennedy's *"Hot in Here"* ringtone by Nelly startled them awake.

"Hey, Mark, sweetheart!" Kennedy answered. "Yeah, give or take another hour, and I'll be ready to leave. Sure. You can meet me outside the bar. Okay, I'll see you in about an hour then, bye-bye." Kennedy hung up the line and looked at Marlow, who picked up her dress and carried it to the bathroom. "Leaving so soon?" Kennedy teased, taking a cigarette from a red lacquer box on a small glass table beside the bed and offering Marlow one.

"No, I don't smoke." Marlow smiled, entering the bathroom and closing the door to freshen up. The bathroom was large and dimly lit but not red for a change; it was more of a golden hue with a black clawfoot bathtub and gold hardware, a stand-alone shower enclosed in glass, and a slew of luxury toiletries in the center of the Moroccan-tiled double basin sinks. Marlow took a quick shower, brushed her hair, and put her dress back on before stepping back into the red room to find Kennedy dressed, holding a glass of cognac, and smoking a cigarette. Marlow smiled at her admiringly and sat on the bed.

"I didn't know if you would be driving, so I didn't make you a drink." Kennedy told her, taking another puff of her cigarette and looking at her alluringly.

"I didn't drive tonight because I wanted to drink like you." she chuckled. I'll have my driver pick me up when I'm ready." Marlow told her, queuing Kennedy to make her a drink.

"Yes, ma'am!" Kennedy responded, impressed with her answer, and poured her a drink. "May I ask what you do for a living?" Kennedy said, handing her the drink and taking a sip of hers.

"I'm the maestro at Phoenix Symphony Hall." Marlow responded before raising the glass to her lips.

"Really!" Kennedy responded, impressed and nodding her head. "That's different," she continued, looking at the time on her phone and drinking the last of her cognac.

"What? You never met a maestro before." Marlow chuckled, taking out her phone to call her driver. "Excuse me for a moment." she said, her driver picking up after the first ring. "Hey Alfred, it's me, Marlow. I'll be ready for pick-up in twenty minutes. Is that okay? I'm at the same location you dropped me off at this evening. All right, I'll see you in twenty minutes," she said, hanging up the phone.

"So, would you like to keep in touch?" Kennedy asked her, rinsing her glass and then putting on her shoes.

"Yes, let's get to know one another and grab dinner sometime," Marlow said, winking as they laughed.

"Yeah, we skipped a step, huh?" Kennedy said before taking Marlow's glass, rinsing it, and putting it away, afterward turning off the lights and pulling the red door behind them.

As they made their way to the exit door, Marlow paused and said, "Hey, Kennedy, just a second. I never asked you what you did for a living."

"Oh, I'm Peyton, baby. Kennedy is my stage name." she winked.

"I like your style." Marlow grinned as they both laughed, then went their separate ways.

Black Hampton Elite

Marsha snatched her driver's cap from the hat rack in the mud room, zipped up her uniform jacket, and drove her black mint-conditioned vintage sports car out of her garage and into the depot to park. She grabbed her bagged lunch and hurried to start her regularly assigned bus so it'd be warm for her first and favorite passenger, Mrs. Thomas. "I can't have that gentle soul standing alone at this hour of the morning." Marsha mumbled to herself before she waved to greet her co-workers.

"Good morning!" the crew shouted back cheerfully while she punched her timecard.

She climbed onto the assigned #2 bus, turned it on, and waited fifteen minutes before pulling out and traveling down 63 Main Street in Sag Harbor to the first stop in front of the firehouse to pick up Mrs. Thomas. Marsha was a muscular, brown-skinned woman of thirty-two years who always kept her wavy shoulder-length black hair in a bun. She was the youngest driver to be assigned this route after the previous driver retired; she was selected because of her pleasant and easygoing attitude. She was ALWAYS on time for the early morning shift and eager to work overtime if they were down a driver. So, it was easy for her supervisor to choose her over the others that applied. She drove the same route for five years, and her passengers adored her.

"Good morning, Marsha!" Mrs. Thomas said, smiling pleasantly and adjusting her sweater over her shoulders. She climbed the bus stairs and handed Marsha a freshly baked plate of chocolate chip cookies after paying her fare.

"Good morning!" Marsha responded with a huge smile, thanking Mrs. Thomas and placing the cookies on the broad sill of her driver-side window before driving off. These small acts of kindness always made her job worthwhile.

Mrs. Thomas was a sixty-eight-year-old woman widower who was the part-time caretaker and companion of Doctor Moore, the oldest black doctor on the island. Doctor Moore had been a general practitioner in one of New York's top hospitals for seventy years; he even had a wing dedicated to him for his service. At the country club near his home, he would be celebrating his one-hundred-and-one birthday in the coming weeks, and Mrs. Thomas asked Marsha if she would like to be a guest.

It was a no-brainer. "Absolutely! I wouldn't miss it! Thank you, Mrs. Thomas!" She replied gleefully, pulling up to the next stop and opening the door for the other passengers.

"You're welcome, my dear." Mrs. Thomas responded,

sitting parallel to Marsha, looking at her lovingly, and readjusting her sweater again.

Marsha opened the doors at the next stop… "Good morning!" the passengers greeted, smiling pleasantly, before sitting and having their conversations. The route was slow and scenic, with its tree-lined streets slightly obscuring the waterfront, boutique stores, and modest cottage homes, creating a relaxing environment for everyone, including Marsha, which was precisely why she requested it. Mrs. Thomas was the last passenger to be dropped off before Marsha's lunch hour and the first to be picked up on Marsha's way back to the depot, where she gave Marsha her phone number and wished her a good evening before leaving the bus. Once she arrived back at the depot….

"Could you work Douglas' route this afternoon? He called out sick," her supervisor Simon asked her, yelling it out while walking across the depot to meet her. Simon was a slim, middle-aged, six-foot, silver-haired Irish man who was extremely fair and kind to his crew.

"Sure. I can work this afternoon for you." Marsha responded gleefully. "What's his route again, Simon?" she asked curiously, meeting him halfway.

"You're a doll!" Simon exclaimed, reminding her that Douglas' route was on the opposite side of the Island, starting at 90 Main Street and ending on Hampton Road.

Marsha freshened up in the restroom and then made her way to the bus to start yet another route. When she pulled up to the first stop after ten minutes, her heart began palpitating, and she was becoming emotionally overwhelmed at the sight of a beautiful, fashionably dressed brown-skinned woman who was third in line and approaching the entrance to the bus. She wore large pin curls in the front of her dark hair, finishing it off with a French roll in the back. She wore a solid black vintage short-sleeve blouse with a cherry applique above her left breast, a black pencil skirt, black patent leather pumps, a red clutch under her arm, and a matching change purse she held in her hand.

"Good God!" Marsha mumbled, spellbound with a dry mouth.

"Afternoon, young lady. Is Douglas off today?" the older gentleman boarding first asked her.

"No, he's sick today, I'm afraid." Marsha responded, swallowing hard, hoping it would moisten her dry mouth.

"Welcome," the woman behind him said, smiling after hearing their conversation. "Good afternoon." the beautiful woman greeted her while taking out coins from her change purse for the bus fare, smiling the entire time. She held on to the pole directly behind the driver's seat since passenger seats were no longer available.

"Good afternoon." Marsha responded nervously as she watched the woman through her rearview mirror. She closed the bus doors and cautiously pulled off. Marsha continued down the route, dropping off one person after the other. The beautiful woman was the last one to exit.

"Thank you." she yelled as she got off at the back of the bus.

"You're welcome! Good night!" Marsha shouted, waiting to see which direction the woman headed in. She made a U-turn and noticed the woman walk onto a concrete paved walkway alongside manicured lawns up to a beautiful white two-story home adorned with blue and white hydrangeas and evergreen gardens around the perimeter. Marsha kept her eyes on the woman until she entered the home. Then she went on her way, picking up and dropping off passengers before driving back to the depot, retrieving her car, and calling it a day.

At home, Marsha took a shower, ate a bowl of ramen noodles, and then called her elderly parents to check in on them. Her mother had been a prestigious sculptor for two distinguished art galleries. One in Sag Harbor and the other in Tribeca, New York. Her father retired from his position as the chief curator of the largest, most visited museum in New York. They built their waterfront cottage home in Sag Harbor, AKA a "haven" for the Black elite in the Hamptons, back in the '60s (due to a lack of available homes and vacation destinations for people of color at that time), where Marsha currently resides after her parents moved to the small town of Oak Bluffs on Martha's Vineyard a few years ago. Her parents kindly demanded that she visit them as soon as possible.

"We're not getting any younger, young lady," her father told her, her mother agreeing with him in the background.

"I'll come up to visit next weekend, all right?" She chuckled softly before saying she loved them and wished them goodnight before she retired to her bed.

The following morning, like clockwork, she did her typical routine, but this time, she asked Simon if Douglas' shift was available because she hoped to see the woman again.

"It's still early, Marsha, but I should have an answer for you when you're done with your shift."

"All right, thanks, Simon!" she told him, hurrying to her bus, crossing her fingers along the way, and praying Douglas would call out. After her route, she drove back to the depot, hoping to hear Simon tell her that Douglas called out. But to her dismay, she was met with an enthusiastic hello from Douglas himself.

"Hey, Marsha! How's it going?" I heard you got yourself some OT yesterday; you're welcome." He joked with a hearty laugh.

"A single girl can always use some extra money every now and again. I don't have a benefactor like your wife does." She responded with the same vigor and a wink while hiding her disappointment at his presence.

"Touché!" he responded, causing a domino effect of laughter throughout the depot from the other bus drivers in earshot.

Marsha visited the bathroom, clocked out, and told her co-workers goodbye before getting into her car and stopping by the gym to pay her membership fee before heading home. Once she got back in her car, she couldn't stop thinking about the woman from yesterday and decided to drive down Hampton Road to see if she was waiting for the bus again today instead of going home. She had to wait awhile because Douglas hadn't arrived in this area yet, so she went inside one of the best local diners near the bus stop for a slice of white chocolate cheesecake and a cup of their fair-trade organic coffee, parking her car in the rear. "I'll work this off tomorrow," she thought, laughing as she sat near the window at the front of the diner, enjoying her unobstructed view of the passengers waiting for the bus while occasionally looking at her wristwatch.

Twenty-five minutes and two cups of coffee later…. There she was, Mrs. Beautiful in the flesh, wearing a vintage yellow swing dress with white polka dots and a pair of white peep-toe pumps with a matching handbag. She wore a stylish straw hat covering up her hairstyle and blocking out the sun rays from her beautiful brown face. "This woman is a work of art." Marsha thought, feeling all fuzzy inside. "I'm coming back here every day until I get the courage to ask her out." she mumbled, staring at her as she boarded the bus.

The following afternoon, after work, Marsha went to the gym for an hour to make up for yesterday's cheesecake. Afterward, at home, she prepared a dinner of sauteed chicken breasts in white wine sauce with sundried tomatoes and spinach over a bed of linguine pasta. While simmering the chicken and waiting for the water for the pasta to boil, she changed into a pair of silk boxers and a T-shirt before calling Mrs. Thomas to ask her for Doctor Moore's celebration details.

Delighted to hear from her, Mrs. Thomas gave her all the particulars of the celebration. "By the way, Marsha, you wouldn't happen to be married, would you?"

"I wish!" Marsha exclaimed playfully, causing them to laugh.

"Okay, that's good to hear." Mrs. Thomas responded

cheerfully before growing silent.

"Why'd you ask?" Marsha asked respectfully, placing the linguine in the water's rolling boil.

"I have someone I'd like to introduce you to. I'll bring them with me to the celebration."

"Oh, lord," Marsha thought, rolling her eyes to the ceiling. "Sounds lovely, Mrs. Thomas. Any friend of yours is a friend of mine.

"Oh, dear… this will be far greater than a friendship."

Marsha chuckled at her humor and said, "Have a good evening, Mrs. Thomas. I'll see you in front of the Firehouse in the morning." After they hung up, she tested the pasta before entering her studio to bring forth one of the clay sculptures she had created. She looked it over for imperfections, then placed it in the Kiln outback to bake it before displaying it on the new taupe marble pedestal. This was a talent inherited from her mother (not to mention being a fine art connoisseur). She acquired a passion for the finer things in the art world on her trips to the museum with her father on Saturday afternoons, thereby hanging several pieces of art in every room of the newly renovated three-bedroom cottage. Marsha was a loner and sometimes shy, having few friends. Her last girlfriend went to college late in life, leaving for grad school in Rochester a few years ago. Marsha visited her on campus twice in the beginning. Still, something about her girlfriend was different; she was starting to become very distant, and they didn't communicate as much after a while. The long-distance was too great, so they decided it best to move on, leaving Marsha heartbroken with no choice but to bury herself in gym workouts, her job, and weekend trips to visit her parent's home. She joined a dating site and chatted with several women before deciding to go on her first date with a woman she communicated with daily for about a month. However, when they finally got together, the woman shared that she was taking medication for schizophrenia. Despite that, she mentioned she'd stopped taking it because of the side effects, which caused Marsha to change her phone number and never communicate with the woman again.

A couple of weeks later, she tried the dating site again, scheduling a dinner date with another woman she talked to for a week. That woman turned out to be a catfish, causing her to give up online dating completely. Since Douglas hadn't called out for the following two weeks, Marsha started driving down Hampton Road to watch out for the beautiful woman waiting for Douglas' bus, sometimes observing her chatting with a few select passengers. However, the woman always appeared to be alone. Marsha decided it best she sat in her car instead of the diner because the cheesecake was addictive, and she didn't want it "showing up" in her midsection, causing her to work out more than she initially wanted to. She often sat there past the scheduled bus time because Douglas would arrive late. Nevertheless, she eagerly awaited the woman's arrival. But the woman was a no-show for the rest of the second week.

"Damn, it! I blew it," Marsha said aloud, hitting the steering wheel and driving off, mad at herself for being too shy to ask the woman out. On the following Friday night…

she began sculpting another mound of clay of a woman's torso for hours while listening to classical music. She suddenly became tired and decided to take a hot shower and go to bed.

On Saturday morning, she drove into town for a little social interaction and to shop for an outfit she could wear to Dr. Moore's birthday celebration, expected to take place the weekend after she visited her parents. After some time, she found a small, welcoming boutique on Madison Street with an array of unisex African clothing. She chose a two-piece white Dashiki outfit trimmed in Kente cloth design across the bust and down both sides of the pant leg. The price was nothing to sneeze at, but it fit her beefy build well.

After spotting a Japanese restaurant at the corner, she realized she was in the mood for sushi and ordered herself dinner. She went with two crunchy rice tuna rolls, teriyaki salmon, and seasonal mixed vegetables with steamed chicken dumplings and shishito peppers. Afterward, she drove home and worked on her sculpture with her dinner and a glass of Bordeaux directly on the pier at the back of her waterfront home. The splash of the waves intoxicated her, and the thought of the beautiful woman waiting at the bus stop ran intermittently through her mind as she sculpted the bust.

The following weekend, Marsha drove the four-hour trip to her parents' house in Massachusetts; they couldn't wait to see her. She parked her car in the driveway of their nine-hundred and sixty square foot, two-bedroom gingerbread cottage and then used her key to enter her parents' beautifully decorated country-style home. Her father was in their galley kitchen shucking clams for the chowder they would have, and her mother was upstairs vacuuming the guest bedroom for her stay.

"Hey, baby!" her father shouted, happy to see her, taking off his shucking glove to hug her.

"Hi, Daddy." She replied gleefully in a childlike voice, hugging him back.

Her mother hurried down the stairs once she heard her voice and wrapped her arms tightly around her while kissing her face repeatedly.

"Hi, Mommy," she said, trying desperately to kiss her mother's cheek, but her mother's head was moving too fast.

"How was the drive over, darling?" her mother asked, unable to contain her enthusiasm, while her father looked on and smiled before taking her luggage upstairs.

"It was pretty good; not as much traffic as I expected." Marsha replied, able to kiss her mother's cheek now. Marsha settled in, and after a hearty dinner and conversations with her parents, she fell asleep on the sofa at the end of watching the movie, Carmen Jones. Her mother didn't want to disturb her, but her father decided she would be more comfortable in bed and woke her up.

The following morning, they had a breakfast of scrambled eggs, hash brown potatoes, homemade buttermilk biscuits, and sausage patties. Her parents hinted that they longed to be grandparents, but Marsha changed the topic, reminiscing about her deceased Army Veteran brother Donald Jr., before driving them around town in her father's car to see the sights. They visited the first-ever lighthouse on Martha's Vineyard. Then, they had Conch fritters and a Conch chowder lunch at the Marina during the annual Fleet Week Bluewater Classic festival. Marsha and her mother were tickled watching her father's intense enjoyment at the boat show.

Marsha's mother gently squeezed her hand lovingly and asked, "Are you still single, baby?"

"Yes, Mommy, Unfortunately, I am." she sighed, her eyes saddened as she gazed downward.

"Don't worry. She'll show up soon," her mother said softly, patting her thigh and smiling, reassuring her.

"From your mouth to God's ears, Mommy," Marsha said softly before kissing her mother's cheek and resting her head on her shoulder.

Her mother looked out into the distance and smiled while her hand patted Marsha's thigh. The next morning, Marsha gathered her things and kissed her parents' goodbye before driving home with fried chicken wrapped in brown paper, a thermos of homemade sweet tea, and more homemade biscuits her mother had packed for her to enjoy on the road.

The evening of Doctor Moore's celebration arrived, and Marsha was excited to attend. She went to the hair salon earlier in the afternoon and had a light lunch at a nearby restaurant before going home and getting dressed. At 7 p.m., she pulled up to the ostentatious country club and parked in the designated area before walking up the left side of the double-stone staircases. She entered the banquet hall, looking around in wonderment as she watched all the distinguished doctors, lawyers, and teachers fashionably dressed and mingling while searching for Mrs. Thomas. "There must be at least two hundred people in here," she thought. Meanwhile, a server approached her and offered her a Champagne cocktail, which she took eagerly, looking towards the wide-open flower-filled terrace and the splendorous garden landscape. She walked onto the terrace smiling and greeting those who greeted her, looking over the natural stone railing and observing some guests playing golf on the lush green lawns while others drank and mingled on the paved stone before it. It was nothing short of magnificent. "My people," she mumbled, smiling proudly as she returned to the main hall. "I wonder if," she began to think, pausing when she noticed Mrs. Thomas walking through the entrance door. She was wearing a gold brocade dress with matching low-heel pumps.

Marsha waved her hand excitedly at her, with her mouth around the cocktail glass, before gasping at the sight of the woman with her. "Oh my god!" She mumbled, nearly choking on her drink as Mrs. Thomas waved back, walking in her direction.

"Hello, dear, you made it!" Mrs. Thomas shouted cheerfully at her; her arms extended to embrace her.

"Yes." Marsha said, her mind blank while staring at the woman wearing a black cocktail dress and red bottom stilettos. She barely wore any make-up, and her simple French twist hairdo and nude lips were the peak of extravagance.

"This is my niece, Quinn," she said, turning to the

woman. "Quinn, this is Marsha," she continued, smiling as she introduced them. "Marsha, this is the person I wanted you to meet. She's also unmarried." Mrs. Thomas whispered, her mouth twisted in Marsha's direction while winking playfully at her as she dabbed her forehead with a handkerchief, observing their body language.

"Hello," Quinn smiled, reaching out to shake Marsha's hand.

Marsha had to wipe her sweaty palm across her pant leg before she extended her hand. "You look beautiful, Quinn." Marsha said, trying to hide her nervous excitement.

"Thank you, I like your outfit!" she replied, taking a martini from a server's tray and immediately taking a sip. "Outstanding!"

Marsha continued to stare but was still at a loss for words. "She's even more beautiful than I remember," Marsha thought, hoping she didn't freak her out with her staring.

"I feel like I've seen you before… Have we met?" Quinn asked while looking at her quizzically, trying to figure it out.

"Excuse me, ladies; I'm going over to say hello to some friends so the two of you can get better acquainted." Mrs. Thomas told them before she walked away, pleased she introduced them.

"You can say we've met before." Marsha blushed, holding her drink with one hand, the other in her pants pocket. "We met when I worked on my co-worker's bus route a few weeks ago." Marsha continued with a smile.

"Oh Yeah!" Quinn responded, lightly touching Marsha's forearm. "I asked Douglas about you a few times."

She giggled, breaking the ice while, at the same time, the servers were passing around platters of cocktail shrimp, salmon cucumbers, Asiago Asparagus spears, pastry blossoms with caramelized onions, and bacon-wrapped scallops. "Oh my gosh, I'm so hungry." Quinn said, taking a small plate and one of everything, causing Marsha to be comfortable enough to do the same after handing the server her empty glass. My aunt Mildred told me so much about you, Quinn told her, as they walked toward the terrace, and she ate her salmon cucumber. "Mrs. Thomas' name is Mildred.

"Okay, that's good to know," Marsha grinned. "I mean, oh, really." she said aloud, raising one eyebrow.

"I heard about you on our drive here." Quinn chuckled.

"Oh wow, really?" Marsha responded, her eyebrow remaining raised and her facial expression perplexing.

"Yes, she did," Quinn smiled. "But I have a question for you."

"Okay." Marsha replied, hanging on to her every word, then biting the tip of her asparagus.

"How old are you, sweetheart?" Quinn asked, eating her scallop, then dabbing the corners of her mouth with her napkin.

"I'm thirty-two; why?" Marsha asked, clearing her throat.

"What did my aunt tell you about me?" Quinn asked her seriously, looking out at the landscape.

"Nothing at all, really. She just asked me if I was married…; I told her no. Then she said she had somebody she wanted to introduce me to and that she'd bring them to the celebration. That's about it." Marsha said to her, hunching her shoulders and biting her pastry just as the master of ceremony announced Dr. Moore's arrival with the outside guests following him inside.

Everyone gathered in a group and cheered him on as he smiled and waved to everyone before taking his seat. The master of the ceremony gave Dr. Moore the mic because he wanted to say a few words. "Thank you, everyone, for coming out this evening; seeing you all is a great pleasure. Some of you I know well, like Doctor Peterson," pointing the microphone in her direction. "Please, raise your hand; we're all friends here." he told her, rubbing his itchy left eye as the guests in the room started to smile at her. "I don't know how many more of these celebrations I have left (he laughs), but I'm truly grateful to have this one." Everyone laughed at his remarks cheerfully, their hearts growing warm. He concluded, "Enjoy yourselves! eat, drink, and be kind to one another." Before he handed over the mic.

"We love you," a woman wearing a white evening gown shouted, and Dr. Moore kissed the four fingers of his right hand and blew a kiss at her affectionately.

Soon after that, Glenn Miller's Orchestra, "In the Mood," began to resound across the room, and everyone grabbed a partner and began to dance, including Quinn and Marsha.

"I look stupid." Marsha told Quinn bashfully, slowing

down her dance moves.

"Have fun looking stupid, sweetheart! Have fun! Nobody cares." Quinn shouted, giggling as she continued to dance, twirling Marsha around as if no one else was in the room.

They continued to enjoy themselves for the next hour, drinking and conversing about their lives until dinner was announced.

"I must powder my nose." Quinn joked, keeping in tune with the scene moments before Mrs. Thomas walked over to them with a large grin and asked… "How are you ladies getting along?"

"Everything is fine, Aunt Mildred; I'll be back in a minute." Quinn smiled, hurrying to the restroom and leaving Mrs. Thomas and Marsha to walk to their assigned seats.

"I'm gonna wait for Quinn, so she knows where we're seated if that's okay with you?"

"Of course, my dear." Mrs. Thomas told her as she cheerfully walked to the table.

When Quinn returned, Marsha escorted her to their table, where they talked and waited for dinner. A few minutes later, the staff walked into the hall carrying platters of food. They enjoyed lobster tails with clarified butter and Beurre Blanc sauce, macaroni with Brie and lump crab, beef steak wellingtons, butternut Squash gnocchi with herbed brown butter, and roast duck with blackberry-orange sauce. And if anyone had a sweet tooth and room for dessert, there were Dr. Moore's favorite crepe cakes with mascarpone cheese and fresh raspberries, dark chocolate tarts, or Ischler Tortchen (Austrian shortbread cookies).

The night's festivities were unfolding slowly but surely, so Marsha asked Quinn for the last dance, to which she obliged. They slowly two-stepped to Michael Franks' "The Lady Wants to Know," with Marsha's arm around Quinn's waist and Quinn's hand resting on Marsha's shoulder. Others danced along while Mrs. Thomas and a few others were onlookers standing around the dance floor's perimeter. Once the song ended, they stared at one another until Quinn asked, "Did my aunt mention how old I was?"

"No, sweetheart. Remember, I told you, she didn't tell me anything. Besides, what does your age have to do with anything?" Marsha asked sincerely, looking affectionately at her.

"Well, after that comment, nothing." Quinn responded, smiling.

"Can I call you sometime?" Marsha asked her hopefully.

"Of course, you can. Perhaps I can cook dinner for you some time at my place." Quinn responded pleasantly, waiting for her response.

"I would love that." she said, her smile wide.

Quinn chuckled sweetly at her reaction, wrote her number down, and handed it to Marsha. "Call me tomorrow, and I'll give you the address." she said softly. Marsha took the number from her hand, holding it momentarily, both smiling at the other. "It was nice meeting you.

Good night, beautiful." Marsha said, kissing Quinn on

the cheek before watching her slowly walk away.

Quinn looked back, noticing Marsha was still watching her, so she smiled softly at her and continued out the door. Marsha didn't dare let her know she already knew her address. "That's just creepy," she thought, elated that she finally had a name to go with the pretty woman she enjoyed watching waiting for the bus.

Mrs. Thomas came over after witnessing the exchange and kissed Marsha on her cheek. "Goodnight, sweetie." "Good night, Mrs. Thomas."

For the following two weeks, Marsha and Quinn talked on the phone daily for hours. Quinn was surprised to find out about Marsha's passion for sculpting and artistry, and Marsha was stunned at Quinn being a famous restaurateur who had been awarded the James Beard award twice.

"That's a big deal, baby, considering it's the "Oscars" of the food world!" Marsha exclaimed, causing Quinn to become even more intrigued with getting to know her.

"I'm curious. How did you learn about the James Beard Award? Are you in the restaurant business and a bus driver?" Quinn asked playfully, awaiting Marsha's response.

"Oh, no!" Marsha exclaimed, chuckling. "Let's just say I have a lot of time on my hands, so I watch television occasionally, and I tend to enjoy watching cooking competitions when I do if I'm not sculpting."

"Well…We'll have to occupy your time with something else going forward." Quinn responded flirtatiously.

"Oh, yeah? What might you have in mind?" Marsha asked in the same flirtatious manner, licking her lips. She longed to see her but was too nervous to say it aloud.

"Well… I've been waiting for the right time to invite you over so that I can cook that dinner I promised you." Quinn responded, making Marsha squeal in silence.

"I didn't want to make you feel like I was rushing you, so I waited for you to bring it up again," Marsha said, her fist balling up excitedly.

"I like that." Quinn said, both at a pause. "Would you like to come over this Friday?"

"I would love to come over this Friday.; I'll bring over a bottle of wine because I might want to stay the night," Marsha giggled, shocking Quinn and causing her to play it out in her head momentarily.

"Okay, sweetheart, I'll see you Friday around seven."

"Seven it is, goodnight, sweetheart." Marsha replied.

"Goodnight." Quinn responded seductively, hanging up the phone softly.

Marsha listened to be sure the line was disconnected, then looked at the receiver lovingly before hanging it up. Afterward, she went into the kitchen, prepared her lunch for the next day, did three sets of abs and push-ups, showered, and went to bed, hoping Quinn would show up in her dreams. No matter how hard Marsha tried, she couldn't fall asleep as the thoughts of making love to Quinn raced through her mind. She tossed and turned the entire night, yet she was bright-eyed and bushy-tailed when she got out of bed for work the following morning, and she woke up two hours earlier than her usual wake-up time. She used the bathroom and took out a pair of black pants and a cream-colored button-up shirt she wanted to wear for her dinner date with Quinn. She was on the fence about whether to pack the dildo she had purchased and planned on using when she joined the online dating site. Nevertheless, she put it in her small brown leather duffle bag with the harness just in case, and then she threw everything in the trunk of her car, ready to make her way to the depot, smiling from ear to ear.

At the end of her shift, she couldn't wait to get home and change out of her uniform for her dinner date when suddenly, she heard someone whistle and call her name to attract her attention on her way to the time clock. It was her supervisor, Simon, hurrying over to her.

"Marsha! Thank God, I caught you." He said, huffing and puffing.

"Yeah, Simon, what's up?" Marsha asked him, smiling but anxious to leave.

"I need you to work a route for me this evening; Harold is running late." He said, putting his hands in the praying position.

"Well, I have plans for this evening, Simon." She informed him, noting the desperation in his eyes.

"It's only one trip. When you return to the depot, Harold will be here, and I'll pay you for the entire shift… What do you say? Please. I need you, Marsha, just one trip." he begged, holding up one finger.

"All right, Simon, let me make a call first, and I'll make the one trip for you." Marsha told him, nervous about upsetting Quinn.

"You're truly a doll!" Simon exclaimed, writing the information down on his clipboard.

Marsha went into the office to call Quinn, telling her she'd be late and the reason why.

"No problem, sweetheart. I got home late myself, and I just started cooking. Take your time; I'll be here." Quinn told her, giggling sweetly.

Her patience increased Marsha's desire to make love to her that much more. "All right, I'll see you a little later." "All right, baby, see you later," Quinn responded before quickly hanging up the phone. Marsha finished the route, said her goodbyes, jumped in her car and went home to shower quickly. Afterward, she sprayed on cologne and brushed her hair, putting it into a new bun.

By 8 pm…. Marsha was pulling into Quinn's driveway, parking directly behind a classic orange metallic two-seated pick-up truck with white-wall tires. "Nice!" she said aloud, nodding and getting out of her car. She walked up the pathway to the front door but didn't ring the doorbell until she picked two hydrangeas from the bush.

Quinn heard the doorbell chime, hurried to the door, and opened it. She looked like a movie star in her chiffon lounge dress and matching duster, licking the forefinger on her left hand and holding the door open with her right.

"Well, hello, beautiful." Marsha grinned as she stepped over the threshold, handing Quinn the hydrangeas and a bottle of white wine.

"Thank you, but I expected to see you in your uniform," Quinn chuckled, taking the hydrangea and wine from her, then closing the door. "You clean up nicely, in any case." Quinn told her, placing the hydrangeas in an empty wine bottle she retrieved from the kitchen's open shelving and placing them in the center of the dining table. "Dinner is almost ready, sweetheart; make yourself comfortable," Quinn told her, walking back to the stove.

Marsha looked around at all the aqua blue and chrome retro appliances with glee before entering the cozy living space, feeling like she was caught in a time machine of Old Hollywood glam with all the art deco decor. The soft teal walls, the accented gold trim molding, and museum-quality art prints hanging on the two largest walls. The sofa and loveseat were soft white velvet with a large gold metal "Jax-style" base holding a piece of thick clear glass and matching end tables. I guess the gold metal Greek key room divider was placed off to the side for aesthetic purposes, as there was no obvious need for it to be there.

"Now I understand why she dresses the way she does," Marsha thought, impressed with it all.

"Dinner is served," Quinn said softly as she walked into the living room and turned on the record player.

Marsha got up from the sofa and followed Quinn into the dining room, where she found a romantic candle-lit dinner. "Oh wow! I didn't expect this," Marsha commented, pleasantly surprised as Quinn chuckled softly before they both sat.

"I hope you like it," she said, passing Marsha the platter of stovetop grilled meat. They dined on chipotle glazed Venison tomahawk steaks in red wine sauce, topped with caramelized onions. There was a large salad bowl of tender baby greens with raspberries, roasted carrots, and pistachios, dressed with a balsamic drizzle and a side of corn on the cob that they'll wash down with the chilled white wine Marsha brought in while listening to the sounds of Bobby "Blue" Bland's "For Members Only" playing softly in the background.

"So, tell me about your parents, Marsha." Quinn asked as she cut into her Venison.

"Okay, well, both of my parents are retired. They were both artists and moved to Oak Bluff a few years ago. I renovated the house to my specifications and stayed here in Sag Harbor. How about your parents?" Marsha asked, washing down her salad with wine.

"My parents didn't want to be parents." Quinn replied matter-of-factly. "And my aunt Mildred couldn't have any children of her own, so she raised me from when I was four years old."

"Oh!" Marsha responded in a surprised tone. "Do your parents live in Sag Harbor?" Marsha asked her curiously, picking up another forkful of greens.

"No, they never lived here. They live in Bridgeport, Connecticut. I speak with them occasionally." she responded, never looking up from her plate and moving the raspberries around it.

"Wow, that's interesting." Marsha mumbled, her tone sarcastic and dry, but then realized the conversation made Quinn uncomfortable. "Trust me, If I didn't have the love of my aunt Mildred and if I didn't get therapy, you wouldn't be sitting here tonight." she told her, looking up from her plate and winking before biting into her corn on the cob.

"Well, I'm glad you were loved and conscious enough to get the help you needed. Thank God for love and therapy!" Marsha roared, both laughing, lightening the mood. After dinner, they cleared the table while laughing and joking as they had over the phone. Marsha helped Quinn load the dishes into the dishwasher before she grabbed the remaining wine and headed into the living room.

"I'm right behind you."

Quinn shouted, afterward flopping down on the loveseat while Marsha sat on the sofa.

"Now, why in the world are you sitting over there?" Quinn asked seriously, chuckling at her.

"I don't want you to feel cramped." Marsha said, her shoulders hunched as she pretended to be bashful.

"Girl, if you don't get your butt over here," Quinn said while playfully rolling her eyes and laughing as Marsha walked over rapidly and practically sat on her lap.

She left no room for either of them to move, causing them to laugh hysterically. Amidst this, Quinn spilled her drink, with some landing on her breasts.

"Oops, let me get that for you." Marsha said seductively, looking into Quinn's eyes before placing her wine glass on the coffee table to lick the wine off her.

"Oooh," Quinn mumbled seductively, "It's your fault, so I expect you to lick up every drop," She continued, her voice just above a whisper as she watched Marsha slowly lick it off. And without looking at her,

Marsha took Quinn's wine glass from her hand, set it next to hers on the coffee table, and kissed her softly; at the same time, Quinn reached out to caress her face tenderly, placing her tongue inside Marsha's mouth, both moaning with pleasure. After their last kiss…

"Hold on to that feeling, baby. I'll be right back!" Marsha said as she sprung up and began hurrying to the front door.

"Where are you going, love?"

Quinn asked with a surprised tone and perplexing look. "I'm going to get something out of my car because if we go any further, baby, I wanna be prepared." She responded with a wink and then rapidly walked to the door. Once outside, Marsha jogged to her vehicle, excited to retrieve her duffle bag, returned with a mischievous look on her face into the living room and placed it on the sofa. "All right, where were we?" She walked over to Quinn slowly, taking her time and smiling before licking her lips.

Quinn crossed her legs seductively and tapped her lips lightly with her forefinger, reminding her where they had left off. Marsha bent down to kiss her passionately, causing Quinn to stand slowly while Marsha gently helped her and removed her robe, letting it fall on the loveseat, then softly kissing her shoulders.

"Let's finish this in my bedroom," she whispered into Marsha's ear, then looked into her eyes lustfully as she raised her head.

"Yeah, Let's do that." Marsha agreed, biting her bottom lip and taking Quinn by the hand. "Lead the way," Marsha told her with a flirty smile.

"Don't forget to bring your "little" bag." Quinn teased, placing her pinky nail between her teeth, chuckling softly because she knew exactly what was in it.

Marsha picked up the duffle bag and followed Quinn

upstairs into her bedroom, which was decorated with tufted pink velvety furniture, including the circular headboard and satin sheets on the round bed, which were also pink. The room was as beautiful and feminine as Quinn was.

Quinn let down the straps of her nightgown, allowing it to fall to the floor, revealing her voluptuous, saggy breasts, tiny greying pubic hairs, and the large keloid scar across the right side of her flat belly. She looked insecure as she waited for the expression on Marsha's face to show up.

"You're so beautiful," Marsha told her, in awe of her body and impressed with her courage. She removed her clothing quickly to embrace Quinn, their breasts touching.

"Thank you." Quinn replied bashfully. "I like how you take care of yourself," Quinn told her as she traced her fingers down Marsha's muscular, blemish-free, taught body. She was mesmerized by her muscle definition each time her body moved.

Their bodies remained pressed against each other until Marsha gently put her hand at the back of Quinn's head to caress the nape of her neck before they kissed slowly and romantically.

Suddenly, Marsha stepped forward to lay Quinn on the soft pink satin sheets, her body on top of hers as they grinded body-to-body, the sheets enabling them to slide slowly from side to side in sweet ecstasy. Marsha gazed into Quinn's eyes as she took her hands in hers, interlocking their fingers and then raising them over Quinn's head as she kissed the front of her body, releasing them only to hold both sides of Quinn's waist in the palms of her hands. She kissed the length of her right-sided belly scar, purposefully repeating, "You're so beautiful."

Quinn reached out to caress Marsha's head and watched her lovingly as tiny sparks pulsated throughout her body. Marsha looked up at her briefly and smiled before returning her moist lips to Quinn's body. She took Quinn's tiny pubic hairs and gathered them between her lips, gently pulling on them repeatedly while inhaling the sweet fragrance coming from between her thighs.

"Come up here for a minute, baby," Quinn whispered, her hand extended.

"Yes, beautiful," Marsha replied softly, moving up toward her, landing face-to-face.

"Thank you." Quinn said to her, looking into Marsha's eyes and caressing the right side of her face.

Marsha kissed her and lifted her body just enough to wrap her arms around her, causing Quinn to moan softly.

At the same time, Quinn was running her hands tenderly up and down Marsha's muscular arms, returning her kiss with so much passion that it surprised her. Marsha's breathing became heavier as the desire to make love to Quinn grew more intense than she had ever experienced before. She extended her tongue and applied it to Quinn's neck, licking her way between her legs, her nose helping to open the gates of her garden, exposing Quinn's pearl. She licked it tenderly, then ravenously, making Quinn cry out in pleasure while pulling at Marsha's hair. Marsha's shoulders were cradled against the back of Quinn's thighs, lifting them slightly as Quinn's hands grabbed and slapped them as she gyrated in pleasure, repeating the words "Sweet lord" as she neared climax. "I'm Cumming, baby!" Quinn softly shouted, climaxing three consecutive times before covering her mouth to muffle her screams.

Marsha held her thighs tightly with the intention of never letting her go while her mouth maintained a firm grip on her pearl.

Quinn screamed… "Okay, baby, please; I can't take it anymore," simultaneously tapping Marsha's arm. Marsha released her reluctantly, hovering over her and watching her body calm down in awe. "Give me a minute," Quinn said, covering her face and blushing once she regained focus. "Would you like a glass of water?" Quinn asked, her lips sticky and dry.

"No, I had plenty to drink, thank you." Marsha teased, reaching over and playfully pinching her cheek. She lay beside her, taking hold of her hand, smiling as they stared at the ceiling.

Moments later… Quinn slid off the bed, saying, "I have to use the bathroom; I'll be right back." Not too long after, Quinn returned to the bedroom, drinking a glass of water, stopping abruptly in her tracks when she observed Marsha in bed, grinning from ear to ear with a harness strapped to her, holding a seven-inch clear dildo. "Is that for me?" Quinn asked seductively, her eyes glued to the dildo.

"Of course it is, baby," Marsha replied, gently stroking it.

"Hmm. In that case, I'm gonna need you to move into the center of the bed for me, baby." Quinn looked at Marsha with dreamy eyes as she swallowed her last gulp of water and placed the glass on the bedside table before crawling onto the bed and wiping her lips. Quinn tongue kissed Marsha slowly while stroking the dildo, then moistened it with her mouth, motivating Marsha to give her dirty direction.

"Oh, my goodness, baby, you look so fucking good sucking on it. I can't wait to put it inside you, girl, damn!" Marsha said in a lustfully aggressive tone.

Quinn's mouth was full, so she could only suck and stare. Marsha started playing with her nipples and making herself moister as she watched Quinn enjoy herself intermittently gagging when the dildo went in a little too deep. Afterward, Quinn swung one of her legs around Marsha, straddling her, slowly lowering her body onto the dildo. Meanwhile, Marsha was holding both of Quinn's cheeks and staring at her lustfully, with her bottom lip in her mouth, withholding her overwhelming desire to thrust the dildo in completely. Once the dildo was completely inside, Quinn began to ride Marsha wildly, her hands gripping Marsha's upper arms for support.

Marsha began to thrust her hips upwards, penetrating Quinn deeper. They both whimpered in pleasure as the squooshy rhythmic sounds of Quinn's juices became louder with every bounce. Marsha continued thrusting Quinn faster and harder, her hands slapping and spreading Quinn's cheeks. Suddenly, she sat up and moved toward the edge of the bed. "Hold on, baby," Marsha said in a deep, sexy voice, cautiously getting off the bed and maintaining her grip on Quinn's cheeks.

Quinn wrapped her arms around Marsha's neck, and Marsha lifted her up and down while thrusting her hips rapidly as they kissed each other fervently. Marsha then moved over to the bedroom wall, pinning Quinn against it for leverage without missing a beat.

Quinn was squeezing Marsha's neck tighter now while assisting her. After some time, Marsha began to tire as the sweat poured down her face. Her thighs tightened and became moist from Quinn's sweat trickling from hers. Quinn climaxed repeatedly but only whimpering and shutting her eyes tightly when she did. Marsha walked back over to the bed, laid Quinn down, and continued penetrating her missionary style, climaxing after every third stroke. She pressed her knuckles into the bed while staring at the expressions on Quinn's face and repeating, "This feels so fucking good, baby." Marsha's last climax was so strong it made her grunt and collapse momentarily onto Quinn, who held her firmly, her eyes tightly shut. "Oh, my God, baby," Marsha said, unbuckling the harness strap and flopping down beside Quinn, allowing her sweat to dry.

Quinn rolled over to her side and watched Marsha, whose eyes were closed. Her body looks like a masterpiece. she thought, moving closer and running her hand across Marsha's abdomen, causing Marsha to look at her and smile.

"You mind if I go downstairs and get a glass of water?" Marsha asked her, sitting up on the bed.

"Of course not! Bring me one too! I'm going to the bathroom and freshen up," Quinn responded quickly and got off the bed.

Marsha chuckled at her response, then went downstairs,

poured two glasses of ice-cold water, and brought them upstairs. In the bedroom, Marsha placed Quinn's glass on the bedside table and began drinking hers, waiting for Quinn to return. She sat at the head of the bed with one leg propped up.

Quinn returned to the bedroom wearing a white feather-trim, see-through chiffon robe. She picked up her glass and took a drink before sitting on the bed beside Marsha, Marsha watching her in awe, thinking how Quinn was possibly the most sophisticated woman she'd ever been with.

"Wow, you're terrific. I haven't had a night like this one ever."

Quinn told her lovingly while lightly touching Marsha's muscular arm.

"I'm glad you approve." Marsha winked playfully and then finished her glass of water. "I loved how you trusted me while giving yourself to me, sweetheart." I also like how you shut your eyes when you're climaxing, too," Marsha winked, licking her lips and leaning closer to Quinn's side.

Quinn looked at her and blushed, her hand slightly covering her mouth.

"Not that it matters, but can I ask you a question?" Marsha asked, remaining on her side, looking at Quinn cautiously.

"Ahem, let me guess," Quinn said, clearing her throat and sitting taller. "You want to ask me my age, right?" Quinn said, looking at Marsha with a pleasant smile.

"Yes." Marsha responded, sitting up gleefully and

waiting for Quinn's response.

"I'm forty-seven," Quinn said, waiting for Marsha's reaction.

"Okay, okay." Did you say forty-seven by mistake, and you meant thirty-seven?"

"Marsha!" she giggled, playfully hitting her arm. "Seriously, is my age going to be a problem for you?" Quinn asked, trying to hide her nervousness.

"Not at all! Are you serious?" Marsha chuckled. "I wouldn't care if you were sixty-seven! Besides, have you looked in the mirror…you're a goddess."

Marsha pulled Quinn closer to her before kissing her passionately and holding her in her arms. Quinn sighed in relief, embracing Marsha tightly.

"Hey, babe, I meant to tell you, this bed is awesome!" Marsha said to her before kissing her on the forehead.

"Thank you. I purchased it from a consignment shop in California a few years ago. I guess you can tell I like all things vintage, huh?"

"Well, not all things," Marsha teased, squeezing Quinn tightly and settling into bed, Quinn's head on her chest until the following morning.

The sunshine blazed through the small opening of the bedroom window curtain, waking them both up. Marsha started stretching and singing good morning to Quinn as she leaped out of bed, hurrying to the bathroom.

"Good morning," Quinn sang back as she rolled over in an awesome mood. "What would you like for breakfast?" Quinn yelled out, getting out of bed.

'Surprise me!" Marsha yelled back, afterward flushing

the toilet, washing her hands, and looking for a towel to dry them on.

Quinn put on her loungewear from the previous evening, removed the sheets from the bed, went downstairs to prepare breakfast, and threw the sheets into the wash before washing up and brushing her teeth in the downstairs guest bathroom. She took out the butter, shredded cheese, eggs, and leftover ham chunks she brought home the other day out of the fridge to make Western omelets for them.

"Quinn, do you have any extra toothbrushes up here, baby?" Marsha yelled out from the top of the stairs.

"I do. Look inside the medicine cabinet to the left." Quinn replied while taking her cast iron griddle pan from the bottom cupboard.

Marsha found the toothbrushes, loaded one with toothpaste, and brushed her teeth. Then, she decided to straighten out the sheets on the bed, but, to her surprise, they were gone, so she picked up her clothes from the floor and put them on, removing and balling up the panty liner from the crotch of her underwear, then pulling them up after throwing the liner in the bathroom trash can before heading downstairs, buttoning up her shirt along the way. Once in the kitchen, she hurried over to Quinn for a quick kiss on the neck.

"That smells so good; what are we having?" Marsha asked cheerfully, sitting down at the table in anxious anticipation.

"I hope you don't have any food allergies because I've decided to make Western omelets and home-fried potatoes.

"I love omelets and home fries!" Marsha exclaimed. "Do you need help with something?" Marsha asked pleasantly, starting to get up from the table.

"You could slice the oranges in the wicker basket, sitting over there on the counter, and then juice them with the juicer sitting next to it."

"No problemo," Marsha replied, sneaking peeks at Quinn as she stirred the onions, red peppers, shredded cheese, and ham chunks into the egg batter. "Can you pass me the ripest avocado over there, please?" she pointed.

"Only if I can get a kiss first," Marsha smiled, holding the avocado behind her and puckering her lips while closing her eyes.

Quinn walked to her, kissed her tenderly, and then returned to her dish, grinning.

"Mm, mm mm!" Marsha commented softly, shaking her head. "Do you have a pitcher for the juice, babe?" she asked, squeezing the last orange and filling the chamber.

"Look in the cupboard above your head, baby, and breakfast is almost ready," Quinn told her. Marsha brought over the pitcher of orange juice. She placed it in the center of the table, next to the hydrangeas, and then walked back to the cupboard for the drinking glasses while Quinn placed the ketchup with the salt and pepper grinders on the table before scooping out the home-fried potatoes and placing them on their plates.

Afterward, she brought over the omelets with the potatoes.

"Dig in," she said as they sat down.

"So, do you have any plans this weekend?" Quinn

asked, looking over at Marsha, her fork slicing into her omelet.

"No, I don't have any plans. I'm probably going to work on my newest sculpture. Why? Do you have any plans?" Marsha asked, putting ketchup on her fried potatoes and smiling. She was hoping Quinn wanted to spend some more time together.

"Well… I have to go into the restaurant this afternoon to check the inventory, and I was wondering if you would like to join me." she said, looking down and adding a slice of avocado to the omelet.

"Of course! "I'd love to go anywhere with you," Marsha told her, grinning, her cheeks full of eggs and potatoes, looking like a chipmunk but feeling like the luckiest woman in the world.

Quinn giggled and looked at her lovingly, delighted that Marsha wanted to spend the afternoon with her. After breakfast, they "monkied around" while cleaning the kitchen. Afterward, Quinn went upstairs to put on some clothes, and when she returned, she was wearing a brown safari short set, a pair of low wedge tan espadrilles, and a matching woven handbag. They decided to drive Marsha's car since she had to return home to change her clothes anyway. On their way there, they chatted like schoolgirl best friends, singing songs on the radio and blushing when they caught themselves glancing at each other. Marsha pulled the car onto her narrow driveway and went to open the passenger side door, but Quinn was already outside of it, so she led her by the hand inside the home. Mildred crossed her mind, and she felt deeply grateful in that moment.

"I love your home," Quinn told her, looking around at the artwork and rustic furnishings.

"Thanks, babe. Please help yourself to something to drink; I'll just be a sec!" Marsha said, quickly kissing Quinn on the cheek and taking off to her bedroom to change clothes.

Quinn walked around the cottage admiring the décor. She touched the sculpture Marsha recently placed on the pedestal. "This is gorgeous," she mumbled as she walked around it, unconsciously looking at the colorful abstract piece for imperfections but couldn't find any.

Ten minutes later, Marsha returned wearing a white one-pocket T-shirt with a blue and white striped sweater hanging loosely around her shoulders, which she folded at the cuffs to keep it in place, a pair of white-washed blue jeans, white canvas boat shoes, and black aviator sunglasses resting on top of her head, and a sliver wristwatch to top off the look. Her biceps were popping, and her jeans almost hugged her muscular thighs, arousing Quinn. "Ready to go, baby?" Marsha asked her, smiling and rubbing lotion into her hands before taking her wallet from under her arm and putting it in her back pocket.

"You look so handsomely nautical." Quinn walked toward Marsha, grabbing her hand. "And yes, I'm ready!"

"Thank you, baby." Marsha replied, gently kissing her before opening the door. "After you." She let go of Quinn's hand and watched her walk out. Then, after she locked the door, she raced to the car's passenger side to open the door for her. They made their way to Quinn's restaurant, arriving Forty-two minutes later. Q's exceptional cuisine was engraved boldly in elegant pewter stone on the face of the brick-and-mortar restaurant.

"Wow, is this your restaurant?" Marsha asked in awe. "It is. Let's go inside." She grinned, opening the car door, and Marsha followed her inside.

"Exceptional!" Marsha commented, staring in amazement at the beautiful black and white interior.

She gasped at the massive artwork hanging on the walls. She later discovered that a local artist donated the artwork and often rented the space to showcase his works and introduce the guests to Quinn's cross-cultural cuisine.

"Good afternoon, Trina," Quinn said to a female staff member who was going to the dining area to prepare for this evening's dinner guests.

"Good afternoon, Quinn," Trina responded pleasantly, stopping in case Quinn needed anything while Marsha watched on with admiration of it all.

"I'll be in my office, Trina, if you need me," she said, walking down the hallway till she arrived at her office door. She unlocked it, and as soon as they entered, she dropped her keys on her desk, turned on her computer, and sat behind it.

Marsha sat quietly on the brown Chesterfield sofa and picked up a culinary magazine to avoid disturbing her.

"Excuse me, babe," Quinn said as she shot up. "I'll be right back...going to review the inventory with the manager and the chef."

An hour later, Quinn returned with two plates of food, handing one to Marsha. "Sorry it took me so long, baby," she said, sitting beside her on the sofa.

"Oh, no worries," Marsha responded, giving the food the once over. "Mm, this looks good. What is it?"

"It's Osso Bucco, macaroni and cheese, and steamed broccoli, baby. It's what's on the dinner menu tonight." Quinn responded.

"Osso Bucco, huh? Is it beef or something?" Marsha asked, tasting the gravy on the fork.

"Yes, it's braised beef shanks. You're going to love it!" Quinn told her, digging her fork into it. They finished eating, had a glass of sparkling water, and played "footsies" in her office while they kissed and whispered sweet nothings into each other's ear.

"Would you like to take a culinary bicycle tour around the vineyard near the restaurant?" Quinn asked.

"That sounds fun, baby. What time does it start?" Marsha asked, putting one plate on the other, preparing to leave.

"They leave every hour, on the hour." Quinn responded, walking over to her desk and turning off the computer and the lights as they left the office. Quinn handed the dirty dishes to a male dishwasher, then told everyone, including the manager, goodbye while walking out of the restaurant.

Marsha drove them to the venue, meeting the tour guide at the gate. Marsha insisted on paying their admission fees; they chose their bikes and went off on tour with a group of others to taste specialty olive oils and artisan cheeses, some mixed with fresh herbs and smeared on baguets for tasting. Marsha and Quinn were flirtatiously feeding each other the snacks the entire time while the others minded their own business. Quinn purchased some items for herself and placed them in her bike's basket; then, she placed a larger order for the restaurant, which the merchant promised to deliver within the coming days. The tour continued to the vineyard, where they were given a history of the wine and the process. Although they could not taste them because Marsha was driving, they did purchase a few bottles to drink later. The tour ended after a few hours, and they returned their bikes and went to retrieve the car.

"I think we should christen your house tonight," Quinn said as they drove toward her house.

"Say less," Marsha responded, making a detour to her home. Marsha pulled up to her driveway, got out, and took her wine from the back seat before they proceeded to the front door.

Once inside, they both kicked off their shoes, and Marsha put the wine into the fridge while Quinn sat on the sofa. "My bedroom is over there," Marsha pointed toward the rear of the home, looking sly as she brought a chilled bottle of wine she had previously in the fridge and two wine glasses leading the way. Quinn chuckled and followed her into the bedroom, sitting on Marsha's king-sized rustic log bed underneath a large black iron candlestick chandelier attached to the wood beams on the ceiling. "Your room is so cozy and romantic." Quinn commented, looking around while Marsha poured them a glass of wine.

"Thank you, baby. I'm glad you like it." She said, handing Quinn her glass, and standing beside her.

"Cheers! Baby, and to many more wonderful evenings."

Quinn blushed and saluted her glass.

"Would you like to listen to some music?" Marsha asked, walking over to the music player on the wooden ladder shelving, leaning against the wall.

"Sure," Quinn replied. Marsha pressed play, and Stevie Wonder's "Golden Lady" came on. Quinn put down her drink and began to dance while slowly taking her clothes off, entertaining Marsha, who was now sitting at the head of the bed watching her with admiration. "You are just… a goddess. And I'll never stop saying it." Marsha told her, slowly shaking her head, loving her in-house entertainment.

Quinn danced over to Marsha, then climbed on top of her and kissed her slowly while Marsha's hand rested on her lower back. Marsha paused their interaction by getting off the bed to remove her clothes while Quinn assisted in speeding up the process. Marsha pulled the linen back to get cozier, but Quinn took charge this time. She gently laid Marsha on the bed and ran her wet tongue down her thighs. Marsha panted lustfully, opened her legs wider, and assisted Quinn's head between them.

"Mmm, you're not wasting any time, huh, baby?" Quinn asked as she opened her mouth wide, diving into Marsha's Ocean of love. She sucked on Marsha ferociously, causing her to squirm wildly at the same time; Marsha was pinching her nipples for the full effect, making her first climax rapid and plentiful, but her second explosion took a while, causing Quinn's neck to cramp, (information she kept to herself). Marsha was exhausted afterward, and Quinn was satisfied and rested in Marsha's arms, both waking at noon the following day.

They decided to go out for lunch since neither wanted to cook. They freshened up; Marsha threw on a pair of black linen pants, a white linen shirt, and a pair of black leather driving moccasins, then drove to a popular local restaurant to have lunch alfresco. They arrived at the restaurant, walked through to the back, and seated themselves moments before the waitress arrived with sparkling lemon water and the menus. "Just let me know when you're ready," the waitress chirped, walking off. They thanked her and then started to look over the menu.

"Wow, this menu is fancy; what are you having, baby?" Marsha chuckled, still looking over the menu.

"I'm going to have octopus ceviche with tomatoes, cilantro, lime juice, and avocado. What are you having?" Quinn asked with a smile.

"I'm definitely having more than that!" Marsha teased, causing them to laugh. "But for real, I'm going to have the steamed mussels with shallots, white wine, and cream served with French fries."

"French fries sound good; I'm gonna get a side order," Quinn told her, raising her hand for the waitress.

"Share my fries. No need to buy a side order, baby." Marsha said, closing her menu.

"Awe, you're gonna share your fries with me? That's so sweet." Okay, baby, I'll share your fries." Quinn said, blushing.

The waitress arrived, got their orders, and returned with their platters within twenty minutes. "Do you need anything else?" The waitress asked them before leaving.

"No, not at this time, thanks." Marsha told her.

"These are steak fries. I'm glad you convinced me not to get another order; they're huge!" Quinn chuckled. They joyfully completed their dinners while discussing their short-term and long-term goals to see their compatibility before exiting the restaurant.

"How spontaneous are you on a scale of one to ten?" Marsha asked, on their way to the car with their fingers entwined the entire time.

"Hmm. It depends on what it is." Quinn laughed. "What do you have in mind?"

"It involves a cruise and the sun, but let's get you changed first."

Marsha drove them back to Quinn's place, where she changed into a white cotton wrap dress with a white bolero sweater for their spare-of-the-moment two-hour sunset cruise around the island. They held hands on the deck, sipping complimentary red wine, listening to smooth jazz, and watching the sun fade. "This was the best weekend I've ever had." Marsha told Quinn.

"Mine also," Quinn responded, kissing Marsha tenderly as the boat pulled into the harbor.

Marsha drove Quinn home, kissed her goodnight, and returned home to prepare for work in the morning. Marsha drove to work Monday morning in a better-than-ever mood, expecting to do the usual, but when she arrived, her co-workers told her that Simon needed to speak with her urgently. "Yes, Simon?" she asked, her voice shaky as she entered the office. "Hey Marsha, did you have a nice weekend." he asked cheerfully.

"As a matter of fact, I did!" she smiled, reflecting in relief.

"Well… I just received some good news. He said, getting up from behind his desk.

"Oh, yeah, do tell?" she continued to smile.

"Congratulations, you've been promoted to shift supervisor!"

Marsha was beaming. She no longer had to drive the bus, and her salary had increased by $25,000!

"Oh, my goodness! I'm speechless, Simon. Thank you!" Marsha exclaimed, her hands crossing her chest.

"You're so welcome, Marsha…; you deserve it." Simon said, coming from behind his desk and softly patting her back as he smiled at her.

Marsha ran into the break room and immediately called Quinn to share the good news.

"That's terrific, baby. Congratulations!" Quinn screamed.

"Thank you, baby, but listen… I gotta go. I have to shadow Simon for the next few days before I can go it alone. I'll call you when I get a break, all right?"

"Of course, baby. Go, go," Quinn told her, kissing into the phone.

Marsha kissed back, then hung up the phone and returned to the area Simon wanted to meet her in. The next four weeks were even better than the first day they'd met. They took Mildred out to dinner several times and thanked her for introducing them, and Mildred congratulated Marsha on her promotion. Marsha and Quinn took turns sleeping at one another's homes, and Quinn went so far as to ask Marsha to design a piece to be permanently placed in the restaurant. Marsha was so overjoyed with the request that she began working on it that very day, completing the large sculpture within two months.

On one weekend, Quinn was remolding and steam cleaning the restaurant, when Marsha visited her parents. She felt confident enough in the relationship to open up to them about Quinn. Marsha stood in the kitchen where her parents were preparing lunch and told them all about her and Quinn's relationship with the sweetest grin she could muster.

"She sounds wonderful!" her mother told her cheerfully, thrilled to hear how happy her baby girl was.

"Bring the young lady over, we'd love to meet her!" Her father added, also thrilled about his daughter's new love.

"Awe, you guys are the best!" She opened her arms widely, suggesting a three-way hug. "Thank you for loving and supporting me…always."

Their eyes filled with tears, then her mother loosened her embrace to kiss Marsha on her forehead while her father stood there smiling at them and wiping his eyes.

August of the following year Marsha brought Quinn to Oak Bluffs to meet her parents as well as attend the annual Black Film Festival she and her parents traditionally attended each year. Quinn was so nervous to meet them, but also honored that Marsha wanted her to, because not only was she in love with Marsha, but Marsha was also the most wonderful woman she had ever met. She was certain that this relationship was going to be her last.

They pulled up to Marsha's parents' home in Quinn's orange truck. Quinn was too nervous to get out, so Marsha opened the passenger side for her, taking her hand and kissing it before holding it and leading her to the front door, which she unlocked with her spare key.

"Mommy, daddy, we're here!" Marsha shouted out then chuckled at Quinn's nervousness. "Babe, stop being nervous, they're going to love you!" She grabbed her hand playfully and pulled her in past the door.

Her parents were in the kitchen preparing a dinner of Cornish hens, wild rice, sauteed greens and apple pie for their arrival. "Marsha! Is that you and Quinn baby?" her mother yelled walking out of the kitchen and drying her hands on a blue checkered dish cloth.

"Yes, it's us mommy." Marsha was smiling hard just as her father shouted "Hello!"

Marsha's parents hugged them both tightly, ridding Quinn of all anxiety. "You look beautiful together." Her mother commented, looking at Quinn lovingly.

"Let's go into the living room and chat, dinner will be ready soon." Her father said leading them into the living room with his hand on her mother's upper back. They took their seats in the living room and started to get to know one another better, laughing and joking while Marsha's father cracked open a few walnuts from the glass bowl on the coffee table, while Quinn ate peanuts from the other. The stove alarm went off, interrupting their laughter and indicating the dinner rolls were ready.

Marsha's parents insisted that Marsha and Quinn get comfortable at the kitchen table while they set everything up. So, the new lovers sat down making googly eyes at each other. Marsha's mother caught them a few times and smiled. Quinn felt so comfortable that she invited Marsha's parents over to eat at her restaurant, and they accepted the invitation with honor.

After the main course, they took the apple pie into the living room and ate them a la mode on folding trays in front of the television, so her mother wouldn't miss her nightly programing of "Murder She Wrote." Afterward, they called it a night, and went to bed. Marsha suggested she sleep on the sofa, but her father refused, sleeping there himself. So, Marsha slept with her mother and Quinn slept in the guest room so as not to be disrespectful.

The following morning, they had breakfast out before going to enjoy the festivities at the Black film festival. Marsha snuck away to have a private conversation with her mother while her father had Quinn holding her stomach from hysteric laughter. Marsha was watching them affectionately.

"She really makes you happy, doesn't she?" her mother asked her.

"Yes, and I'd like to think I make her happy too"

"I would bet a million dollars you do." Her mother said softly while tenderly rubbing her arm, then hugging her.

"I knew you would like her." Marsha continued

"So, do you guys' plan on having a family, so I can finally get me some grandbabies?" her mother teased.

"Well, if things keep going the way they are, I just might!" Marsha chuckled, winking at her.

Her mother embraced her tightly again, kissing her on

the cheeks while Marsha caught Quinn watching them and smiling before she blew her a kiss as she rested her chin on her mother's shoulder.

"My heart has finally found a home mommy." She said before allowing her eyes to close, relishing the moment.

www.ingramcontent.com/pod-product-compliance
Lightning Source LLC
Chambersburg PA
CBHW071247300726
48975CB00002B/578